My friend Martha Bolton has created the perfect presidential candidate—a back-to-basics, plain-speaking, humble, and wise Amish man named Josiah. As a writer for Bob Hope, Martha wrote plenty of humor about the political scene (from the Reagan years to the Clintons'), and even wrote for a certain real-life presidential candidate from Little Rock. So if you're looking for a fascinating read or just an escape from the current political scene, this book is it!

—GOVERNOR MIKE HUCKABEE, TV host
and bestselling author

A great read that challenges you to think outside the box! Josiah comes to life via his interaction with Congressman Mark Stedman in a unique and interesting way. Martha Bolton brings forward a character who is believable and who embodies many of the back-to-basics traits that Americans crave.

—CONGRESSMAN MARSHA BLACKBURN,
United States House of Representatives

With a fascinating premise, Martha Bolton crafts a delightfully heartwarming story, poignant for these political times, yet laugh-out-loud funny. Bolton breathes new life into the Amish fiction subgenre!

—BEVERLY LEWIS, *New York Times* bestselling author
of *The Fiddler*

Josiah for President is a compelling tale of an unlikely friendship, and an even more unlikely agreement. Heartwarming and funny, Martha's book will leave you cheering for the underdog, while believing there is still hope for America's future.

—MICHAEL CATT, senior pastor of Sherwood Baptist
Church and executive producer for Sherwood Pictures

With Martha Bolton's help, I was nearly elected president myself some years ago, so when I heard she was writing a novel about an Amish man who runs for president, I wasn't surprised at all. You're going to love how Martha's wit, creative imagination, and heart clearly come through these pages. And Martha, if Josiah ever really does run for president, tell him I'm available to serve as his vice president!

— MARK LOWRY

Were one to look up the definition of "great top comedy writer, talented, sensitive, and truly genuinely nice person," surely a picture of Martha Bolton would appear. She is a brilliant talent, having written for the likes of the great Bob Hope all the way to my shows, whether in Las Vegas or the U.S.O. Tours in Beirut or Afghanistan. She's the best, and I am honored to know her.

— WAYNE NEWTON

Martha Bolton's writing never disappoints. *Josiah for President* demonstrates her ability to get the reader turning each page to discover what happens next. It is a gripping and most timely novel.

— LORD TAYLOR OF WARWICK, House of Lords

Martha Bolton is one fine writer. I don't know much about writing — normal writing, that is — but I do know what I enjoy reading. Everything on the page is crisp and pulls you right through the story. It's like wine. I know nothing about wine either except that when I take a sip, I know whether I like it or not. Martha's writing, to me, is delicious.

— GENE PERRET, author and writer for Bob Hope and *The Carol Burnett Show*

Martha Bolton has woven a stunning story—compelling and finely detailed. I couldn't wait to pick it up each time! It was riveting! Next—*Josiah*, the movie! Martha is a real talent—I'm her biggest fan!

—JUDI FELDMAN, former personal
and production assistant to Bob Hope

Martha Bolton and I shared the longest laugh of either of our lives over lunch one day in California. It was one of those laughfests that kept going—lasting several hours at least, with other patrons even getting in on it, including Dick Van Dyke, who was dining a few tables away. Martha and I became fast friends and have been ever since. I love Martha's writing style; I love Martha; and I love her new novel, *Josiah for President*. It's a fresh take on politics and a real twist for Amish fiction. You're going to love it! And her!

—LANI NETTER, Lani Netter Productions,
wife of Gil Netter, producer of *The Blind Side*

Martha Bolton is one of my favorite nonfiction authors and her first attempt at a novel may be her best work yet. I hate clichés, but I'm gonna use one here—this is a real page-turner. I mean that in an, "I can't put this thing down" kind of way.

—BRAD DICKSON, former staff writer
for *The Tonight Show with Jay Leno*

In the complex political world of positioning, negotiations, strategies, and world policies, the wisdom of a two-thousand-year-old book guides Josiah and rallies a public hungry for a simple truth. Martha Bolton has created an inspirational modern-day parable that is a reflective example of the things that really matter in our nation's condition of political and economic distress.

—RICK ELDRIDGE, studio executive and film producer

Josiah for President by Martha Bolton is the definitive novel of the twenty-first century and seamlessly combines humor and humanity. A long-time writer for my cartoon feature *The Lockhorns*, as well as for comic legends, including Bob Hope, Martha Bolton has maximized her genius for comedy and her brilliant insights on American politics.

Josiah for President is both timely and timeless. It describes a perfect storm of events leading to the White House, motivated by real people we grow to love. I was unable to put the book down. For a totally uplifting read, *Josiah for President* is number one on any list. Thank you, Martha.

—BUNNY HOEST, president and CEO
of Wm. Hoest Enterprises, Inc.

Well done! Blending the Amish and D.C. cultures together is a truly unique idea with so many possibilities for tension and fun. Martha has created easy-to-visualize scenes while always showing respect for Amish culture and values. This could so easily be adapted to a movie.

—PAUL ALDRICH, comedian and songwriter

JOSIAH
for President

MARTHA BOLTON

ZONDERVAN®

ZONDERVAN.com/
AUTHORTRACKER
follow your favorite authors

ZONDERVAN

Josiah for President
Copyright © 2012 by Martha Bolton

This title is also available as a Zondervan ebook. Visit www.zondervan.com/ebooks.

This title is also available in a Zondervan audio edition. Visit www.zondervan.fm.

Requests for information should be addressed to:
Zondervan, *Grand Rapids, Michigan 49530*

Library of Congress Cataloging-in-Publication Data

Bolton, Martha, 1951–
    Josiah for president / Martha Bolton.
      p. cm.
    ISBN 978-0-310-31872-9 (softcover)
    1. Presidents—Election—Fiction. 2. Amish—Fiction. 3. Political campaigns—
Fiction. 4. Political fiction. I. Title.
PS3552.O58779J67   2012
813'.54—dc23   2012027194

Cover design: Curt Diepenhorst
Cover photography: Mike Heath
Interior design: Beth Shagene

Printed in the United States of America

JOSIAH
for President

To Melva ... my sister, my friend
For your giving, caring, loving, courageous heart

CHAPTER 1

★

AMERICA WAS SICK. SHE NEEDED A MIRACLE. BUT THE MIRACLE was slow in coming—and long overdue. Congressman Mark Stedman had been certain he *was* that miracle. All he'd needed was a chance ... and a little help.

The fifty-year-old congressman with sandy blond hair and blue eyes stared out the window of his limo and saw—perhaps for the first time in his twenty years in the nation's capital—how the accent lights fell just short of lighting all the way to the top of the 555-foot Washington Monument, the tallest structure in D.C. The obelisk was visible for miles at night—on this crystal-clear night in particular—but other than the aircraft warning lights, the very tip of the monument remained in shadow.

We couldn't even get that right, Mark thought, almost scolding himself. It was the irrational judgment of the disappointed and disillusioned. Words of the wounded ought never to be taken as gospel.

"You sure about this, sir? Your decision, I mean." The driver had obviously been itching to ask the congressman the question on everyone's mind since Mark had made his official announcement.

"As sure as anyone can be about anything these days," Mark said, then turned back to the window and continued staring at the monument as it shrank in the distance.

The driver glanced at Mark in the rearview mirror again, his eyebrows pushed together in a frown. He was clearly unsatisfied with the answer, but he said nothing. He turned his attention back to the road, leaving Mark alone with his thoughts as the luxury car maneuvered through the streets of Washington. The traffic was surprisingly light — unusual for the nation's capital this time of year. Spring, with its cherry-blossom pinks, magnolia whites, and trees of every shade of green imaginable, enticed people from all over the country to visit the capital of the United States in all its glory. But where were they on this day? Perhaps at home sitting in front of their televisions, catching up on the latest news in the world of politics. Or, more likely, after almost a year of being subjected to endless debates and negative campaign ads, staying as far away from the political mecca as possible.

It wasn't until the limo passed the Lincoln Memorial that Mark spoke again.

"What is it about this town?"

"What's that, sir?" The driver glanced in the rearview mirror again.

"You lived here long?"

"All my life."

"And it hasn't eaten you up yet?"

The driver eyed Mark in the rearview mirror, seemingly uncertain whether Mark expected an answer to the question or whether he was just venting. Perhaps thinking of his tip, the driver opted for diplomacy. "No ... but then I'm not in the trenches every day like you are, sir."

The Lincoln Memorial, another impressive D.C. monument, lit up the sky. Its thirty-six massive columns, symbolizing the thirty-six states in the Union at the time of Abraham Lincoln's death, stood in bold testament to the spirit of the man immortalized inside.

Honest Abe, sixteenth president of the United States, had been a hero of Mark's for as long as he could remember. He'd learned about him in grade school and had been fascinated with Lincoln's complicated life, both public and private, ever since. What was it about the lanky, witty, compassionate, and honest-to-a-fault law-yer that had caused him to rise from virtually nothing to become one of America's greatest presidents? Where did that kind of inter-nal strength come from, that ability to stand resolute in the face of scorn and ridicule and do the right thing? Whatever the source of that strength, it had struck a chord within a younger Mark, and his admiration of Lincoln held the seed that eventually drove the adult Mark into politics.

Tonight, though, Mark wondered if that seed had fallen on good soil. Perhaps he had been chasing a dream that was never intended for him. Maybe he should have been a plumber instead. Or a dentist. Or pursued any other occupation, for that matter. The presidency was too lofty a goal; politics too costly.

No one can say I didn't do my best for America, he thought.

Twenty years in Congress was a remarkable feat by anyone's standards. During those two decades of service, Mark had man-aged to champion plenty of good legislation for the country. Even when he threw his hat in the ring and signed up to run for presi-dent, he had believed he was doing the right thing.

Why shouldn't I give the presidency a try? he'd thought. *I have solid ideas on how to fix the country's problems and get her back on the right path.*

Lately those ideas had gotten held up in Congress, but as presi-dent, Mark could more easily move them along and bring them to fruition.

At least, that had been his plan.

It was the perfect time too. President Holt, the incumbent, had both surprised and — in some circles — pleased the nation by choosing not to run again. There were both positives and nega-tives to President Holt not seeking a second term. The positive? He was leaving the field wide open for both parties. The negative? He was leaving the field wide open for both parties.

It seemed that everyone was tossing their hats into the ring now. Of course, some of them weren't serious candidates — the alligator wrestler from Orlando, the reality-show star, the ice trucker from Anchorage. But among the more viable candidates were some very impressive men and women.

With the abundance of choices and the indecisiveness of the voters this go-round, a newcomer from either party could easily swoop in and take over the reins and responsibility of leading America. Mark was by no means a newcomer to Washington politics, but he'd never run for president before either. If he ever had a chance of winning a presidential election, though, this would have been the perfect election cycle.

But it was all history now. Because he hadn't pulled in the numbers necessary to stay in the race, Congressman Stedman had joined the long list of Washington's also-rans. That and a fistful of quarters wouldn't even get someone a parking space in this town. And with the economy tanking the way it was, who had a fistful of quarters anyway?

Monday-morning quarterbacking would say it was the polls that had killed Mark's presidential chances. The polls and party officials. The polls, party officials, and a severe lack of campaign funds. The polls, party officials, a severe lack of campaign funds, and his no-show at the last debate.

But that last one hadn't been Mark's fault. He hadn't even been invited.

"Not fair," he muttered to himself.

It wasn't fair, of course. A lot of things in Washington weren't. Mark—and every other candidate who had ever been passed over by party officials, the news media, or anyone else with the power to disrupt one's political hopes—had to accept that simple fact. If a candidate didn't pull in the polling numbers, he or she didn't get a microphone in the debates. Simple as that.

Shoot, even when you do get a microphone, someone still tries to shut you out, Mark thought. He recalled the 1980 presidential debate when the moderator told the Great Communicator —then-candidate Ronald Reagan—that he would cut off his microphone, and Reagan had snapped back, "I'm paying for this microphone!" *Maybe I should snap back.*

"Politics aren't for the thin-skinned," Mark said out loud, realizing he could use a few more layers of skin himself.

The driver nodded. "Definitely not for me," he agreed.

The debate snub had bothered Mark more than he had let on. And it had most certainly cost him any chance of increasing his poll numbers. If he wasn't taken seriously by the debate committee and his own party, it was a campaign death sentence.

He sighed and sat back. "Not for me anymore either, I suppose," he said. "Maybe it was just as well."

The congressman couldn't put his finger on it, but something had changed in Washington in recent years, and it was a change that left him with an unsettled feeling in the pit of his stomach. Both sides of the aisle had seen politicians who'd been sent to Washington to make a difference gradually lose their passion — the very passion that had gotten them elected in the first place.

It seemed that something was changing within the country too. Apathy had settled in. Many folks had lost the strength and the desire to stand up for anything. If an issue didn't affect their own lives or the lives of their immediate families, they ignored it. Malaise, or collective depression, had taken hold and spread faster than any swine or bird flu.

"Not sure how much people care anymore," Mark said.

"We're all just trying to survive," the driver said.

Mark had hoped to have a shot at returning his country to her greater self. He firmly believed that America was still an exceptional and noble nation, a grand experiment that still proved grand more than two hundred years later. Had she made mistakes? Yes. But what country hadn't? More than anything, Mark wanted her to survive.

At her core, America's heart was good, and she remained a symbol of freedom for the world to see and draw hope from. Mark had simply wanted to do what he could to jump-start patriotism again and help bring America back.

"I had a good plan," Mark said. "A plan to get Americans back to work and America back on course."

And he did. Only now he'd have to do it from his home in Wisconsin. He'd have to be one of those retired politicians who help from the sidelines, trying their best to keep their names in the news and their relevance intact.

Washington isn't my problem to fix anymore. I've put in enough years serving this country. It's time to let someone else take up the charge.

All Mark wanted to do now was get a good night's sleep. He had earned it.

The driver pulled up to the Willard Hotel—an upscale, historic hotel in the heart of D.C. Mark couldn't help but notice the media poised on the curb, awaiting someone's imminent arrival.

"Who's the story tonight?" he asked, curious.

"I believe you are, sir," the driver said.

The doorman opened the limo door, and Mark stepped out and began making his way through the crush of reporters with their microphones and camera flashes, assaulting his privacy.

"Congressman Stedman, when did you know you were going to drop out of the race?"

"Who will you be throwing your support to, sir?"

"Does your decision have anything to do with the fact that you were shut out of the recent debate?"

"Do you have anything to say to your supporters?"

The questions overlapped each other as Mark tried his best to get through the crowd, smiling however insincerely. He had never felt comfortable with this sort of thing, and on this night, he practically loathed it.

He hadn't foreseen any of this. He had truly believed he had a shot at winning the White House. Folding this early in the game was both a surprise and a disappointment to him.

When he'd been jostled enough, he gave in and took one of the reporters' outstretched microphones.

"As you know, earlier this evening I withdrew my candidacy for the office of president of the United States. I will simply repeat what I said at my press conference today: after much thought and prayer, and after consulting with my family, whom I love every bit as much as I love my country, I determined that withdrawing from this campaign was the right thing for me to do.

"That's all I have to say at this time."

With that, he nodded to the crowd, then turned and walked into the Willard. Reporters, hungry for that one last tidbit of information or clever sound bite, attempted to tail him through the entrance into the lobby of the grand old hotel, but they were effectively deterred by attentive doormen.

The Willard was a landmark. Known as the "residence of presidents," it had welcomed every commander in chief since Franklin Pierce. Abraham Lincoln had lived here before his inauguration. Mark Twain, Charles Dickens, Harry Houdini, P. T. Barnum, and Emily Dickinson had all stayed at the Willard. It was here that Martin Luther King Jr. wrote his famous "I Have a Dream" speech back in 1963, and Julia Ward Howe penned "The Battle Hymn of the Republic" while staying as a guest at the hotel in 1861. The hotel had history.

But on this particular night, Mark wasn't thinking about dreams or patriotic hymns. He was too busy processing the what-might-have-beens of his own life as he checked in and received his room key. All he wanted was to be done with this day.

Exhausted, he stepped into the elevator and waited as the doors closed, securing his peace if only for a brief moment. He was alone now, with only his reflection in the mirrored walls that surrounded him. He pitied that man in the mirror, the one who had given his best years to a country that didn't seem to know what it wanted now.

Fickle people.

Mark reached a new low. He had never blamed the voters before.

But ultimately, that's where the blame belongs, he thought.

If the numbers had been there, Mark wouldn't have been at this junction in his life. He would have been speaking at yet another rally or out delivering wisdom to all who would listen.

But he wasn't at a rally or a debate or even a television interview.

He was in an elevator, talking to an audience of one.

And even that audience was growing disinterested.

There were no words to encourage the tired, disheartened man who stared back at Mark from the mirror, and it saddened him to think that man in the mirror had nothing more to give.

The elevator arrived at Mark's floor, and he stepped out and made his way down the long hallway to his room. A luxurious suite appeared before him when he inserted his key into the door and opened it. Politics did have its perks. Mark was able to find a bit of solace in the fact that his bed had been turned down, mints had been placed on his pillow, and soothing music was already playing.

He sighed in surrender to his new political reality, grabbed the room-service menu, and began thumbing through it. It had been a long day. Mark wasn't sure he was hungry, but he knew he needed nourishment. He hadn't had a thing to eat since breakfast, and while he knew he could stand to lose a few pounds, he was sticking to an unwritten rule — never diet when you're down. *Depression* meant "buffet" in six languages. Why fight it?

Mark picked up the room phone and ordered a steak cooked medium rare, a loaded baked potato, and a salad with a double helping of bleu-cheese dressing.

Maybe this is what Lincoln ordered when he stayed here, Mark mused.

After his food arrived, and mostly out of habit, Mark turned on the television to watch a bit of the national news before calling it a night. He knew what he was in for, yet he was drawn to it. It was human nature — the same irresistible pull that compelled a driver to slow down and gawk at a three-car pileup. Or roadkill. Humanity was drawn to misery.

Why?

"Now that's a mystery that won't ever be solved." Mark chuckled wearily to himself.

Even if he was the roadkill for the night, he chose to watch the news programs anyway. His reasoning was simple: if he was being maligned in the news, it would be best to know about it as soon as possible so he could respond in a timely manner. So he could get his side of the story out quickly. That was the best, and sometimes the only, way to save a reputation.

But on this night, a part of Mark had lost interest even in that. The past twenty years — not to mention the presidential campaign — had taken their toll. Things had gotten rather nasty, and even though mudslinging dirtied both the thrower and the receiver of the sludge, Mark was worn out from all the ducking. It didn't even matter who was right anymore. People were going to believe what they wanted to believe; no amount of defense was going to change that. Lies were far more entertaining than the truth, and — as far as Mark could tell — most folks just wanted to be entertained these days.

As expected, he was the lead story on all the evening news shows. He settled on the third network broadcast he came to and turned up the volume.

"Congressman Mark Stedman dropped out of the presidential race today, narrowing the field yet again. Most political pundits say he was never a serious contender, garnering less than 10 percent in recent polls. His absence in the race will hardly be noticed."

The words stung.

"How could anyone even have known I was running when I was shut out of the process?" he barked at the reporter on the television screen before hurling a dinner roll her direction.

The bread bounced off the screen and onto the floor. He'd

wanted that roll too; that's how frustrating the system had been for him lately. Mark had never felt like an outsider in Washington prior to this election year, prior to declaring his candidacy for president. He had always been a team player, never stepping too far out of line to be a bother ... or make a difference. But ever since he decided to run for the highest office in the land, everyone he met seemed to want a piece of his hide. Even some of his long-time friends had turned on him. Not unusual for Washington. This city had a bad habit of eating its own.

"Who cares?" he said as he turned off the television and finished his dinner. He'd never liked that reporter anyway. Mark was proud of his record, whether or not anyone else recognized his accomplishments. He also knew he would have made a good president. Maybe even a great one.

It was a moot point now.

After taking the last bite of what might very well have been the best steak of his life, Mark flopped across the bed and tried to wish the day's events out of his mind. It worked, or at least something did, because within minutes, he was snoring peacefully, safe from the scrutiny of political analysts, the disloyalty of party leaders and friends, and the barbs of his opponents. He was in such a deep sleep, not even his nightmares could bring him to consciousness.

But a cell phone did. On the seventh ring.

Rising bleary-eyed, Mark squinted at the caller ID. "Cindy." He smiled.

"Hi, hon," he said sleepily after hitting the Answer button.

"Did I wake you?"

"No," he lied. "Everything okay? What time is it?" Mark wasn't sure if it was day or night; the curtains in his room let through no light.

"Everything's fine. I just miss you," she said.

Mark glanced at the alarm clock. It was twelve minutes past midnight. It felt much later. "Miss you too, babe."

Cindy Stedman was one of the benefits that had come from

Mark's political career. The daughter of Richard Henton, newspaper tycoon and a major contributor to Mark's earliest political endeavors, Cindy had caught Mark's eye when, as a college intern, she was helping with his mayoral campaign. During the campaign, Mark had fallen madly in love with Cindy—her contagious laughter, her tanned olive skin, the way her auburn hair glistened in the sunlight. Best of all, he loved how she never took herself too seriously—a quality absent in Mark. He knew he needed someone like Cindy in his life. And Cindy had believed in him unconditionally, both as a budding politician and her future husband.

Mark had ended up losing the mayoral campaign, but he had won Cindy's heart. And he had gained name recognition for the next time around, when he won the state congressional seat by a respectable margin. Mark had always credited the Henton family and Richard Henton's generous support with this victory and the turnaround of his political career.

After a brief courtship, Mark and Cindy married in a lavish ceremony suitable for a couple of their status, though neither of them had felt all that comfortable with the pomp and circumstance. They were private people at heart, thrust into the limelight —one by heritage, the other by calling.

That had been a long time ago.

"You're all over the news here, you know," Cindy told him. He could tell by her voice that she was both proud of him and disappointed over this latest turn of events.

"I wish it had turned out differently," he said. "You would have made a wonderful first lady."

"They probably wouldn't have liked my decorating style." She laughed.

Cindy had always been nontraditional, not afraid to make waves if necessary. Maybe that had been the secret that kept their marriage exciting—Cindy's unpredictability. Mark still found her as appealing as he did when they'd first met. She never ceased to fascinate him.

"It'll be good to be home," he said, wondering if she knew how much he meant that. It had been a grueling campaign. The last leg of his cross-country tour had him stomping through fourteen different cities in six days—a demanding schedule by anyone's standards.

"Everyone's disappointed, you know," she said. "Wisconsin loves you. People really believed you could have won it."

The words were soothing to Mark's wounded ego. But there was still that bothersome little thing called reality. It sure got in the way sometimes.

"It takes more than home-state loyalty and a good record to get you elected these days," he replied.

What exactly *did* it take to get elected in this current climate? Politics had become anything but conventional lately.

"Used to be all you had to do was meet and greet, kiss a few babies, hit at least one debate home run, and you had a good shot," he said. "But now, one minor slipup can cost you your entire political career."

He was right. In the past, even a scandal was survivable. Members of both parties could attest to that. But in recent years, with political enemies looking under every rock to find something disreputable on anyone daring to step into the election process, the outcome was often anyone's guess.

"It's over now," Mark said. "I'll be home soon."

"Wish you were flying."

"Me too," Mark agreed.

There was something appealing about the ability to arrive at one's destination within a few hours by plane. Who had time for road trips anymore? The country was in a hurry. The speed of nearly everything had increased—communication, cooking, travel. Even childhood only lasted about ten years these days—the age of Mark's youngest son, Marcus. After that, there was very little a parent could do to slow down the passage of time. Still, Mark tried to keep up with his son's world. Marcus owned all the latest iWhatevers, ensuring a strong father-son, techno-gadget relationship for years to come.

Lately Mark had been wishing he could spend more time with his son. He knew they were growing apart, a natural outcome of too much time spent on the road. Maybe now it would be possible to have some real one-on-one moments with the boy who looked so much like him. His teenagers, Carrie and Seth, had already built their walls. They lived in the same house, but barely. Maybe Mark would do better with Marcus.

But first he needed time to process the past few weeks. It had been a whirlwind, and whirlwinds left a good bit of destruction in their wake. Mark had to analyze the damage and put back together whatever he could. Then he could move on with his life.

Driving would delay his return home, but it was exactly what he needed to recover and regroup.

"A road trip will give me a chance to wind down," he told Cindy. "Maybe it'll be good for me."

"Well, drive safe," she said.

"I will. I love you."

"I love you too. I miss having you here next to me."

"Hold that thought till I get home. We'll celebrate."

"Celebrate, huh? Well, Congressman, I'm impressed."

"With ...?"

"You remembered."

"Remembered?"

"Our anniversary. It's a few days out, but it'd be nice to celebrate early. See, the counseling *has* helped."

Mark was fully awake now.

"Anniversary?" The word tumbled off his tongue.

How could I forget the most important date in my life?

Aloud he said, "Twenty-six wonderful years."

"Seven," corrected Cindy. "Twenty-*seven* years. But at least you remembered the date."

"You're going to love your present," he quickly assured her, wondering what time the hotel gift shop opened in the morning.

"Still no regrets about your decision?" Cindy asked.

"To drop out of the race or to marry you?"

"Both."

"No regrets at all about marrying you. As for the other ..." Mark hesitated and then picked up an Elect Stedman bumper sticker, looking at it thoughtfully. "The country wasn't ready for my message."

"Their loss," Cindy said.

Mark loved Cindy more than anything, but he knew she hadn't necessarily been able to tell these last few years. She had stepped back and given Mark his space — the space he said he needed to run a presidential campaign. But it seemed the more distance she had allowed to come between them, the more distance his job required. Or took. *Robbed* might have been an even better verb. Mark was certain that although she wouldn't admit it, Cindy was happy he had dropped out of the race. She would gladly give up the White House to have her husband back.

"We'll celebrate both," Mark said. "Our anniversary *and* the end of the campaign."

"It's a date, Congressman."

After hanging up, Mark lay awake for a while, staring up at the ceiling. Cindy deserved better from her husband. Now that the campaign was over, Mark vowed to himself that he would start putting Cindy first in his life again.

Yes, it would be good for both of them if Mark Stedman finally came home to stay.

CHAPTER 2

★

"H E WOULD'VE BEEN A SPOILER!" HARLEY PHILLIPS SAID AS HE gleefully slammed the morning's *Washington Post* down on his desk with such force it startled his secretary, Marcia Clayton. "Stedman did the right thing. Divide and the other side conquers!"

Harley Phillips knew politics. He should. He'd been a Washington congressman for as long as most people could remember; some speculated he'd been one all the way back to Lincoln's day. Although that was an obvious exaggeration, Harley was indeed a Washington mainstay. His longevity in Congress was legendary, following in the ranks of Ted Kennedy, Robert Byrd, Strom Thurman, and so many others who'd had a knack for winning reelections for decades on end.

Harley was overjoyed that Stedman had finally succumbed to the political process and had withdrawn from the campaign. Anyone with half an ounce of political savvy knew the Wisconsin congressman didn't stand a chance of winning this election.

"If you can't win, get off the racetrack!" Harley would often say of his opponents.

He was highly competitive, and he knew it. The dream of victory consumed him.

"I have nothing against Stedman personally," Harley said. "And our Gridiron routine was the best."

"The Washington press corps still talks about it," Marcia said.

"Of course they do. It was classic. Went viral on YouTube, you know. No one can accuse me of not being a team player."

"No, they can't, sir," Marcia said.

"But camaraderie has to step aside in an election year. It's every candidate for himself," Harley said.

"Or herself," Marcia added.

"Yes, well, perform in the polls or get out of the way! That's what I say. And Mark Stedman has finally gotten out of my way. Now we can all go about the business of electing the electable."

"That's right, sir."

"Who needs upstarts coming to Washington trying to change the status quo? It's taken years to get things to my liking in the House. I don't need Mark Stedman from Wisconsin suddenly getting the notion to start changing things by becoming president!"

Truth be known, Harley hadn't taken kindly to Stedman's presence in the House ever since the junior congressman first appeared on the House floor. And even though Mark had two decades of experience behind him now, Harley still referred to him as "Junior." And it wasn't meant as a compliment.

Yes, things were going Harley's way. Just how he liked it. As long as the country was headed in the same direction Harley Phillips was headed, he was a happy man.

———

Mark ignored the morning sun that peeked around the drapes for as long as he could, but he finally surrendered and opened his eyes. The numbers on the alarm clock surprised him —8:30!

"How could I sleep in this late?" Mark scolded himself. "I should have been on the road already."

He quickly threw on his clothes, tossed his belongings into his suitcase, and was out of his room in ten minutes flat. After taking the elevator to the lobby, he stopped by the front desk to check out. He didn't even bother with breakfast. If he got hungry, he'd grab a bite on the road.

Mark rolled his suitcase to the exit doors of the Willard (no sense bothering a bellman for one piece of luggage) and handed his parking ticket to the valet.

"I'll have it right up for you, sir," the valet said, as he took the ticket, then ran off toward the parking area.

Mark hoped the morning rush hour would be over by now, and he was eager to get far away from D.C. as quickly as possible.

The air was unseasonably thick with the kind of summer heat and humidity that Washingtonians always said they'd grown accustomed to, but no one really had. Mark pulled the collar of his shirt away from his sweaty neck and wondered how it could be this uncomfortable this early in the day this early in the year. It was April and not even ten o'clock in the morning!

An older couple stood near him, awaiting the arrival of their car as well. "Gonna be a hot one today," the man said, making friendly conversation.

Mark Stedman turned and nodded. The man immediately recognized him.

"Congressman Stedman?"

Mark smiled, and the man extended his hand. "Sir, it is an honor!" he said with sincerity. "You sure had our vote!"

The woman smiled, nodding her head in agreement. Then she reached into her purse and pulled out her camera, an action that didn't escape the scrutiny of her husband.

"Now, Agnes, we don't want to bother the congressman," the man said, noticeably embarrassed by his wife's potential breach of privacy.

"No problem," Mark said, motioning for Agnes to come stand by him.

A doorman offered to take the photo so that Agnes and her husband could be in the shot.

"This is very kind of you," Agnes said, bubbling with excitement. "Thank you so much!"

The doorman directed the couple to move in closer and then snapped a photo that was likely destined to be enlarged and framed and hung on the couple's wall as soon as they got home.

"Thank you, Congressman," the woman said to Mark.

"Happy to do it!"

And Mark meant it. He often felt uncomfortable with large crowds, but he was skilled at working the one-on-ones. He enjoyed making new friends wherever he went. It often happened exactly like this—a chance meeting of mere seconds. But Mark knew he could have sat down with this man and woman, total strangers, and it would have been like talking to old friends. Mark could read people that quickly and usually that accurately. These were his kind of folks.

"Sure wish you would've stayed in the race," the man said. "A bunch of us in Sarasota were going to vote for you. You were the best of the whole lot."

Mark smiled. "Thanks!" Validation felt good to anyone, especially the wronged. "Wasn't meant to be, I guess."

"Will you run again?" Agnes asked.

"I don't know, but I'll tell you one thing I learned a long time ago: never say never."

"Well, we sure hope you'll consider it," the man said. "The country needs a back-to-the-basics president like you ... especially now."

Mark knew what the man meant without his having to elaborate. Over the years, the country had developed a severe distrust of many of its elected officials in both parties. Some of that distrust had been rightfully earned; some of it was guilt by association. Regardless, most folks would say they were looking for a new kind of leader this election year. What that was, and who that was, was anyone's guess.

The valet drove Mark's government vehicle up to the hotel

entrance, exchanged the keys for his tip, and then opened the door for Mark.

This trip would be Mark's last approved use of his government vehicle. The previous night the limo service had picked him up, but now he was taking the remainder of his personal belongings home in his government car. He would later drive it back to Washington to turn it in and then fly home to Wisconsin. He had some government duties and loose ends to tie up before he could say he was totally free from the political scene. How long his absence from politics would last was a question even he couldn't answer. But for right now, he looked forward to the respite.

Mark waved a friendly good-bye to his new friends.

"I'm still gonna vote for you!" Agnes promised, holding her camera close to her heart.

"My name won't even be on the ballot," Mark laughed.

"That's okay. I'll write it in!" she said.

"I suppose you could," Mark replied, impressed with such loyalty, "but you'll be my only vote." They all laughed.

"The next time you run, we want to help," the man said, handing Mark his business card.

"Don't say that to a politician," Mark said. "We'll hold you to it!"

"I hope you do."

With a final good-bye, Mark drove away from the Willard. Next stop Wisconsin.

CHAPTER 3

★

ONCE ON THE BELTWAY, MARK REACHED OVER AND TURNED on the car stereo. Music always made the drive seem shorter to him, and if he needed anything on this particular day, it was to get home quickly, home to the waiting arms of his beloved Cindy. He may have forgotten that their anniversary was rapidly approaching, but Cindy was his everything. In the tumultuous sea of politics, she was what kept him afloat. He hadn't told her that, not lately anyway. Mark had been so busy with the presidential election—and before that, all his congressional duties—time had slipped through his fingers, and he simply hadn't had any leftover hours, or minutes even, for the more important things. But Cindy was what mattered most in Mark Stedman's life. He knew that in his heart, and she knew it too. He was certain of it.

Besides, he told himself, *I will never again forget our anniversary.*

A noble promise, but one he would probably unintentionally break. Mark was terrible at remembering dates—a shortcoming that drove his staff to the brink on more than one occasion. But an anniversary was different. Some men only got one chance to forget something that significant. And Mark was determined not to ever blow it again.

The gift! Mark suddenly remembered. He was already on the road, but he told himself he would stop somewhere along the way and get Cindy something. Something meaningful. He recorded a note to himself on his iPhone, just to be safe.

Even though Mark had forgotten their anniversary—which he had—and even if Cindy had known about it—which she didn't—she no doubt would have given him a free pass. She was forgiving like that. Oh, she would have kept it in the back of her mind for future leverage, to be sure. Cindy Stedman was forgiving and unconditionally loving, but she wasn't stupid. A forgotten anniversary could be worth several movie nights out with the girls or one good shopping spree, at least ... within reason, of course. Cindy could never be accused of being frivolous, but she did enjoy keeping up with the latest styles.

While stopped at a light, Mark opened his cell-phone calendar and scrolled through the rest of the month of April. It was full of appointments:

Meeting with Governor Hennessey—11:00 a.m.

Lunch with Keith Stevens—12:15 p.m., Capitol lunchroom.

Banquet—7:00 p.m., Library of Congress.

And that was just for tomorrow, April 12! The remainder of the month was every bit as packed.

Mark made a call to his campaign manager, Carl Wilson, who was back in Wisconsin.

"Clear my schedule, Carl," he said. The light turned green, but Mark continued, "Take everything off the books."

"All of it, sir?" Carl said. "But some of these events are ..."

"Clear it all. At least through May. And start the process of shutting down operations."

"Everything, sir?"

A car horn brought Mark's attention back to his driving. "I'm coming home," he said. He waved an apology to the driver in the car behind him and proceeded down the beltway, recalling the Hang Up and Drive legislation he'd voted for in Congress.

Mark concluded his instructions to Carl and told him he would be in touch. Disconnecting the call, he sighed as he thought about his decision to drop out of the presidential race. Mark had received comments from some of his supporters saying they felt he had let them down, had abandoned the country when the country needed him most.

"What choice are you leaving us voters?" they had asked. "Harley Phillips? Mitch Caldron? Randolph Sutter? Anne Kurtzfield? Governor Karen Ledbetter? Seriously?"

By most accounts, neither party had much to offer voters this go-round. It was a lackluster lineup, to say the least.

Mark prided himself on being a man of his convictions. He might brush his convictions to the side on occasion, but he would never fully surrender them. He stood firm and refused to let lobbyists influence his vote. He was a vocal champion of term limits, balanced budgets, and green causes. Not a cookie-cutter politician, Mark marched to the beat of his own opinions rather than the political correctness of the day. He had courage, or so he thought. One thing was certain — he was the shot in the arm that the presidential campaign needed, the missing link of excitement. But party officials wouldn't support him, and he had grown tired of the fight.

Mark Stedman was tired, *period.*

He turned on the radio to listen to some soothing music, but a special news bulletin caught his attention instead.

"According to a recent poll, 80 percent of the American public believe Washington is broken," the reporter said.

"Don't blame me," Mark admonished the reporter. "I tried."

There were plenty of good people in Congress who had tried too. People who loved this country and had sacrificed a lot to serve it. The change in their spirit hadn't happened overnight; it had happened gradually. A frustration here. A disappointment there. Filibusters, gridlock, media reports slanted one way or the other. It was no wonder that the dreams they'd brought with them when they first came to Washington had turned into doubts, passion had become passiveness, and possibilities had settled into limitations.

And now their apathy reflected the nation's apathy. When they tried new ideas and solutions, the ideas and solutions backfired on them. Or were ignored. Who could blame them for not sticking out their necks again and continuing to try?

"What was it all for, anyway? Twenty years ... It's time to move on."

Mark Stedman had seen the change happening to him, too, but he fought against it. That's why he had entered the presidential race—to take on the apathy that was turning into an epidemic. But the antidote to apathy is a fire in one's belly, and Mark had allowed his fire to slowly go out.

Other politicians would be joining his exit from Washington politics; it was just a matter of time. Only theirs might not be by choice. No seat in Congress was safe these days—House or Senate. The president's reelection wouldn't have been guaranteed in this kind of political atmosphere. No wonder he decided not to run. Elected officials were one misstep and one long election night away from being sent home. "Lie low" was the mantra of politicians this election year.

But not a lot got done when one was lying low.

Wall Street wasn't helping matters any either. Its breath-snatching market swings were the lead story most nights on the evening news. Not since the Great Depression had there been such volatility in the market. A four-hundred-point drop, a three-hundred-point gain, a five-hundred-point nosedive—often in the same day! The big board was having seizures. It was the kind of financial environment that sends stock in antacid companies soaring.

The only thing predictable about the stock market lately was its unpredictability. No politician with any thoughts of survival wanted to be the one calling for the lifeboats the same hour the stock market was shooting up six hundred points. Nor did any politician want to be the one telling the American public that the country was on the road to recovery just as Wall Street hit a sinkhole, and 20 percent of America's wealth was swallowed into oblivion.

Lie low.

This was the time to sit on the sidelines and let things settle down before voicing an opinion on anything. One could hardly blame the politicians, who were diving for cover instead of governing, concerned over their own fortunes and comfy retirement plans. In this kind of atmosphere, it was every politician for himself. Or herself.

"What was I thinking when I decided to run for president in this kind of mess?" Mark Stedman thought out loud. It was a suicide mission. Who needed it?

In his gut, Mark knew that if voters had only listened to him, if he had only been given the chance to explain his solutions, he could have made a difference. But he hadn't been given that chance. And now he was headed home.

Mark was surprised at how small the Washington skyline appeared in his rearview mirror. In all his years of service, it had never looked more insignificant and inconsequential than it did at this moment. There was so much more to him than the politics of D.C. He could see that now. Still, his departure from the capital city seemed surreal. It felt odd to leave this other life behind. There was a sadness to his leaving, but Mark didn't dwell on it or turn around to go back. Instead he drove onto the expressway and headed west.

———

"Did you read this?" Harley Phillips asked Stacy Creighton, his campaign manager, as he waved a weekly news magazine in front of him. Stacy nodded his head, but Harley was sure Stacy had no idea what article he was talking about.

"Eighty percent of Americans say Washington's broken! Eighty percent! You agree with that?" Harley said.

"Yes, sir, I do." Stacy hurried the words out of his mouth as he always did before Harley could take his hesitation as a form of weakness.

"So do I. It is broken!" Harley said. "And I'm just the guy to fix us!"

Harley came from a long line of politicians who had red tape coursing through their veins. Harley's father had been governor of Mississippi for two terms, and his grandfather had been Speaker of the House for close to a decade, dying of natural causes before he could serve out his full term.

Harley Phillips thought he knew exactly what was wrong with America and, like Mark and all the other candidates running for president, he was convinced that he, and he alone, was the answer. Washington was broken because it hadn't done everything *Harley* had been proposing it do throughout his years in Congress. He had more know-how and experience than any other politician in Washington, and he knew what was best for the country. But Congress hadn't listened to him, and now just look at the shape they were in.

As president, Harley would have more power to get his plans enacted. It was his time, his season, and at long last, his rightful turn. Harley Phillips would be sworn in as president of the United States come the following January, if he had anything to say about it. And he planned on saying plenty.

———

THE DRIVE FROM D.C. TO WISCONSIN WOULD TAKE ABOUT FOUR-teen and a half hours, according to Mark's semi-trustworthy GPS, which he'd mounted on the dashboard of the car. He'd never learned to operate the ones that came with the various government vehicles. He preferred to use his own, despite the fact that he had never gotten along with the lady navigator inside his device. He wasn't sure why, but she seemed to have it out for him. He figured she must have different political views than he did. That had to be what put her in a perpetually testy mood. Whatever it was, she was far more vocal than Cindy had ever been when it came to backseat driving. Mark especially resented the lady's interference in areas where he clearly knew more than she knew, like on this journey between Washington and Wisconsin. It was a run he had taken hundreds of times. He could drive it in his sleep —and had on more occasions than he'd ever tell his insurance company. As long as he stayed on the highways, he was fine. So who could blame him for ignoring the pesky meddler-in-a-box on this particular trip?

No techno-genius, Mark preferred tracking his trip the old-fashioned way—from Cracker Barrel to Cracker Barrel. When he got hungry, he'd park the government vehicle in the rear of the restaurant (no sense bringing added attention to himself) and throw on a ball cap. No one would even realize that a former presidential candidate was in their midst. He'd be just one more customer sitting by the fireplace asking for another basket of cornbread. Besides, while there, he could pick up a present for Cindy in the Cracker Barrel gift shop.

Mark continued to ignore the bothersome Lady of the Dashboard. He mainly just kept her around for emergencies anyway. So when she strongly suggested that he take an alternative route some scarce one hundred miles outside of D.C., he couldn't follow her logic.

"This isn't the time to go sightseeing," Mark said to the Lady. "I'm on a mission to get home to my family."

Maybe I can finally catch some of Marcus's Little League games or we could go on some long overdue family outings that might even entice Carrie and Seth to join. It's never too late for a family man to get to know his family.

Mark wanted the shortest route available and that didn't involve country roads, so he ignored the voice and drove west on the interstate. West was the direction he needed to go. Anyone with a basic knowledge of geography knew Wisconsin was northwest of the District of Columbia.

"Take the next exit and head northeast to avoid road construction ahead."

"I don't see any road construction," Mark said.

It didn't take long for Mark to realize how much the Lady of the Dashboard did know. He was quickly stuck in a bumper-to-bumper trail of red lights that stretched for miles ahead of him. All four lanes of the expressway were being funneled down to one —never a good sign—and motorists had begun communicating in the language of their car horns.

Great, Mark thought. *Who approved this?*

Mark wasn't in the mood for "Men at Work" or—more likely he figured—"Men *Not* at Work."

After what seemed like hours, Mark grew desperate and reached over to punch new information into his GPS. He didn't care if the Lady of the Dashboard threw in an "I told you so." He was ready to listen to her now, ready to take whatever detour she recommended.

"Take the next exit and ..."

Mark followed her instruction and moved over to the far right lane, but he still had to wait ten additional minutes before being able to exit the highway. It would have taken even longer, but as soon as he was close enough, Mark pulled onto the shoulder and drove on it until he reached the off-ramp. A few people honked as he passed them on the right, but no matter.

"I'm on official government business," Mark said under his breath. "Party officials wanted me to get out of town, so I'm obliging them." The chuckle Mark got over that self-deprecating comment almost made the traffic jam worth it.

Once off the highway and out of the congestion, Mark settled back to enjoy the lush green landscape that now surrounded him. Wherever this detour was taking him, at least it was pastoral and peaceful. It was also leading him away from an angry thunderstorm that appeared to be brewing to the south. The greenish tint to the clouds made them look especially menacing, not unusual for spring in the northeast.

"Okay, I confess," Mark said to the Dashboard Lady, though it pained him to do so. "You were right."

Mark Stedman may have had his faults, but he wasn't above giving credit where credit was due.

Before he got too far down the unplanned path, Mark called Cindy using his headset so he could keep his hands on the wheel and eyes on the road. It was Mark and Cindy's agreement to always inform each other of their whereabouts while traveling. One couldn't be too careful these days.

Most people liked Congressman Stedman, but it was a rare politician who didn't receive at least one death threat from some misguided zealot or anonymous lunatic. There were already some politically active bloggers who had taken an especially tough stance on the congressman and some of his voting history, and a few who seemed to simply ramble on and on about all things Stedman. That came with the territory, Mark figured. Neither he nor Cindy wanted to dwell on the dangers of a life in the political limelight, but it was worth taking a few precautions.

"Hi." Cindy's voice sounded in his ear.

"Hey, hon," he said. Unfortunately, it was Cindy's voice mail. This wonder of modern technology had tricked him before. The recording was so clear, it sounded exactly like Cindy. But Mark was surprised that he'd fallen for it again.

"This is Cindy. Please leave your message at the sound of the beep," the recording continued.

Mark hung up, preferring to wait and talk to Cindy live. He figured Cindy would see his name in her Missed Calls list and call him back as soon as she could.

Wanting to be certain that the storm was indeed moving away from him, Mark fiddled with the stereo, searching for a station that would give him a weather update. The last thing he needed was to get stuck in the middle of nowhere in a flash flood. Or a tornado. One tornado had already dropped unexpectedly into his life this week with that obvious debate snub, and its devastating aftermath had destroyed his political aspirations and hopes. He didn't need another one.

Mark continued scanning the stereo for a weather station, but the result was mostly static. Eventually Mark found one local station that was talking about everything *except* the weather. He listened for a few minutes, never hearing which way the storm was heading. He did, however, learn whose tractors were on sale that weekend.

He scanned the stations again, ultimately landing on a news radio station. He hoped they would cover the weather at some point. After a few minutes of inconsequential news, he heard his name and turned up the volume.

"While Mark Stedman is being tight-lipped about who he'll be endorsing, the question on everyone's mind is what's next for the former congressman who resigned from his post to run for president," the announcer said.

"Getting as far away from Washington as I can!" Mark replied. His habit of talking to himself was the result of driving too many places alone. He hadn't done this in front of anyone, but it was something he felt quite comfortable doing within the confines of his car. Sometimes he'd even debate against himself, presenting both sides of an argument rather eloquently. That was how he knew he could have delivered a masterful performance in the presidential debate. But it was not to be.

Not in the mood for any more political commentaries from the news station, Mark reached over and turned off the stereo. It hadn't been much help anyway. As far as the weather was concerned, he'd have to revert to doing it the way his father had taught him — by simply reading the clouds. And so far, he had dodged the bullet.

With each passing mile, the countryside grew more and more tranquil, fertile, and breathtakingly beautiful — and more and more remote. As much as he hated to do it, he was now forced to blindly follow the directions of his GPS. The Lady of the Dashboard knew more than he did about this area, and without a single gas station in sight or an impossible-to-refold map in the car, he had no other choice.

Her voice guided him north and then west through the heart of Pennsylvania, continuing in the direction of Wisconsin by way of a long and out-of-the-way trek through Lancaster County. In all the years he had traveled between D.C. and Wisconsin, Mark had never taken a side trip through Lancaster County. He was both pleased and annoyed to be doing it today.

CHAPTER 4

★

THE LADY OF THE DASHBOARD WAS REALLY BEGINNING TO GET on Mark's nerves. He was starting to relax, taking in the beauty of his surroundings, when her irritating voice suddenly broke through the silence yet again, telling him in no uncertain terms to make an immediate right. Not to turn two hundred feet down the road, not to turn at the next stop light, but *now.* Mark ignored her, but the lady was insistent. The only problem was, if he executed the right turn here—where she demanded he execute it—he would end up in the middle of a pond. Unless the woman was on Harley Phillips's payroll, Mark figured her wires were probably in a wad, or at the very least, crossed.

Mark typed his destination into the device once more, but the woman merely told him to drive into the pond again. She sounded like a broken record and was clearly wrong, but Mark knew she'd never admit it. He had no choice but to give the misbehaving device a good whack to the side of the screen, hoping to knock some sense into it.

It worked ... sort of.

"Recalculating," the lady said, and then changed her directions. "Continue straight ahead for a quarter mile and turn left."

True, these new directions didn't take Mark into a pond now. This time they would land him in the middle of a cornfield.

Mark Stedman thought fondly of the old rabbit-ear-TV-antenna days when a twist here, a tweak there, and a slap to the side of a television set would bring the picture back. A creature of habit, he was always trying his old-school methods on today's new technology to make it behave, but it didn't always work.

Another whack to the side of the screen.

"Recalculating," the voice said. "Continue going straight for one mile."

Mark looked straight ahead. In just one hundred feet, the road ended. He bit his lip. The Lady of the Dashboard obviously didn't know what she was talking about. He drove the hundred feet and stopped in front of a sign with two arrows. One arrow pointed to the left, and the other arrow pointed to the right. Neither gave any hint as to what lay to the left or to the right; however, if Mark were to drive straight ahead, as the lady was instructing him to do, he would drive right into a herd of cattle.

Mark banged on the device again and reprogrammed his destination. He was beyond frustrated. Unless he wanted to end up in a pond or being charged by a sizable and short-tempered bull, he had to come up with another plan. No one was behind him or crossing the road in front of him. It was just Mark and the Dashboard Lady out there on that lonely stretch of country road.

Perfect, he thought.

"Look, lady. You told me to turn right, and you were wrong. You told me to turn left, and you were wrong. Now you're just messing with my head! Well, listen here—I'm not driving into a pond or a cornfield or through a herd of bovine. So you got another plan?"

Mark waited, but there was no answer.

"Yeah, I didn't think so!" he said.

Mark sat for a moment, alternating his gaze from the left to the right. There was no clear choice—green, rolling hills one way; green, rolling hills the other way. He could just toss a coin to determine his direction.

"Recalculating," the lady's voice interrupted the moment.

Mark could feel his blood pressure bubbling to the boiling

point, so he made a Plan B himself. He wanted to rip the GPS off the dashboard and toss it — along with the monotone, nagging lady inside it — out his window, where no one, except the bull that was staring intently at him from across the field, would see it. Mark was sure that the bull wouldn't blame him for his actions. Being the only male in the herd, chances are he'd also had to deal with a nagging cow or two in his life.

Mark was a reasonable man, though, so he gave the Dashboard Lady one last chance.

"All right. This is it, lady! You brought me all the way out here to the middle of nowhere. Talk to me. What do I do now, genius?"

"Continue going straight for two miles."

Straight? Once again she was leading Mark into the bull's territory.

"Obviously, I'm on my own," Mark sighed, accepting his fate.

"Recalculating," the lady promised again.

"I'm ignoring you," Mark said.

"When safe, turn around and proceed east."

"I don't care what you say. I'm doing it my way now!" Mark said, turning left.

"Recalculating."

"You had your chance!"

"Recalculating. Proceed west."

Mark ignored the confused navigator, continuing his drive until all he could hear was static. The Dashboard Lady had completely lost connection with him now; he couldn't listen to her even if he wanted to.

"The silent treatment now? That's what you're giving me?" Mark said. It was the final straw. "Okay, that's it! You've let me down for the last time!"

He gave in to his primal instincts, leaned over, grabbed the GPS, ripped out its cord, and threw it out the window. The nagging, recalculating, obstinate, intrusive voice was silenced forever!

Mark felt vindicated—as only a chronically nagged driver can—but only briefly.

While he'd been exacting his overdue vengeance, he had taken his eyes off the road. When he looked forward again, he was careening off the shoulder of the road and straight into a ditch!

Mark slammed on the brakes, but it was too late. He rode the ditch and steered the car up the slight incline on the other side, crashing into a fencepost that stood unyieldingly in front of him. The black government car rested, mangled and steaming, on the wrong side of the ditch.

Mark's week was not improving in the least.

Other than a few cuts and bruises and feeling understandably shaken up, Mark was uninjured. His blood pressure, however, had soared to new heights, along with his temper.

"Great," he said, pounding his fist on the steering wheel. "Just great!"

The engine was coughing and sputtering, but at least it was showing some signs of life. But Mark couldn't get the wheels to budge in the least. They seemed to be frozen in place, making a loud grinding noise every time he attempted to turn the steering wheel. He wiped some blood off his bottom lip, and got out of the car to assess the damage. As he had suspected, the axle was badly bent. He tried turning the steering wheel to see what was happening underneath the car, but the damage prevented the wheel from moving at all. Steam was now starting to spew from the radiator as well, indicating a possible puncture. The car might be fixable, but it certainly wasn't drivable in its present condition.

Mark turned off the engine and pulled his cell phone out of his pocket so he could make a call. No network. He walked around a bit and looked again. No success. Annoyed, he shoved the phone back into his pocket.

"No reception," he said out loud. "Seriously, God? Did I need this?"

He meant no disrespect to the Almighty. He had grown used

to talking to God that way—open, honest, as a friend or, more frequently, as a whining child to his long-suffering Father. Not that he wasn't thankful too. There were plenty of things in his life to give thanks for, but there was a lot in Mark's life that left him dissatisfied. His dissatisfaction, however, was almost always voiced in private prayer. Privately, he had no problem saying whatever came to mind or telling God exactly what had annoyed, confused, angered, or hurt him throughout the day. God wouldn't audibly answer him, of course. But he would answer. Sooner or later, he would answer. And on this day, God seemed to be saying, "Yes, Mark Stedman, you *do* need this."

Mark was far from happy about his current predicament. His wrecked government car was in a ditch, he had no cell-phone reception, and there wasn't a single house in sight. It did seem like some divine joke was being played on him, and he wasn't in the mood for it.

Just then, Mark looked down the road and thought he saw a glimmer of sunlight bouncing off something in the far distance. Could it be a car coming down the road toward him?

Now that would *be a miracle,* he thought.

Mark kept his eyes on the object as it moved closer—one inch at a time, it seemed. He watched and he waited. And he watched and he waited some more. When the object got closer still, Mark stood in the middle of the road waving his arms at it like a wild man.

And yet he still couldn't make out what it was. It was too far away.

"Enough of that," he grumbled and then sat back down by the side of his wreck. It was much too hot to be standing out in the sun, flailing his arms. He would wait until the object got close enough, and then he'd flag it down. Where else would it be going, anyway? With no houses in sight, the car—or whatever it was—would have to pass right by him. Eventually.

When the object was closer, Mark stood and waved his arms

again, whistling and hollering. He could see it clearly now. Only it wasn't a car. It was a horse-drawn buggy moving at an incredibly leisurely pace. Whoever was in there certainly wasn't in a hurry.

Mark watched as the buggy approached. He had to admit he was a little jealous of whoever was living life so patiently, able to take so much time to enjoy his surroundings, seemingly without a care or a stress in the world. Oh, for the freedom and additional hours in the day to do such a thing.

When the buggy got close enough, a bearded man inside pulled back on the reins.

"Whoa!" the stranger said, bringing his horse to a stop. Glancing over at the mangled car in the ditch, he asked, "You hurt?"

"No, but it looks like I'm going to need a tow. Know of any close by?"

The man, who was clearly Amish, looked at Mark for a brief moment and then smiled. "I don't personally have much use for an automobile tow," he said.

"Sorry." Mark apologized for his tactless error. "No, I don't suppose you would. No disrespect intended."

"None taken," the Amish man said. "Got a couple of draft horses that might be able to pull you out, though."

Mark laughed. "Calling a tow would probably be quicker, don't you think?"

"S'pose it would."

Get the car towed to town, get it fixed, and I'll be on my way.

"It'd be quicker, all right," the man said, "if the shop was open today."

"It's closed?"

"Had a wedding in the family. Down in Kentucky. Sign on the shop said they'd be back in a couple of days."

"Anyone else around here work on cars?"

"They're the closest."

"You really think your horses could manage it?" Mark asked, grasping at any straw.

"Between the two of them and the two of us, we might be able to do it. They're strong horses."

Mark laughed to himself over the thought of a couple of draft horses pulling a car—a government car, no less—out of a ditch. But then he remembered a YouTube video that had made the rounds among his office staff. It had been of an Amish man and his team of horses pulling a semitruck out of a ditch. So it was possible, he supposed.

"Well, if you're sure it's no trouble."

"Can't speak for the horses, but I don't think they'd mind. Get in—I'll take you up to my house, and we'll hitch 'em up."

"Thanks," Mark said, as he climbed into the buggy. "I sure do appreciate it."

The Amish man snapped the reins, and with a click of his tongue, the buggy started down the road. Mark thought the stranger was friendly enough, but since he had never talked at length with an Amish person before, he wasn't quite sure how to start up a conversation.

What should I talk about? he wondered.

"Name's Josiah," the Amish man said, breaking the silence.

"I'm Mark." Mark was pleased that the man didn't appear to recognize him. He wouldn't have to answer a string of questions about why he had dropped out of the presidential race or what his future plans might be. There were precious few occasions to enjoy anonymity, so when one came along, Mark savored every minute of it.

"My wife's probably got dinner ready," Josiah said. "You eaten yet?"

"No, but I don't want to impose on you and your family. Maybe if I could just call Triple-A from your house, I'll be ..." Mark stopped, realizing too late what he was saying. That was twice. "Sorry," Mark apologized again. "It's been a long week."

"There's a Mennonite family with a phone 'bout five miles down the road or so. They let us use it for emergencies. I'd be happy to run you over there so you can make a call . . . if you don't trust my horses to pull you out."

"It's not that. I just wouldn't want to put you out any."

"No bother at all."

"Well, where would the tow be coming from?"

"Town. We're in Lancaster County, but it's fairly spread out. Town's 'bout ten miles down the road from my house. But like I said, it's no bother."

Mark didn't want to offend the man by not taking him up on his generous offer of the "tow horses." It was the politician in him. And there was something else in him that wanted to see the horses do it.

"Ten miles, huh? Well, if you're sure you don't mind."

"Wouldn't offer it if I did. Might save you some money too. Nothing wrong with that, *jah*? We could have your car out of there in no time. Your choice, though. How bad do you figure the damage is?"

"Axle is broken, and the radiator's probably got a leak," Mark said.

"I could probably help with some of that."

"You got the tools?"

"Got my farm tools. Might be able to hammer the axle back in place. You'll need help with the radiator though. I've got a Mennonite cousin in Bird-in-Hand who fixes those. But first things first."

"Well, whatever it takes to get me back on the road."

"You late getting somewhere?"

"Yeah, home. About twenty years too late." Mark didn't say much more as they continued down the road. He figured it was the only way to guarantee his foot staying out of his mouth — a trick he'd learned early in his political career. He didn't know enough about the Amish to avoid any more verbal gaffes. Sometimes silence really could be golden.

It was Josiah who finally broke the awkward silence.

"I apologize if you're someone I should know," he said.

Oh no. Here it comes.

"Are you a new neighbor?"

"No. Just passing through."

"Where's home for you?"

"Wisconsin."

"You *are* lost," Josiah said, then clicked his tongue again to get his horse to pick up the pace a bit.

———

JOSIAH'S BUGGY HORSE, DAYBREAK, HAD BEEN A LOYAL FRIEND and service horse to the Stoltzfus family ever since Josiah bought her at a Lancaster town auction. She was a former harness-racing mare, which accounted for her graceful gait and high step. It had taken a while for her to fully switch from her former life to that of an Amish buggy horse, and on more than one occasion, she'd taken Josiah for a good race through the streets of Lancaster, leaving him hanging on for dear life, his broad-brimmed hat flying off in the wind. Eventually, though, Josiah had managed to get DayBreak to settle down and leave the racing to the automobiles of the English.

Josiah took good care of all his horses, but DayBreak was his favorite. They had a special bond. Not only had Josiah almost lost her the night she was delivering her foal, but he'd personally nursed her back to health after someone — most likely an unaware tourist — had given her some junk food to eat. Josiah didn't harbor ill will toward the misguided visitor, even after having to stay up all night for three nights out in the barn with DayBreak. He merely figured whoever had done it simply hadn't realized that buggy horses have their own diet, and it's best to leave their feeding to their owners.

"Well, all I can say is I sure hope she's happy."

"Who?" Josiah asked, puzzled.

"That nagging woman."

"I'm sorry. I thought you were alone. Did you drop off someone before I found you? I don't mind going back to pick her up if you need me to."

Mark laughed. "No. I'm alone. I'm talking about my navigational device. Sorry, it's a car thing," he corrected himself quickly.

"Oh, I see. Your GPS," Josiah said.

"You know about them? I didn't think the Amish knew about such —"

"We read approved books. And talk to tourists."

"But you don't use them, do you?"

"DayBreak here's my GPS," Josiah said, nodding toward his horse. "Knows these parts better than I do."

"Well, you're better off. A lady's voice speaks through my GPS and gives me directions ... and gets me lost. She nags at me to follow her crazy directions, and then when I don't, she'll just keep telling me to 'Recalculate' until I want to throttle her. It's her fault I'm in this mess."

"She told you to drive into the ditch, eh?"

"No. But she sure caused the accident," Mark replied. His tone of voice made it clear that he wasn't about to take the blame.

"But you were the one driving, *jah?*"

Mark gave a half nod.

Josiah continued. "You know, we Amish have a saying," he said. "Don't blame the horse when you've got the reins."

"Touché," Mark said.

"Too what?" Josiah wondered about this man who used funny words and was twenty years late getting home to his family. But Mark seemed friendly enough.

"Touché. It means 'you're right.'"

"Well, getting lost can sometimes be a *gut* thing, *jah?*"

"Don't tell me that's how you ended up here."

"No. But it's how my wife did. Although my wife and I both grew up Old Order Amish. I met her when her family was passing through our community on their way to the big auction. They took a wrong turn and had to stop to ask directions. I saw Elizabeth sitting in the buggy and talked to her for a bit. She told me where she lived, and after that, we wrote letters and eventually married."

"It was meant to be, huh?"

"I believe it was, *jah*. So that's why I say when we lose our way, it can sometimes be a *gut* thing. Maybe there are reasons you're here, Mark."

Mark laughed again. "Yeah, I took my eyes off the road and drove into a ditch."

Josiah turned the buggy up his driveway. It led to his quaint house, which was built on top of a slightly sloping hill. The house was freshly painted white, and Elizabeth's garden was growing off to the side of it. Their goats and sheep grazed in the field next to the barn, along with their draft horses that watched the buggy's approach from their vantage point.

"I'm serious now. You're welcome to break bread with us," Josiah said as he continued up the drive toward the house.

"Thanks, but I know what my own wife would say if I brought home unexpected company for lunch."

"We always have room at the table for more. And by the way, in these parts, we don't call it *lunch*. It's *dinner*," Josiah said with a friendly laugh. "Supper's our evening meal."

———

MARK LIKED PEOPLE WITH A HEALTHY SENSE OF HUMOR, PEOPLE who didn't take themselves too seriously. He wished he could be more like that himself. If he had to end up in a ditch in the middle of nowhere and hitch a ride with a stranger though, he was glad it was with someone who was as easygoing as Josiah.

"I stand corrected again," Mark said. "Dinner it is. Thank you for the invitation."

Three children, all dressed in typical Amish clothing, were playing in front of the house.

"Your kids?" Mark asked, as they moved up the driveway.

Josiah smiled and nodded. "My quiver is full."

"Quiver?"

"It's a Bible thing."

"Guess I missed that part," Mark said, noting to himself to look it up later.

"It means I've been abundantly blessed with children. Mary Ann's inside helping her mama in the kitchen. She's our teenager."

"I got a couple of those kicking at my quiver too. Don't see 'em much. Even when they're home, they've got their faces glued to the latest techno-gadget. Sure do miss the younger years."

Mark was serious. He did miss when his children had been so young and innocent, when he and Cindy—rather than their kids' peers and the media—were the major influences of their decisions. He missed those times when his kids would squeal with delight and run to him when he returned home from Washington, throwing their arms around him while calling, "Daddy! Daddy!" He missed when he'd tuck them in at night and read them a bedtime story. Actually, Mark couldn't recall reading his children any bedtime stories, but he felt justified giving himself poetic license for that pseudomemory. Whatever he did or didn't do as a father, he still missed the younger age.

"You've got to enjoy all the stages of life, my friend," Josiah said.

"I know. It's just that in our world there's a lot that competes for a teenager's attention."

"Our Mary Ann doesn't have a lot of free time. Too many chores to tend to."

"And she *does them*?"

Josiah smiled in answer.

"Oh, you *are* blessed!" Mark said. "You are very blessed, indeed."

Josiah gave a knowing nod.

"But it's easier for you," Mark continued, trying his best to rationalize his own life, family dynamics, and his shortcomings as a father. "You're protected from the outside world here."

"You can be as protective as you want, but all families have their burdens to bear, *jah?*"

"But this whole cocooning thing that the Amish do ..."

"Cocooning?"

"You know, protecting your kids from outside influences, especially negative ones. You do that, right?"

"We separate ourselves from the world, but we don't think of it as a cocoon."

"No, no. Don't get me wrong," Mark said. "I think it's great. I'd love to cocoon my kids like that. Keep 'em out of trouble."

"But a butterfly leaves the cocoon and flies away one day. That's not our goal. We prefer staying close, even when they're adults," Josiah explained. "We believe in community and families who truly care about each other."

"I want my teenagers to grow up and stay close too," Mark said. "At least within a few states. Or countries."

Josiah eyed Mark a moment, as if to make sure he was joking.

"Don't get me wrong. I love my kids," Mark said, "but those teen years sure give me heartburn."

Josiah pulled back on the reins, stopping the horse by the hitching post near the house. He started to get out of the buggy, then hesitated for a moment, turning away and looking back toward the road.

"Our oldest child was killed last summer," he finally said. "We were coming home from the auction in the buggy. It was dark. The driver of the car said he didn't see us."

Mark didn't know what to say. Somehow he managed, "I'm sorry. It's a parent's worst nightmare—outliving one of your kids."

"We live apart from your world, sir. But your world doesn't always live apart from us. But we don't question God's will."

"You really believe it was God's will that your child died?"

"Nothing happens outside of his knowledge and ultimately his will."

"But how in the world did you get through a loss like that?"

"By believing the same things I did before it," Josiah said, and then he stepped down from the buggy and tied his horse to the hitching post.

"Dat! Dat!" the children called to Josiah as they ran to him. Josiah greeted each of them with a gentle hug or a pat on the head and then began the introductions.

"This here's Esther. She's ten."

Esther looked up and smiled at Mark.

Josiah pointed to the boy next. "Joseph is our middle child and our only boy. He's eight."

Joseph nodded at Mark and then turned to his little sister. "He's not gonna bite you," Joseph told her, pushing her a little closer to the stranger.

Josiah took Beth's hand. "Beth is our baby. She's six."

Beth smiled shyly and then grabbed ahold of her daddy's pant leg as if it was her tether to life.

"Now you kids go on inside and get washed up for dinner."

The kids obediently ran into the house, Josiah and Mark following. When they reached the front door, Josiah held it open for Mark.

"Welcome to our home," he said. Mark stepped through the doorway and, for the first time in his life, entered the world of the Amish.

Seeing Josiah Stoltzfus outside of the buggy for the first time, Mark took the time to study his rescuer. He guessed Josiah was approximately fifty-five years old. He was taller than average and had a thin build, and he was bearded, which, according to what he understood of Amish culture, meant he was married.

The house was simply furnished, with handmade chairs and benches. A dining table was at the far end of the living space. Kerosene lamps were strategically located throughout.

"We call this our family room," Josiah said. Unlike Mark's Wisconsin home, there were no family portraits on the wall nor a high-definition television in the center of the living room. Hooks lined the wall on one side of the room and an assortment of Amish clothing hung from each hook. Beneath them sat several baskets filled with various sewing projects. The aroma of home cooking filled the room. It was a smell that took Mark back to his grandparents' farm.

"Fried chicken?" he asked.

"Mama makes the best," Joseph said.

A pretty woman stepped into the room, wiping her hands on her apron. She appeared to be in her late thirties, with soft, golden, curly hair and a petite frame.

"This is my wife, Elizabeth," Josiah said. "Elizabeth, this is Mark ..." Josiah hesitated and then turned to Mark. "I'm sorry. Did you tell me your last name?"

"Stedman. Mark Stedman." Mark stretched out his hand toward Elizabeth.

Elizabeth gently took it and nodded. "Welcome," she said.

"Mark will be joining us for dinner."

"How nice," Elizabeth said, smiling without a hint of imposition. "Well, it's already on the table. Please, come."

Josiah led Mark into the kitchen as the children took their places around the dining table.

"Did you make this?" Mark said, admiring the fine woodwork.

"I made the table," Josiah said. "God made the wood."

The children giggled and whispered among themselves the same way kids did in any home where an unexpected stranger had just appeared. To children, everything seemed funnier when there was company. But Mark knew he wasn't in a home like any other. There were no reality shows playing here, no pop music bouncing off the walls. This home was filled with genuine laughter and actual conversation. And it all felt good.

———

HARLEY PHILLIPS'S GO-TO GUY WAS HIS SON-IN-LAW, BART. BAR-tholomew Rasmussen Templeton III, to be more accurate — and a lot more boring. Had Bart not been family, Harley never would have hired him. The two were polar opposites — politically, socially, and physically.

Bart was a rule follower. He didn't color outside the lines, tear the tags off his upholstery, or leave a single button unbuttoned on his shirts. He was dependable, trustworthy, faithful, cooperative ... and grossly underappreciated.

Bart didn't have any real authority in Harley's campaign, but he drew a paycheck.

And he got in the way ... at least that was Harley's assessment.

Contrasting Bart's lean frame, Harley was clearly a health-club dropout. He was married, but his faithfulness was more by default and ongoing rejection than because of anything else. But Harley had more on his mind these days than flirting with interns and secretaries. What satisfied him most was being the victor in a good political challenge. He took a special liking to watching his opponents squirm. It exhilarated him. Surrender and weakness repulsed him. Give Harley Phillips a worthy adversary, and he was in his element. Mark Stedman had proved no match for this political gladiator. With Stedman out of the picture, Harley moved on to the next worthy opponent who stood in the way of his prize.

"Bart! Get in here!" Harley Phillips demanded.

Bart hurried into Harley's office, pen and notepad in hand, just as Harley slammed a letter down on his desk

"What is it, sir?" Bart said.

"You wanna explain this?"

"Explain what, sir?"

"This letter!"

Harley slid the letter across the desk toward his son-in-law with such force that it sailed right off of the desk. Bart reached down, picked it up, and read just enough to get the gist.

"Oh, this? Yes. I don't know what happened on this, sir, but ..."

"You dropped the ball. That's what happened, Bart! You dropped the blasted ball!"

"You want me to see if they can fix it, sir?"

"Of course I want them to fix it! What do you think I want, Bart?"

"I'll take care of it right away, sir."

"Well, see that you do!"

Bart took the letter and left the room. When he arrived at his desk, he made a call.

"Three thousand four hundred and seventy-five," he said into the phone, tapping his pencil forcefully on his desk, nearly snapping it in two.

"What?" the person on the other end of the line said. It was Bart's wife, Stella Rose Phillips-Templeton.

Bart gritted his teeth. "That's how many times I've allowed your father to walk all over me. I know he's your dad, but there are limits, Stella. And I'm close to reaching mine."

Stella was the love of Bart's life — and the only reason he tolerated his father-in-law. Bart ran everything through her first so she could sufficiently come to his defense in any and all situations involving her father. If Harley wanted to complain about some action of Bart's — which he usually did — he would back off once he discovered that Stella had first approved it or, in some instances, even suggested it.

But Harley did have a flair for the dramatic. Launching the letter into the air like that, making Bart retrieve it from the floor after it landed, wasn't necessary. It was ridiculous. But then, Harley had a master's degree from the University of the Ridiculous. With his well-honed theatrical skills and his love for making scenes, he might have even been valedictorian of his class.

"Your dad wants to know why he wasn't included in the speaker lineup for Friday night. What do I tell him?" Bart asked.

"The truth. It's because he ran thirty minutes over the last time they gave him a microphone," Stella said.

"I know that, and you know that, but you don't really want me to remind Harley of that, do you?"

"He should know the truth."

"Not from me."

Bart could practically hear Stella click her tongue and roll her eyes. "Put my dad on the phone," she said.

Bart put Stella on hold and dialed Harley's extension. When he told Harley that Stella wanted to speak with him, Harley immediately took the call. Bart conveniently "forgot" to disconnect from his end.

"Hey, darling," Bart heard Harley say. "What's up?"

"Dad, we tried getting you on the platform at the foundation dinner, but the committee is still upset over your antics last year."

"Going over my time? Nonsense! They're leaning their support toward Anne Kurtzfield; that's what this is all about. She's been creeping up in the polls since Mark Stedman dropped out of the race. I wasn't born yesterday. I know the truth!"

"It was your speech, Dad. The schedule's tight, and they're saying you're unpredictable."

"Unpredictable? That's bunk! I can be as predictable as they want me to be. What do they want? Forty-five minutes? Thirty? I'll talk for as long as they want. How many minutes? Just tell me."

"None. No minutes. They said no, Dad."

"Tell them to call me. We'll talk about it."

"It's their final decision, Dad."

"There are some places I could cut my speech. No problem. I'll shorten it."

"You're not hearing me, Dad. It's a no."

"That's their final decision?"

"That's their final decision."

"Well, then, I guess I'll just have to accept it," Harley said. Bart could hear the insincerity dripping from Harley's voice.

Stella waited a beat, then said, "You're still going up on the stage, aren't you, Dad?"

"You bet I am! I'm not rolling over and playing dead for Kurtzfield. If the committee is setting her up to be the front-runner, they're going to have to steamroll over me to do it!

"It doesn't matter to me what that blasted committee says. I wouldn't have gotten this far in my career if I'd let other political opportunists push me to the side. And I'm not about to be pushed aside now. The stakes are too high. I *have* to be up on that stage. Every vote counts!"

"So I guess I'll see you there, then?" Stella asked with a sigh.

"Are you kidding me?" Harley said. "I wouldn't miss this for all our money in China!"

"Well, then, all I'll say is watch the sound bites. Like that one."

"I'll only say what I mean to say, sweetie," Harley replied before hanging up the phone.

From the next room, Bart heard Harley add, "And I do mean to say plenty!"

CHAPTER 5

★

M ARK COULDN'T REMEMBER THE LAST TIME HE SAW A HOME-
cooked spread quite like this — fried chicken, mashed potatoes with gravy, corn on the cob. It was nothing short of a feast.
And it wasn't even a holiday. Nor had this Amish family been
expecting any company. It was merely lunch. Or rather, dinner.
The congressman couldn't wait to dive in.

Mark and Cindy Stedman's lives had become a series of micro-
waved meals, fast food, and delivered pizzas. Mark was proud of
the fact that his family still ate together — or at least on the same
level of the house. One family member might be in the living
room watching television, another might be at the computer in
the den, and yet another sitting at the counter in the kitchen, but
there was still a *sense* of togetherness.

But it's nothing like this! Mark thought.

Mark sat down at one of two empty place settings, briefly wondering why there was an extra one. The feast before him canceled
out any mathematical errors on the table setter's part, though.
Mark's mouth was already watering.

"We always give thanks to the good Lord for his plentiful
bounty," Josiah said.

"Oh yes, of course," Mark said, wishing he'd thought to bring
up the matter himself.

Josiah took Elizabeth's hand in his right and Mark's hand in his left, and the children followed suit around the table. All of them bowed their heads.

"Dear Lord," Josiah began, "we thank you for providing the food that we are about to eat. Thank you for the health that you have given us to work the land and reap the harvest, and we pray a special blessing upon our new friend, Mark, who has found himself here with us this day. We know his journey here was not outside your plan. Amen."

By the time Mark raised his head, the bowls of food were already being passed around. This family had thankful hearts, but they also appreciated eating well.

"Take as much as you like," Elizabeth told Mark when the potatoes arrived in front of him.

"These look delicious! It *all* looks delicious!" he said.

"Does your wife enjoy cooking?" Elizabeth asked.

"Yes," Mark lied. But then he clarified, "Well, she watches cooking shows on TV."

That part was true, but watching a cooking show didn't make someone a cook any more than watching an airplane take off made someone a pilot. Besides, an Amish woman like Elizabeth wouldn't know about cooking shows on TV. Mark felt the need to explain further, to at least try to be more truthful. Unlike in his world, where perception was everything, there was no need to put on a facade with these folks. He would probably never see them again anyway. For once, he was free to be real.

"Well, to tell you the truth, my wife and I are both on the go so much, running in different directions, she doesn't have a lot of free time ..."

"You have kids?" Elizabeth asked.

"Three," Mark said proudly.

"You spend a lot of time with them, *jah?*"

"About as much time as they'll allow, which is about as much time as I can take of their racket. Don't imagine you have a lot of garage bands here, huh?"

Josiah glanced over at the empty place setting at the far end of the table. An extra place setting complete with dinner plate, glass, flatware—perfect and untouched. Mark watched as Josiah took Elizabeth's hand once again. Now Mark understood.

Tears welled up in Elizabeth's eyes, but she quickly composed herself. "I would be happy to send some of my favorite recipes home with you for your wife," she said, dabbing her eyes with her apron.

"I'm sure she'd like that," Mark said. "Thank you."

"More chicken?" Josiah asked, passing the platter Mark's way again.

"Can't pass up chicken this good!" Mark said as he grabbed another drumstick. He took another scoop of green beans while he was at it.

"So what line of work are you in, Mark?" Josiah asked.

"Well, I suppose you could say I'm unemployed." The truth of that statement surprised Mark. He hadn't been unemployed in decades, and it felt strange to be saying the word now. Strange and liberating. He knew he would go into another line of work, maybe even get his own talk show or become a news contributor, as other politicians had done after leaving Washington.

"Well, if you need work, I could use some help baling hay this week," Josiah said.

Now there was one option Mark hadn't considered. Baling hay?

"It might take a spell to get your car fixed up, anyway," Josiah added.

"How long's a spell?" Mark asked.

"Well, a spell's always longer than you thought but not as long as you feared. We'll get you fixed up as soon as possible."

"Me baling hay, huh?" Mark couldn't help but laugh. "Talk about a photo op! Can't get more back to basics than that."

"Just offering you some work … if you need it," Josiah said. "No offense."

"No, no. I appreciate it. But I should probably explain. I'm a politician," Mark said. "A currently unemployed one."

"A politician?" Josiah said, obviously surprised. "I don't think I've ever met one before. Most of 'em don't come around here much."

"I guess since the Amish don't typically vote, you're not on our radar."

"No, I don't suppose we are. But we do vote. 'Bout 10 percent of us do, anyway."

"Well, now that you mention it, I did campaign in South Bend, Indiana, not long ago when I was preparing for the upcoming Indiana primary. Met some Amish folks there. Or maybe they were Mennonite. Don't really know the difference. They were from Shipshewana, I believe."

"There are differences, but the ones you'd notice most are that Mennonites drive automobiles and have phones. At least the modern Mennonites do."

"But you're Amish?"

"Old Order."

"Meaning?"

"We live separate lives from the world. No cars, no phones . . ."

"No stress," Mark said.

"Well, we do enjoy our peace and quiet," Josiah said. "So were you a Washington politician?"

"U.S. congressman. From Wisconsin. Stepped down to run for president. And now I've stepped down from that to . . . well, to go back home, I guess. Hence, unemployed."

"President, you say? Well, well. But why'd you drop out of the race? The election isn't until November."

"I know, but sometimes you've got to pay attention to what the polls are saying. I was polling at the bottom, so I got out."

"Well, I don't know much about politics," Josiah said, "but how do you lose an election that hasn't even taken place yet?"

"Josiah, my good man," Mark said. "I've been asking myself that same question ever since I left Washington."

———

"THAT WAS SOME GOOD EATING!" MARK SAID, WISHING HE'D GOT-ten a longer belt the last time he'd gone shopping for one. His current belt was suddenly one belt hole and one Amish dinner short of fitting.

"You're welcome to share our meals anytime," Elizabeth said, gathering up the dishes.

"But you don't have to drive into a ditch to join us," Josiah said. The comment caused the children to giggle.

"No worries there," Mark said.

Josiah headed toward the door. "Well, are you ready to head on out there and get to work on that car of yours?"

"Let's do it!" Mark said, even though his body was screaming for a nap.

Mark started to help Elizabeth clear off the table, but Josiah stopped him.

"The kids'll do that," he said.

And they did. Before Mark could even insist on at least clear-ing off his own plate, the children had already taken it from him. Out of the corner of his eye, he saw the two youngest having a bit of a tug-of-war over the last brownie in the basket, and he smiled to himself, almost relieved. *Nobody's kids are perfect 100 percent of the time.*

"You kids share that now," Josiah said, interrupting Mark's thought.

"Do we have to, *Dat?*"

Josiah didn't answer. He just waited until Joseph obediently broke the brownie in two.

"Come on, Mark," Josiah said. "We've got some work to do."

Mark followed Josiah out of the house, and they walked down to the barn. Mark was both frustrated and amused at the turn of events in his life. Only a day before, he'd been knee-deep in Washington politics, and now look at him. He was in a barn with an Amish man, getting ready to hitch up some horses to pull his government car out of a ditch. Life could be full of surprises ... and irony.

"You ever hitched up a horse before?" Josiah asked.

"When I was younger," Mark said. "My granddad had a farm. Taught me some about horses. More about life."

"Can't get that kind of learning from your universities, *jah*?"

"I tell people I attended the Graduate School of Grandpa. The times I spent with him are some of my best memories."

"Here in our community, our elders are our compass."

"Used to be more like that in our world. Wish it still was."

"What changed?"

"Nobody wants to be old anymore. It's all about youth. Too often the elderly get pushed aside. But it's a real shame—all that wisdom's just going to waste."

"Getting buried with 'em at their *leicht*?"

"*Leicht*?"

"Funeral. It's Pennsylvania Dutch. Our native language," Josiah explained. "So what else did you learn from your wise grandfather?"

"The value of hard work. He'd always tell me, 'Corn won't grow in your bed, Mark.' Would never let me sleep in."

Josiah laughed. "What else?"

" 'Plant a potato, reap a potato.' That was another one of his favorites."

"Sounds like your grandfather was a *gut* influence on you. And now your own kids will reap what he sowed. And what you've sowed into their lives too."

Mark nodded, hoping Josiah was right, and also hoping that he'd sowed enough good seed in his own children's lives. In many ways, Josiah reminded Mark of his grandfather; that's partly why he was enjoying his company so much.

"Well, hitching up a horse is like riding a bike. Once you learn, you never forget how to do it," Josiah said, grabbing a couple of harnesses off some hooks on the barn wall.

"Here, take this one," Josiah said, handing one of the harnesses to Mark.

The men made their way to the pasture, where a couple of strong, muscular draft horses stood near the white fence.

"So how many acres you got here?" Mark asked, looking around at Josiah's spread.

"A couple hundred."

"Is that right? That's a good size. But a lot of hard work, huh?"

"Nothing wrong with that."

Josiah grabbed the halter of the first horse. "This here's Samson," he said, patting Samson's nose. The horse backed away slightly at the intruding presence of the stranger.

"Easy, boy. Easy." Josiah calmed Samson before slipping the harness over his neck. "Come on, Sam. Just got a little side job for you. That's all."

With Samson harnessed, Josiah walked the horse over to Mark and handed him the reins. "You hold on to Samson here while I get the other one."

"What's the other one's name?" Mark asked. "Delilah?"

"How'd you know?" Josiah smiled.

"Seriously? Samson and Delilah?" Mark laughed. "I love it!"

Josiah harnessed Delilah and then swapped reins with Mark. "Here. Delilah's gentler. But I still wouldn't turn my back on her."

"True to her name, eh?" Mark asked.

Josiah gave a slight raise of an eyebrow, then pulled back his shirtsleeve and showed Mark a crescent-shaped scar on the middle of his forearm.

"And she's the gentle one?" Mark said, tightening his hand on the reins just a bit more.

"Hold tight to the reins and make her earn your trust," Josiah said.

Mark and Josiah led the horses over to the makeshift "towing" equipment that was out by the tool shed. Once the hitch was set, Josiah clapped his hands together and said, "All right, let's do it," and the two men started down the road toward the broken car.

CHAPTER 6

★

"**B**ART!" HARLEY PHILLIPS BARKED FROM HIS DESK. BART ROLLED his eyes, dropped what he was doing, and walked into Harley's office.

"Whatcha need, Dad?" he asked, almost gasping as soon as the word, *that* word, slipped out of his mouth. He knew Harley cringed whenever Bart called him that, but Bart didn't fully understand why. Harley *was* his father-in-law, after all.

"How many times have I told you not to call me that at the office? It's Mr. Phillips or Harley. Not *Dad*!"

"Sorry, sir, I forgot."

"At home. And only in front of my daughter. You can do it for her. But don't do it *here*!"

"Okay, Harley," Bart said with a slight shrug of his shoulders. Sometimes he didn't understand Harley. Actually, he hardly ever understood Harley. But for his wife's sake, he kept trying to give his father-in-law the benefit of the doubt. He knew that Harley had risen through the political ranks the hard way. And anyone who got kicked around enough would start biting back, even at friendly hands. Sometimes one *only* bit friendly hands. It was safer. The dog bites the cat, so the cat attacks the mouse. Not fair for the mouse, but safer for the cat.

Bart also knew that Harley saw his son-in-law's passiveness as a defect. Harley would often tell Bart that he was Harley's Achilles' heel. The weak link in an otherwise smooth-running operation.

Bart couldn't remember, but that might even have been Harley's wedding toast at Bart and Stella's reception. Still, Bart hung in there and took the bad with the good — the good being Stella, his wife and Harley's beloved daughter.

"So have you found anything on Kurtzfield yet?" Harley asked.

"Like dirt?"

"No, I mean like where she buys her clothes. *Of course I mean dirt!* Anything turn up?"

"Not yet."

"Well, keep digging. Everybody's got *something*!"

Bart nodded in fake agreement and then walked out the door, almost bumping into Marcia, who was on her way in to speak with Harley.

"So what kind of mood's he in?" she asked.

"His usual," Bart said.

"Oh?" Marcia said, clearly disappointed. "I was hoping for human."

They both tried to restrain their laughter so Harley wouldn't hear them.

"He's after Kurtzfield now."

"Of course."

"Can I ask you something, Marcia?" Bart said.

"Sure."

"What is it that drives politicians to go after each other's dirty laundry the way they do?"

"Maybe because it makes their own laundry smell a little better," Marcia said and then, taking a deep breath, stepped into Harley's office.

———

CINDY HELD HER CELL PHONE TO HER EAR AND TRIED CALLING Mark again. The line didn't even ring. Instead, a prerecorded voice came on telling Cindy the person she was trying to reach was unavailable.

Cindy wouldn't let her mind go to the unthinkable—that something had happened to Mark on the road. He was probably on one of those stretches of highway where reception was poor or, more likely, nonexistent.

Comforting herself with that assumption, she hung up and, vowing to try again later, returned to her project of mailing out thank-you notes to everyone who had helped with her husband's campaign. It was a daunting task, even for a flailing campaign like Mark's. But it was necessary. Keep the donors happy and loyal —the first rule of politics. You never knew when you might need to call on them again.

AFTER WALKING A GOOD DISTANCE, MARK AND JOSIAH, EACH leading a horse, turned onto the last stretch of road where the wrecked government car sat useless, straddling the ditch and the slope of the small hill, waiting to be rescued and restored to her former self—or at least as close to original condition as possible.

"Well, there she is, right where I left her," Mark said, pleased that the car hadn't been stripped. He'd once parked a car in front of a Manhattan hotel, and someone had cleaned it out in five minutes flat. The only thing left had been the cigarette lighter— obviously a health-conscious thief. But this car was perfectly safe. Apparently, the crime rate in Amish country was about as high as the number of blizzards in Los Angeles.

"I still can't believe I drove off the road like that," Mark said.

"You'd be surprised how many times I've seen this," Josiah noted. "Cars, trucks, you name it. Folks get to looking at the scenery instead of watching the road, and they veer right off it."

"And end up in the ditch, huh?"

"It's a hard, fast rule of life, Mark. If your wheels are pointed in the direction of a ditch, and you don't turn 'em back to the road, the ditch is where you're gonna end up."

When they reached the car, Josiah told Mark to hold on to the horses while he took a few minutes to assess the situation. Josiah walked to the rear of the car. Then he walked to the side of the car. Then he stood in the ditch and looked up at the car. Then he returned to the front of the car and shook his head.

"So how's it look?" Mark asked. "Think your horses can pull it out?"

"It'll be a workout for 'em, but *jah*, they're up to it."

Mark looked down the ditch until he spied his unruly GPS, its cord dangling in shame. He walked over to it.

"Well, I'll tell you one thing," he said. "*She's* fired!"

Mark kicked the ornery navigational device and sent it skipping along the pavement until it came to a stop close to where Josiah was standing. Josiah watched for a few seconds while Mark enjoyed the satisfaction of that action, and then he calmly walked over and retrieved the GPS.

"I'd appreciate it if you'd fire her in your own yard," he said, handing the contraption back to Mark. "You said yourself, it's beautiful country here. We'd like to keep it that way."

"Sorry," Mark said. "You're right. I suppose the lady does deserve a decent burial."

"Just trying to be a good steward of the land," Josiah said.

Mark tossed the device onto the backseat of the car. "If it helps, I voted for every anti-littering law and conservation bill that came up in the House."

"That so?" Josiah asked, looking half pleased and half doubtful.

"Yes, I did," Mark said, desperate to win back Josiah's respect. He couldn't explain it—perhaps it had something to do with his grandfather—but for some reason, Josiah's opinion was important to Mark. "I surely did."

Josiah turned the horses around and guided them as they backed up to the front bumper of the car.

"Come on, Samson," Josiah said. "Back on up! You, too, Delilah. Let's go. That's it. Line 'er up."

The horses dutifully obeyed, and once they were in place,

Mark hitched them to the vehicle. When the hitch was secure, Mark put the car in neutral. Josiah moved behind the animals, gave a click with his tongue, and called out, "All right. Let's go!"

He gave the reins a snap, and the horses began pulling with all their might, but the car didn't budge. Not even an inch.

"What if I got behind it and gave it a push?" Mark said.

"Couldn't hurt."

Mark walked into the ditch and placed his hands on the rear of the car. When Josiah urged the horses forward again, Mark pushed. Samson and Delilah pulled with everything they had, and Mark pushed as hard as he could. It was teamwork in the purest sense of the term. But that didn't budge the car either.

"One more time," Josiah said. "Samson's got the strength, but he's got to get the right footing."

Josiah snapped the reins again, and the horses started pulling again. "Steady, steady ... You're doing it! Don't quit on me now."

"Don't quit on us now!" Mark echoed.

The words had a familiar ring to the congressman. Don't quit —that was what both Mark's grandfather and his father had always told him. Don't quit had even been Cindy's mantra over the years. Now Mark found himself a quitter. He had left the presidential race, left Washington, and was leaving his life's calling of serving his country. It seemed a bit hypocritical for Mark to be telling a couple of draft horses not to quit when he couldn't even take his own advice.

As he pushed and the horses pulled, Mark recalled his last meeting with party officials Sam Lynch and Randall Baxter. There hadn't been much budging then either. It was over the debate situation, and it hadn't gone well ...

"Give me one reason!" Mark said. "One reason why you're not backing me on this! I deserve to be in that debate, Sam!"

"Deserve?" Sam snapped back. "How do you deserve *any* attention when you're only pulling in 10 percent of the vote?"

"The polls can be wrong. You know that."

"So what do you really have? *Thirty* percent? Forty? Did someone do the math wrong, Mark?" Sam said.

"Mark, you're not a contender this time around," Randall interjected. "Give it another try in four years."

"I was a solid 15 percent and still climbing three weeks ago!"

"And Super Tuesday blew you out of the water, Mark," Sam said.

"There's still no clear winner," Mark insisted. "It's anybody's game."

Sam shook his head.

Mark was determined, but even he knew the party was going to have to side with a winner.

"Look, it's a matter of time," Sam said. "Might as well face it, Mark."

"Go home. Spend time with your family. There's no way for you to win it now," Randall echoed. "It's over."

"Harley's all but sewn up the nomination," Sam pointed out.

"Not from where I sit," Mark said.

"Then you'd better scoot your chair back into reality, my friend, 'cause we're withdrawing our support," Randall said matter-of-factly.

"You've been sliding in the polls for weeks. That's momentum in the opposite direction," said Sam. "You're at 10 percent now, Mark. Ten percent. And you've never even made it past 15 percent. You've been as low as three. We can't continue to commit our resources to a train wreck!"

"This debate would've done it for me, Sam! I could've hit a home run!" Mark snapped.

"Not with your batting average, Mark!" Sam snapped back.

"Look, your campaign just never caught traction," Randall

said, trying to soften the escalating tension in the room. "Nothing personal. Just politics."

"So you shut me out?"

"You shut yourself out, Mark. You weren't pulling in the numbers. It's over, Mark. It's been over for weeks. I'm simply ending the pain."

"Wait and try again next time," Randall assured him. "This run gave you national exposure. In four more years, you'll do better right out of the gate."

The words offered no comfort to Mark.

"Look, the bottom line at this point is that we're going to have to go with our front-runners," Sam said.

"Harley Phillips?"

"He's got the best chance of winning this election." Randall held up a copy of the latest polls. "It's him or Anne right now. You may very well be the best candidate, Mark, but you can't fight the polls."

"So the country gets to suffer through four years of Harley or Kurtzfield before it gets the chance to turn things around?"

"All right. I'm not going to waste any more of our time on this," Sam said. "We're not telling you to drop out of the race. We're just withdrawing our support. Continue if you want, but it's all on your dime."

"Withdrawing the party's support will be the final nail in the coffin, you know that," Mark said.

"Your campaign died a long time ago, Mark," Randall said. "It hobbled up to Super Tuesday and has been on life support ever since. Trust me. I'm giving you good advice here. Let it go, give it a decent burial, and resurrect it again in four years."

"And in the meantime, decide who you'll be throwing your support to," Sam pressed. "The sooner we announce that, the better bounce we'll get in the polls."

"Bounce for who? Harley Phillips?"

"If you've got any party loyalty, yes. He's got the best chance. But it's your decision."

"I'm still in the race, Sam! Those are my voters!"

"Throw us a bone here, Mark," Randall said. "We've got to start closing the gaps or the other side's gonna whip our tail come November!"

"Think about it, Mark," Sam pleaded. "To continue your campaign would be a mistake."

"Like we've never elected a mistake before?"

"Withdraw, Mark," Sam said. "For the good of the party."

"I'm in it for the long haul, gentlemen," Mark said flatly. *"I won't quit!"*

"Don't quit now!" Josiah said, coaxing the horses and snapping Mark out of his stinging memory. "That's it! Pull ... pull!"

Mark joined in, "Come on, Delilah! Keep going, girl! You're doing it!"

The horses were pulling with the full force of their muscular legs and backs, giving it every ounce of strength they could muster.

"Think they need a break?" Mark asked, huffing and wheezing, trying to return some air to his own lungs.

"No, but you might."

Mark nodded, then changed his mind, "No, it's okay. I'll be fine. Let's do it."

"You sure?"

"If Samson and Delilah can keep going, so can I."

Josiah snapped on the reins again, and the horses gave it another try. Samson dug his rear hoofs into the side of the hill and pulled and grunted and then pulled and grunted some more. Delilah stayed right beside him, a worthy companion, taking up whatever slack Samson might have left.

Then it happened. The car started to give way, only slightly at first, but it was movement.

"That's it! It's coming!" Mark said, excited to think his problems might soon be over.

"Keep pushing!" Josiah called to him. "Push!"

The horses could have handled the task more easily, but the position of the government vehicle was a peculiar one. The car couldn't simply roll back onto the road. It had to roll back through the ditch and then onto the road. It could be done—at least Mark hoped it could—but it would require a bit of extra effort.

Mark pushed, the horses pulled, and before long, their determined teamwork and steadfast persistence paid off. The car rolled out of the ditch and onto the road. They'd done it.

"Well, I'll be!" Mark said. "If I hadn't seen it for myself, I never would've believed it!"

"I told you they were strong," Josiah said, giving the horses a congratulatory pat and granting them a well-deserved rest. "Sometimes you've just got to work together and give it all you've got, *jah*?"

Mark wiped the sweat off his brow, then added, "And not quit."

"*Jah*, never quit," Josiah agreed. "Now you're starting to sound like one of us."

Mark laughed. "I could do this. Get back to my roots. Live off the land," he said. "Need a politician around here?"

"We Amish don't really get involved in national politics, and we don't proselytize, but you'd be welcome as far as I'm concerned," Josiah assured him. "The Plain life is a lot of hard work, though."

"I'm used to hard work."

"We rise at sunup."

"I could manage it."

Josiah laughed like a man who had heard all this before. No doubt from tourists passing through who got caught up in the beauty and peacefulness of the surroundings and couldn't wait to get home, sell everything they owned, and buy a farm. But most likely, after the first year, all that would have happened is that they would have lost the farm, their retirement money, and a whole lot of sleep.

"You might want to ponder that for a spell," Josiah cautioned. "Spend some time working on a farm first."

"Well, since I've gotta be here while my car's getting fixed up, maybe I'll do some of that now. Get a better feel for this lifestyle."

"You serious?"

"Nah. My kids would never give up their cell phones. Speaking of which, I've gotta find some way to check in with my wife. She'll be worried. Where'd you say that emergency phone was?"

"At the home of a Mennonite family 'bout five miles down the road. Want me to run you up there?"

"Sometime today, if that's all right."

"Sure. We'll take good care of you, Mark."

The two men walked next to the horses and started down the road. It was quite a sight—Josiah and Mark leading the two draft horses, who were towing the government vehicle behind them. Mark wondered what Sam and Randall would say if they could see him. Or Cindy, for that matter. In fact, where were that woman and her husband from the hotel? This was the shot she should have taken with her camera. If Mark had reception, he would've sent them a photo himself. Why, just thinking about the mileage Mark could get out of a photo of this made his head spin. But then he remembered how the Amish preferred their photos not be taken, and he dropped that daydream.

"You know, Josiah," Mark said, admiring the Amish man's fortitude and ingenuity, "my whole presidential campaign was based on getting back to basics, but you're the one who's actually doing it. I couldn't even get myself out of a ditch on my own!"

"We all need help sooner or later," Josiah said. "No shame in that."

CHAPTER 7

★

The rest of the way back to Josiah's home, the men talked about life, family, and the differences between their two worlds.

"You ever wonder what it'd be like to live on the outside?" Mark asked.

"Oh, I get a taste of it every tourist season. Cars back up for miles. My buggy rides right past them."

"Can't be worse than D.C. You should see the gridlock we have some days, especially around the Capitol. Everything comes to a standstill."

"So I hear. Both outside and inside, *jah*?"

Mark laughed. "So you follow what happens in Washington?" he said.

"Mostly just what affects our lives here. But we pray for those of you in charge."

"We appreciate it," Mark said. "Well, I should say *they* do, since I'm not there anymore."

"Think you'll ever get back in it?"

"Right now I'm just glad to be going home."

Josiah nodded thoughtfully. "Well, let's see if we can't straighten out that axle somehow and get you back on the road."

"You're really helping me out. It's very kind of you."

"That's what neighbors are for, *jah*?"

"Neighbors. I'm from Wisconsin, remember?"

"That could either make you a stranger or a neighbor from Wisconsin."

Mark thought about his grandfather again and how helpful he'd always been to strangers. Like Josiah, he, too, would have gladly helped someone stranded by the side of the road. Mark could remember his grandpa taking food out of his own refrigerator and giving it to a family in need. It was a memory he would never forget, because he'd been eyeing the bowl of banana pudding and then had wondered where it disappeared to.

But the world had changed since his grandfather's day. Those kinds of people seemed to be few and far between now.

These days, Mark figured, the Good Samaritan would need a Release of Liability form to be signed by the injured man and notarized, three litigation attorneys on retainer, an LLC for his roadside assistance business to protect his personal assets from sue-happy opportunists, a waiver of liability from the inn where he took the man in the event further injury should befall the injured man while there, a check as up-front payment, and a clean bill of health proving he hadn't inadvertently exposed the victim to any communicable diseases.

It's not the same world anymore.

But maybe it still existed here at least. The Amish man hadn't asked for any money at all. He didn't require assurance of legal protection or a health clearance. So what was different about these people?

"So how do you do it?" Mark asked.

"Do what?" Josiah said, turning to check on the car being towed behind them.

"How do you manage to preserve an unguarded, do-the-right-thing-no-matter-what-the-cost attitude when it seems to be on the verge of extinction everywhere else?"

"It's really no secret, Mark," Josiah said. "If you put yourself in the other person's shoes, you'll be inclined to do the right thing."

To Mark, doing the right thing was a matter of courage as

much as it was an issue of integrity and character. It took both courage and faith to help a stranger. Riding by Mark earlier would have required neither of the Amish man. Mark had always been private about his own faith, opting for political correctness rather than running the risk of offending anyone. He wasn't naive, though. He knew that having a faith, some kind of faith, was often a political plus. He simply didn't want to pigeonhole himself by aligning with any one particular group, so he never stated a specific denomination in any interviews. He was all things to all people. Still, he was curious as to what exactly his benefactor did believe.

"I don't mean to sound ignorant, but what do the Amish believe?" Mark asked.

"We try our best to keep God at the center of our lives," Josiah replied.

"I admire that, but it must be easier for you. You don't have all the distractions."

"See those trees over there, Mark?" Josiah said, pointing to a cluster of maple trees at the edge of a creek off in the distance. "Some days I like to ride out there and just sit under those trees and talk to God. Or read my Bible. You got a favorite place to read?" Josiah asked.

"The Bible?"

"Jah."

"Well," Mark said, thinking for a moment. "I guess I do most of my reading on the road. Most of the hotels I stay in have a copy of the Bible."

"Ah, but there's nothing like reading your own copy, Mark—getting the binding all flexible and worn in. It's a *gut* feeling, *jah*?"

Mark could tell that Josiah wasn't judging him in the least, but Mark still felt guilty. He knew he hadn't cracked open his Bible, or any Bible for that matter, in months. Maybe even years. He wondered if there was a special punishment for those who lied about such things, but he plodded on. "I read every time I get the chance—a chapter here, a chapter there," he said. "Politics doesn't give you a lot of time for Bible reading, with everybody vying for your attention the way they do."

"I hear Lincoln spent a lot of time reading his Bible ... both before *and* after he became president," Josiah commented.

Why is he bringing up Lincoln? No one can live up to that standard.

"I've actually seen Lincoln's family Bible at his childhood home in Kentucky," Mark said, steering the conversation off the uncomfortable subject of his own reading habits. "He was one honest politician, I'll tell you that. Told it like it was."

"You're honest, too, *jah*?" Josiah asked.

"Of course," Mark said, almost as a defensive reflex. Mark might not have been as honest as Honest Abe, but he usually did try to tell the truth whenever he was backed into a corner. And he was a lot more honest than Harley Phillips. Or Anne Kurtzfield. Or Governor Karen Ledbetter. Or most of the other presidential candidates, for that matter. He might not have been the best candidate to ever try to fill Lincoln's size-14 shoes, but Mark Stedman would put his record up against any current politician's.

"I know you're honest," Josiah said. "If you weren't honest, you would've told me someone ran you off the road back there instead of telling me the truth—that you got in a fight with your GPS."

Mark laughed at Josiah's good-natured ribbing. The laughter felt good.

———

CINDY STEDMAN HADN'T SPOKEN WITH HER HUSBAND SINCE THE previous night, and she was growing concerned. She'd seen his call on her Missed Calls list earlier in the day, which helped, but he hadn't left a message. She'd tried to call him back several times. This time she called Carl.

"You haven't heard from him either?" she asked.

"I'm sure he's fine, Cindy."

"Well, let me know as soon as you find out anything," she said before hanging up.

Cindy told herself that Mark would return her calls as soon as he could. He was on his way home; that was all that mattered. It wouldn't be long now before their lives would return to normal—whatever "normal" had come to mean in the Stedman household. She couldn't wait to hold him in her arms again, and she relished the thought of finally not having to share her husband with his constituents, the political pundits of Washington, or the media.

Taking Carl's encouragement, Cindy tried to go about her day, praying a sort of continual prayer that her husband would check in soon and put her mind at ease like they had promised each other they would. Beyond that, she relaxed and trusted.

For about twenty more minutes.

Then she surrendered to her anxiety and called his number again.

She finally reached Mark's voice mail and left another message, reminding herself that there were stretches between Washington and Wisconsin where cell phone reception was iffy at best. Mark would get her messages eventually and call her back. He was dependable like that. She would have to trust that he was all right.

———

"I've got to say, I admire your pioneer spirit," Mark said as Josiah guided the horses up another road, where a house gradually came into view. "Doing without so many modern conveniences."

"Well, we're Plain people."

"Plain?"

"That's what we're called. We prefer living simply."

"And self-sufficiently. Living off the grid. Not an easy thing to do these days."

"We depend on ourselves. And each other. And God."

"People in my world used to do more to help each other. But everyone's so caught up in their own lives these days, just trying to survive, you know. Don't have the time to worry about anyone else."

"Not a lot of barn raisings in your world?"

"Yeah, I've heard of those. What's that about?"

"Well, if a neighbor's had a fire or some such event, we all step in and raise a new barn or house for them. Sometimes as quickly as one day."

"*Extreme Makeover* Amish style, huh?"

"What?"

"Nothing."

"Well, it's a social event too. We get to catch up on all the latest doings, and it feels *gut, jah*, to help out a friend?"

"But aren't there some in your community who take advantage of your goodness?"

"What do you mean?"

"Well, you got any, you know, folks who sit back and let everyone else do the work?"

"We Amish grow up learning the value of hard labor. Every community has a few who will try to take advantage, but most of the time it evens out. One neighbor needs help today, and tomorrow he'll be the one helping another neighbor out. Most decent folk want to give back to show their gratefulness."

"So many folks have helped me out over the years with all my campaigns ... I could never repay them all."

"You've had a lot of barns burn down, have you, Mark?"

"Dreams, mostly. But I've had a lot of good things happen too. There were people who opened the right doors for me. They took a risk and gave me a job or position. You don't get to the places I've gotten to without a lot of help along the way."

"See, there are good people in both our worlds." Josiah removed his hat, wiped his brow with his shirtsleeve, then placed his hat back on his head. "Now tell me some about your world, Mark."

"Well, what would you like to know?"

"Since I've never talked to a Washington politician before, tell me about that. Is it as hard as it seems?"

"You ever built a barn and have half the community sit back and criticize your work? 'It leans too far to the left. Now it leans too far to the right. The rafters are crooked, and the ceiling looks like it's about to cave in.'"

"Well, I like to think I'm a better carpenter than that." Josiah laughed.

"But people say those things even after you've done your best, no matter what the barn looks like. What do you do then?"

"Well, I guess I'd have to ask myself one question."

"What's that?"

"Whose barn is it?"

"Well, it's theirs, but ..."

"Then I think I'd listen to 'em."

It wasn't the answer Mark wanted to hear, but he took it in. He knew he was in the presence of a true Washington outsider — someone whose opinions hadn't been jaded by the media, self-seeking politicians, and disgruntled activists. He also knew he'd appreciate the free advice once he let it settle in his stomach.

A snake slithered across the road, causing the horses to stop in their tracks. Josiah calmed Samson and Delilah, then assured Mark, "It's not poisonous."

"How can you tell?"

"Its head. Most poisonous snakes have a triangle head."

"You've seen enough to know the difference?"

"When you live off the land, you deal with what's on the land. And they were here first."

Maybe this isn't such a perfect life after all, Mark thought. He watched the snake slither into a ditch. "I remember my grandpa killing a snake once. It'd been eating his chickens. Your farm got a lot of snakes?" Mark asked, concern furrowing his brow.

"Built the house right on top of a den of 'em. Didn't realize it at the time, and I've been apologizing for it ever since — to the snakes and Elizabeth. But they leave us alone. Hang out by the driveway mostly."

Mark's eyes widened as they neared said driveway, then Josiah let loose with a hearty laugh.

"I'm just joking with you," Josiah said. "No snake den under the house."

Mark was relieved. He didn't like snakes, even avoided the reptile exhibit whenever he and his family visited the zoo.

"They'll leave you alone if you leave them alone," Josiah assured him.

"Well, as much as I like the beautiful scenery, I gotta be honest with myself. This kind of life probably isn't for me."

"I won't lie to you; it's hard work."

"Don't mind that," Mark said, "but I'm not so sure I could give up everything I'd have to give up ... A car for one."

Josiah turned and looked at the disabled vehicle behind them.

"Oh, you might be surprised at what you can do without, my friend," Josiah said, grinning.

Out in the yard, Elizabeth stood smiling at the humorous sight of the horses pulling an automobile. She held a couple of tall glasses of ice-cold lemonade for the men and had a bucket of water for the horses.

Josiah waved to his kids, who were watching from the porch as the car, horses, and men made their way up the driveway and over to the horse pasture. Josiah hitched Samson and Delilah to the fence near the bucket of water, and Elizabeth handed each of the men their lemonade. Mark guzzled it down in a few thirsty gulps.

Josiah then unhitched the car from the makeshift tow, took the harnesses off the horses, and turned them loose in the pasture. The animals had certainly earned their rest.

Mark and Josiah walked over to the vehicle and reassessed the damage. The axle was indeed bent, and the radiator had a bad crack in it.

"Well, we've got our work cut out for us," Josiah said.

Mark was actually looking forward to getting his hands dirty by working on the car. It would take his mind off recent events, and he might even get some good anecdotes to include in his banquet speeches, which he'd already been considering increasing now that he had more time on his hands. But first things first—he needed to find some way to call Cindy.

"That phone you told me about, the one you use for emergencies ... you think we can head over there soon so I can call my wife?"

"Oh, sure, sure. I can take you down there now, if you like."

"You sure you don't mind?"

"Can't have your wife worrying about you now, can we?"

Josiah took Mark down to the Mennonite home. The family was quite friendly and told Mark he was welcome to use their phone whenever he needed to. Mark thanked them, then he called Cindy.

"Hello?" Cindy said cautiously, not recognizing the incoming phone number on her caller ID.

"Hey, sweetheart."

"Mark? I've been trying to call you. Is everything okay?"

"Yeah, I'm fine," Mark said. "But I drove into a ditch in Lancaster."

"*What?* Are you hurt?"

"No, just the car is."

"What were you doing in Lancaster?"

"There was traffic so I took a detour. Well ... it's a long story. The GPS was no help."

"Is the car drivable?" Cindy asked.

"Not yet, but an Amish man came along and helped pull it out. Well, him and his horses."

"Why didn't you call me?"

"There's no cell reception out here. I'm using their neighbor's phone. A Mennonite family's."

"How long do you think it will be until your car is fixed?"

"Don't know for sure. It's pretty messed up, but we're working on it."

"You've got an Amish man fixing your car? You're kidding me, right?"

"It's quite a story. I'll tell you all about it when I get home. Believe me — it's going in my memoirs."

"Well, hurry home. I miss you."

"Miss you, too, hon. Oh! And get a hold of Carl and explain the situation, would you?"

Cindy promised she would, and Mark hung up the phone. He thanked the Mennonite family and offered to pay them, but they graciously refused.

"So what line of work are you in?" the Mennonite man asked Mark.

Mark glanced over at their television set. "Well, I'm unemployed at the moment," he said. If the family recognized him, they hadn't let on. And if they hadn't recognized him, well, that was just one more jab at his already sorely wounded ego.

"Well, if you're looking for work, I operate a cheese factory in town and could use some help come summer."

"Mark lives in Wisconsin. He's just passing through," Josiah answered.

"I see," the man replied, walking Josiah and Mark to the door. "Well, feel free to use the phone anytime."

"Thanks," Mark said.

Mark and Josiah walked to the buggy and climbed in. Since it was five miles back to the Stoltzfus house, Mark took advantage of Josiah's wisdom one more time.

"Josiah, you're one of the few people who has ever gotten my undivided attention for this long. I don't have a cell phone that works, my car's broken down, and I can't even use my laptop. Maybe for the first time in my life, I'm in a place where I'll listen."

"Listening comes easy out here," Josiah said. "It's quiet and peaceful."

"Well, as an outsider looking in, do you think I did the right thing by getting out of the race? I realize you don't know much about me, but from what you do know, I'd be interested in hearing what you think."

"Is it what you wanted to do?"

"Drop out of the race? No. I still feel as though I've got unfinished business. Like I haven't done everything I was supposed to do in Washington. But the votes weren't there for me."

"Well, one thing about me, Mark. I speak my mind. You may not agree, and you don't have to, but since you asked, I'm going to tell you what I think. Is that okay?"

"Absolutely. I need someone to shoot straight with me. Tell me how I can help my country when it seems like my country doesn't want my help anymore."

"Well, what was it that lady in your GPS said? Recalculate? That's what you need to do, Mark. Get back on the path that was intended for you, whatever path you believe that to be. Only do it smarter next time."

"You're saying I should regroup and run again in four years?"

"I'm not telling you to do anything, my friend. But if you truly believe you were meant to be president, then you'll know when it's the right time, and you'll do what you need to do."

Mark knew he should listen to the Amish man's advice. He had paid good money to political advisers and life counselors who hadn't helped him as much as Josiah was currently helping him with his good old-fashioned common sense.

"How'd you get so wise?" Mark asked when they finally reached the house and climbed out of the buggy.

Josiah smiled. "Not all wisdom comes from television, *jah*?"

Mark smiled and walked to his car. "So what do you think? Think we can fix it?"

"We'll do what we can, and if we run into any major problems, we'll bring in the higher authority."

"You're going to pray for my car?"

Josiah chuckled. "I was referring to the radiator shop in Bird-in-Hand. But I think I can fix your axle."

Josiah walked into his shed. A few minutes later, he came back out with a handful of farm tools and began to work on the car. Mark laughed to himself at the obvious difference between this simple Amish farmer's way of fixing things and the overpriced auto body shop he usually went to back home. He hoped he was doing the right thing by letting this farmer help him.

"Don't know how much we'll get done before dark. You're welcome to stay here tonight."

"That's very hospitable of you," Mark said, both eager to get on the road and fascinated by this Amish man. "I'd be happy to pay you."

"Won't charge you to stay in my home," Josiah insisted. "But how 'bout if I fix your car, you help me bale hay when we're done? Sound fair?"

Mark knew the Amish man had already helped him out above and beyond the call of neighborly duty, even by Amish standards. Josiah was going to pound the axle back into shape by hand. Helping the man bale his hay was the least Mark could do.

"More than fair," he said.

"Then it's settled," Josiah said, and the two men shook hands in agreement.

"Now this is the way to do business," Mark said.

Josiah smiled. "If you can't trust a man's handshake, you can't trust the man."

———

ELIZABETH WAS IN THE KITCHEN PREPARING DINNER WHEN Josiah and Mark began working on the car. The sound of pounding metal pierced the calm of the countryside, but it was a good sound. Labor made its own symphony, and it enticed Elizabeth to watch from the coolness of her open kitchen window. She loved her ruggedly handsome husband with an unconditional love.

"The secret to a good marriage is understanding that both parties have faults," Bishop Miller, the bishop for their community, had told them on their wedding day. "If you see the flaws of others through the lens of your own, love comes easily."

Elizabeth had always tried to follow that advice whenever Josiah left the gate open, allowing their goats to wander away. Or when he stayed too late working out in the field so that her meat loaf, the one he had specifically requested, got cold. Or when her wringer washer had gone without a new roller for far too long. Whenever those little irritants of life that wives in both the Amish and English communities had to contend with popped up.

Elizabeth called to the children, who were outside playing by the side of the house. "Come on in," she said. "You've got chores to finish up before supper."

The children hustled into the house without so much as a single whine, and Elizabeth closed the kitchen window to keep the mosquitoes out. The insects tended to step up their invasion once the sun began going down.

———

OUT BY THE BARN, IT WASN'T LONG BEFORE JOSIAH TURNED THE conversation back to Mark's presidential run.

"So what do you think went wrong?" Josiah asked.

"I took my eyes off the road and ran off into a ditch."

"I mean with your political campaign."

"Guess I ran that into the ditch too. Or maybe I should say I was pushed off the road."

"What do you mean?"

"Politics can get dirty. You've got to watch your step ... and your back. But I would've had a chance if they had included me in the debate."

"You got left out of a debate and you called it quits?"

"Hard to recover from that. Especially when your numbers are slipping anyway."

"I'm no expert, Mark," Josiah said, "but I think I know what part of your problem might've been."

"Well, tell me, because I don't have a clue what went wrong."

"I think you ran on things you didn't really believe."

"What do you mean?" Mark said, unsure where Josiah was going with this. "I believed my message."

"If you did, you wouldn't have quit."

"I quit because I couldn't get enough people to believe it with me."

"When you know what you believe, it doesn't matter how many listen or believe it with you. You just go on saying it because *you* believe it. And you say it again. And again. And sooner or later, this one realizes that what you're saying makes sense. And then that one. And before you know it, you might just find yourself winning an election. But you've got to convince the people that *you* believe it first."

I do believe my message ... don't I?

Josiah and Mark continued working on the car, pounding and bending the axle, trying to bring it back to its former operational self. It wasn't easy.

"You did a good bit of damage, Mark," Josiah said.

"Still think you can fix it?"

"I think so. This part anyway. We'll take a break for supper, then come back out and work on it some more. I figure we'll have another hour of daylight then before turning in."

"Supper? I'm still full from dinner."

"In our world, Mark, we work hard and we eat well."

Josiah and Mark washed their hands and then joined the family around the table for the evening meal. It was another big spread, nearly as large as the last one.

"You eat like this all the time?" Mark asked, indiscreetly loosening his belt in a preemptive move.

"The Lord is good," Josiah said, holding out his hand again.

Mark took Josiah's outstretched hand and young Joseph's as

they bowed their heads to pray. After grace had been said, the plates started making their rounds.

"You know, I've got a daughter about your age," Mark said to Mary Ann, Josiah's teenage daughter.

Mary Ann perked up with interest. "Does she like to cook?" she asked.

"She used to. She used to make little cupcakes for her mom and me with a toy oven we'd bought her for Christmas."

"They grow up fast, Mr. Stedman," Elizabeth said. "Don't miss any of it."

Mark nodded and tried not to look in the direction of the empty place setting again.

———

"I DON'T KNOW HOW MUCH MORE I CAN TAKE," BART SAID TO Marcia after Harley barked his latest order at Bart before retreating to his office. "The closer we get to the election, the worse he gets. I'm about ready to quit!"

"You can't quit, Bart. You're family. Turn your back on family when they need you — even the bullies of the bunch — and there's always a price to pay."

"It can't be any more than what I'm paying now."

"You'd better think about this, Bart. What else would you do? Jobs aren't that easy to come by these days."

"Anything would beat this!"

"'You want fries with that?'" Marcia said, changing her voice and acting out Bart's possible future.

"Hey, if it means getting Harley off my back, where do I sign up? No self-respecting person would allow himself to continue being treated like this."

"Have you talked it over with Stella?"

"I don't run everything by my wife."

Marcia didn't respond. She just looked at Bart.

"Okay, I do," Bart said. "But this time I've got to do what's best for me. And believe me, this isn't it."

"Then go on. Call her up and tell her that," Marcia said, holding the phone out to Bart, knowing full well he would balk.

"Oh, I'm going to tell her ... but not on the phone. At home. As soon as I walk through the door."

"Okay," Marcia said, unconvinced.

"You don't think I'll do it, do you?"

"Sure I do."

"You don't think I have the courage."

"I didn't say that."

"You think I can't tell Stella exactly what I think of her father."

"I know you can. I just don't think you will."

"And you probably don't think I'll tell Harley right to his face what a jerk he's been?"

"You're right, I don't."

"Well, then, you'll just have to wait and hear all the details of how I put Harley Phillips in his place when you come in to work tomorrow, won't you?" Bart said with a confident smirk.

Smirks had never come easily for Bart, but as he said, he had reached his limit with his father-in-law. He wasn't going to put up with being used and abused any longer. Family or not, enough was enough was enough!

CHAPTER 8

★

"Have you had enough?" Elizabeth said as she passed the platter of roast beef to Mark. "Or would you like a bit more?"

"More, please," Mark said, taking a large helping. "I don't know where I'm putting it, but this is too good to pass up. Another delicious meal, ma'am."

Elizabeth thanked him, and then, one by one, the children asked to be excused. Without being told, they took their plates to the kitchen.

"I don't know what your secret is for child rearing," Mark said, "but if you could bottle it up and sell it, you'd make a fortune!"

"It's no secret," Elizabeth said. "We live simply and teach our children to work hard and to love and respect God, others, and the land. In that order. And then we hope and pray it was enough."

"Well, they sure are good kids. You've done something right."

Josiah smiled. "We've just done the best we know how."

"That's all any of us can do," Mark said. "Even when you do all the right things, there still aren't any guarantees."

"Life doesn't give us guarantees on much of anything, Mark. But like I said, you just do the best you know how. So what do you think? You ready to get back at it?" Josiah asked.

Mark took one last bite of mashed potatoes, savoring the taste of it, and licked a bit of gravy off his fork before getting up to follow Josiah out the door.

Back at the car, Josiah and Mark resumed their unconventional repairs on the bent axle, trying to shape it back into place. The sound of metal on metal echoed off the barn walls, as did the intermittent sound of their laughter.

"So, what about you?" Mark asked. "Aside from encountering tourists every season, have you ever gotten a taste of life on the outside?"

"I got a small taste of it in my *rumspringa* days. After that, I knew this was where I'd be most content. My heart is here."

"Rumspringa?"

"It's a period of time when Amish young people experience the outside world before deciding whether they want to join the Amish church."

"So our world didn't hold any interest for you, then?"

"Look around you," Josiah said, gesturing to the green, rolling hills that surrounded them, and to his wife, who was playing with their children by the porch. "Tell me what I'm missing."

Mark nodded in understanding.

"How about you?" Josiah asked. "Any regrets about becoming a politician?"

"Only that I didn't do enough. I was driven when I first came to Washington. Driven and focused on making a difference. But I lost something along the way . . ."

"And what's that?"

"My vision, I guess. Happens to the best of us. We come to Washington with grand ideas of how we're going to change things, change the way the place operates. But instead of changing Washington, something changes inside of us. We get that addictive taste of power, and before long, we're not voting our conscience."

"Power's not all it's cracked up to be. The Amish have known that for years."

Mark smiled. "Don't get me wrong. Most of us use our power for all the right reasons — to help our country, fix her problems, and protect our freedoms — but we . . . well, to tell you the truth, I don't know which we lose first — our vision or our way."

"One's just as important as the other—where you're heading and how you get there."

"Yes, but we get so frustrated with the system. It wears us down, and then some of us just stop fighting it. It's easier to go along with the majority than to stand for something alone."

"A vision worth having is a vision worth holding on to," Josiah said, giving the axle one final good strike before calling it a day. "We'll finish this up tomorrow. The sun's about gone, and it looks like there's a storm fixing to roll in too."

Without street lights and neon signs, it got rather dark in the little Amish community, so the men started wrapping up their work.

"Thanks again for all your help," Mark said.

When the men walked into the house, they found Elizabeth sitting on the sofa making some repairs to a pair of Josiah's pants. Mark sheepishly looked at her and asked, "I don't suppose there'd be any of that shoofly pie left over from supper?"

"Oh, I reckon I might be able to scrounge up a piece," Elizabeth said as she put down her sewing and got the men another slice of the popular Amish pie made from molasses. It was every bit as good as it had been earlier. And the slice after that one was even better.

"So what does your wife think about you quitting the campaign?" Josiah asked once the kids had said their prayers and were off to bed, their playful sounds hushed for the night.

"We've both accepted the fact that this wasn't our time."

"And what would make it your time, Mark?"

"Well, for one thing, the party would have to back me 100 percent. And I'd have to do a better job of fund-raising."

"It takes a lot of money to run for president, does it?" Josiah said.

"More than I ever realized. I was outspent four to one! These days, it's all about fund-raising."

"It's about a lot more than that, my friend."

Mark knew what Josiah meant.

"It seems campaigns have become more about who can buy the cleverest, or nastiest, campaign ads."

"It gets pretty competitive, huh?"

"It can get downright mean-spirited. Everyone jockeying for position. Some will do or say whatever it takes to get elected."

"So they don't just want the best man to win?"

"Only if that man or woman is them," Mark said. "I tried to be a different kind of candidate, but as you can see, I'm out of the race."

Carl had once tried to talk Mark into doing a bit of mudslinging himself, but Mark was proud that he hadn't stooped to that level.

At least I can sleep at night.

Mark prided himself on giving others the benefit of the doubt. The atmosphere of trial by rumor and innuendo that seemed to prevail in the politics of the day had left a bad taste in his mouth. As unreliable as most rumors were, he was surprised to see how quickly folks turned on someone they had believed in for years, sometimes decades. Loyalty these days was wafer thin, and many a stellar career had been destroyed by the unproven and unchallenged words of its rivals.

Elizabeth showed Mark to the guest room and told him he was welcome to take a bath before turning in. Mark looked at his watch. It was eight o'clock.

Is she serious?

His normal routine was to work on his computer, then catch the late-night comedy shows, turning in somewhere a little closer to midnight. But there would be no late-night comedy shows tonight because there was no TV.

Mark sighed, figuring he could use the rest anyway.

After taking his bath, Mark lay down on the bed and stared out the window at the stars in the sky. It had been a while since he'd actually taken the time to look at the stars. He was pleased to know they were still there, just as they had been on his grandpa's farm so many years ago.

CHAPTER 9

★

A SPRINGTIME THUNDERSTORM HAD PASSED THROUGH LAN-caster County overnight, leaving the grass even more lush and the roads cleaner, if that were possible. After a hearty break-fast, Mark and Josiah got an early start on completing the repairs to the government car's axle. It was looking better. They still had the cracked radiator to deal with, but the axle would soon be cor-rected. As much as Mark was enjoying the company and hospital-ity of his new friends, he was eager to get home to Cindy.

Carrying a metal bucket, Mary Ann walked by, heading to the chicken coop. She waved to Josiah and to Mark.

"You're up mighty early, young lady," Mark said, impressed with such a responsible teenager.

Mary Ann smiled and continued on her way.

"She's going to feed the chickens."

"She does her chores before school?" Mark asked, amazed.

"She already milked the cows. They all have morning chores," Josiah said. "It teaches them responsibility."

Mark thought of his own kids and wondered what their record was for hitting the snooze button before finally dragging them-selves out of bed and getting dressed for school. He was sure it was something for Guinness's book of world records.

BART CAME TO WORK IN THE MORNING LOOKING UNUSUALLY well rested and unstressed.

"So how'd it go?" Marcia asked.

"Great!" Bart said.

"So you did it?"

"You should've heard me. I said, 'Harley, you have talked down to me for the last time! If I have to endure your constant barrage of put-downs, I will not remain in your employ. You are an overbearing, opinionated, condescending, egomaniac bully, and I wouldn't vote for you if you were the only name on the ballot and you offered me the job of my choice on your cabinet!"

Bart beamed with satisfaction. He had finally done it!

"Wow!" Marcia said, looking quite impressed. "You said all that to Harley?"

"Harley? Are you kidding? I said it to my therapist. I stopped by there on my way home yesterday, and she had me do some role playing. Baby steps."

"I should've known," Marcia said, shaking her head. "No one stands up to Harley Phillips and stays around long enough to tell it."

Bart knew it was safer for him to tell his woes to a paid listener who charged him one hundred dollars an hour to hear his complaints. That way his job stayed intact, his marriage wouldn't suffer, and his blood pressure wouldn't trigger the alarm on his portable blood-pressure machine.

Harley stepped into the room. "What have you heard? Did you get me booked for that speaking deal? Am I on the list?"

"The foundation event?" Bart asked. "Well, I tried, but they're still saying there's no time for you to speak."

"What difference does it make?" Marcia added. "I thought you were going to crash it anyway."

"I will if I have to, but I'd rather be included on the program. I don't want it to look like I invited myself," Harley said.

"But you are inviting yourself," Marcia pointed out.

"Keep working on it," Harley said to Bart, seemingly undaunted by Marcia's barb.

"There's nothing to work on, sir," Bart said.

"Listen, Bart. Tell them they can give me the light or play-off music or whatever cue they want. Just get me up there!"

Bart knew the foundation event was especially important for Harley. It was a gathering of some of the nation's most influential leaders and philanthropists. The Montgomery/Stead/Ross Foundation Dinner was an event his father-in-law not only needed to attend but also needed to be included as an honored guest on the program. After that last go-round when Harley had monopolized the program, the event planners didn't want him anywhere near the microphone again, presidential candidate or not. They had said as much to Bart when he'd tried once again to persuade them to reconsider. To some program officials, the thrill of having a presidential candidate on your stage paled in comparison to disrupting their already-set committee plans.

How could Bart convince the event chairman that Harley was ready to concede a few things now—his never-ending speech being one of them? Bart knew that Harley had already taken the editing pencil to his impassioned, forty-five-minute, off-the-cuff remarks and pared them down to a mere twenty minutes. But the committee didn't know that. Nor did they care.

"I can get it down more," Harley said. "Ten minutes. *Ten minutes!* That's all I'm asking for. Tell them ten minutes. I'm still the front-runner in most of the polls. Does that mean anything to anyone around here?"

"I'll ask them one more time," Bart said.

"Good. Good." Harley looked pleased. "They'll come to their senses, I'm sure of it. Still no word on Stedman's supporters?"

"Last I heard, Congressman Stedman was driving home, sir. Probably wouldn't make an announcement this soon anyway. You're not actually counting on his endorsement, are you, sir?"

"If he knows what's best for this country, I am. Look, I know he and I don't always see eye to eye, but Stedman loves America. He'll do what's right."

———

JOSIAH HAMMERED THE FINAL BLOW TO THE TWEAKED AXLE OF the government car. Aside from an assortment of dimples and dents, the car looked almost as good as new. Almost.

"You should be able to steer her now," Josiah said.

Mark checked the car over, impressed with his and Josiah's handiwork.

"We should open up a shop — Buggies and Bureaucrats." Mark laughed. Then he made a make-shift funnel and poured some of the horses' water into the radiator. He sat down in the driver's seat and turned the key. The engine choked and sputtered, eventually turning over, but steam immediately started billowing out of the engine. Mark turned the steering wheel slowly to the left and then to the right.

"Can't go anywhere till the radiator's fixed," he said.

"Can't help you there. But like I said yesterday, I've got a Mennonite friend who lives over in — "

"Bird-in-Hand, right?"

"Good memory."

"Hard to forget a name like that."

"Well, I've got some errands to run with Elizabeth later, so I'll run you up to the phone now so we can see if my friend Jake can help you out."

The two men got in the buggy and rode back to the house of the Mennonite family with the phone to place a call to Jake's Radiator Shop in Bird-in-Hand, Pennsylvania. Jake himself took the call and promised to have a tow out to Josiah's place as soon as possible. Mark also asked the Mennonite family if he could place another call to his wife. They were more than obliging.

"Hi, hon," he said when Cindy answered after the first ring.

"Please tell me you're on your way home."

"Got everything fixed except the radiator," he said. "But we've got a tow on its way now. As soon as that's repaired, I'll be heading out."

"Okay. Get here as soon as you can. We miss you," Cindy said.

"None of this was in my plans. But it's working out. Could've been worse, I guess."

Life can always be worse, he thought.

"Bye, hon," Mark said. Once again, he thanked the Mennonite family and then climbed back into the buggy with Josiah.

The tow truck arrived at Josiah's place shortly after Mark and Josiah arrived in the buggy. Mark suggested he ride with the driver into town and then leave from there as soon as the work was finished.

"You could do that," Josiah said. "But aren't you forgetting something, my friend?"

Mark looked at him, puzzled. "What's that?"

"Don't you owe me a day of baling hay?" Josiah said, raising an eyebrow and giving a friendly grin.

"You're right. I'm sorry," Mark said, embarrassed. "Guess I forgot."

Mark intended to fulfill his part of the bargain; he truly had just forgotten. He hoped Josiah would understand and believe him.

Mark and Josiah watched as the tow-truck driver hitched up the car and hauled it away. Then Mark turned to Josiah, "Well, let's get started on that hay."

"Can't today," Josiah said. "I've got those errands to run with Elizabeth and the children. You're welcome to join us, if you like. Or you can stay here. But we'll start baling first thing in the morning."

Mark really wanted to get on the road, but he couldn't very well take all of Josiah and Elizabeth's hospitality for granted and not help with the baling as he'd promised.

"That's fine. Tomorrow it is. If it's all the same to you, I think

I'll stay here and take care of some business." He had retrieved his briefcase from the car before the tow truck showed up and had plenty of paperwork to take care of. It would certainly keep him busy for the rest of the afternoon, or until Josiah and his family returned from their errands.

———

THAT NIGHT, MARK ENJOYED ANOTHER DELICIOUS AMISH MEAL, this one topped off by homemade peach cobbler.

If I had to get stranded, I sure picked the right place to do it, he thought.

"So what time should I set my alarm for?" he asked as they all got ready to turn in.

"'Bout 4:30 should be fine," Josiah said.

Mark tried to not let the chagrin show on his face. *Four thirty a.m.? Is he joking? Who gets up at 4:30 in the morning?*

Roosters, that was who.

———

IT WAS MOSTLY DARK OUTSIDE WHEN THE COCK-A-DOODLE-DOOS started coming through the open window in the room where Mark was sleeping. Apparently he'd been so tired the previous morning, he'd slept through the barnyard symphony. But this morning he heard it loud and clear. He pressed his pillow over his head, trying to drown out their cackling chorus. It didn't work. The crowing continued, and roosters didn't have snooze alarms.

Mark stumbled out of bed and made his way down the hallway to the bathroom. He splashed some water on his face, slapped himself a few times, and then returned to his room.

He hadn't brought any outdoor clothes with him — he hadn't planned on baling hay on his way home from Washington, D.C. — and the only semicasual clothes he had were the pants and shirt he'd worn the day before. Elizabeth graciously offered to wash those on the washboard so they'd be dry by the time the men were done with their work. In the meantime, it was decided that Mark would borrow some of Josiah's Amish clothes for the fieldwork.

"Good thing you're my size," Mark said when he walked into the dining room wearing the traditional Amish pants, shirt, and suspenders.

The kids looked up and gave a slight giggle at the sight of the man from Washington in their Amish clothing.

"Children," Elizabeth reprimanded, biting her lip as if to hold back a smile herself. The kids obeyed and stopped their giggling.

Mark was still surprised to see the children up so early in the morning. Up and wide awake, ready to start their day. Some mornings he didn't see his own kids' opened eyes until he was dropping them off at school. But it was too early in the morning for deep philosophical thoughts about his family dynamics. He greeted the children and sat down at the table.

Josiah's clothes fit Mark adequately. He missed having a pocket in the pants, but Josiah had already explained that Amish pants didn't typically have pockets. Mark did like the suspenders, though. So much so that he entertained the thought of buying a pair for himself to wear under his suits.

"That bacon sure smells good," Mark said.

"It'll be on the table shortly," Josiah said. "We'll eat a hearty breakfast first and then commence working at sunrise."

"I sure appreciate all you've done for me," Mark said.

"Glad to help," Josiah responded. "Believe me, my friend, today you'll earn your breakfast."

Mark waited for Josiah to say the traditional prayer.

"Would you like to say grace today?" Josiah asked Mark.

"Sure," Mark said, trying to recall some of the eloquent words he'd used in invocations delivered before Congress and at other special events. No words came to him, though, except honest and simple gratefulness for this good family who had shown him such kindness. "Lord, thank you for this meal before us and for this kind and loving family who are helping me more than they realize."

After the prayer, Elizabeth carried a platter of scrambled eggs from the gas stove behind them to the table and placed it between a bowl of white gravy and a platter of hashed brown potatoes. Mark could get used to this kind of home cooking.

"You ever baled hay before?" Josiah asked.

Mark nodded. "With my grandpa. It's been a while. But I imagine it's a bit different on an Amish farm. You use a tractor?"

"No, but we do use a hay baler. Our horses pull it."

Mark was curious to see how it was all done.

After breakfast, Mark followed Josiah out to the barn through the low-lying fog that hugged the landscape. The temperature was pleasant. It was the start of a beautiful day in Lancaster County. The morning air felt good to Mark, who tended to spend most of his time indoors, sitting behind a desk—a Washington "insider" by all definitions.

Josiah and Mark hitched up the team of draft horses, and then connected the hitch to a wheeled cart on which Josiah would stand to steer the horses. The hay baler followed that and would bale the hay into rectangular bundles. Mark would then take the bundles off the conveyor belt and stack them on the flatbed wagon that followed behind the baler.

"Now if everything goes according to plan, we should be done by this afternoon," Josiah promised.

"Sounds good," Mark said with a nod.

"You ready?"

"Let's do it!"

Josiah clicked his tongue and snapped the reins. The horses snorted, then took off toward the field.

"According to the *Farmer's Almanac*—and my knees—there won't be a drop of rain today," Josiah said.

Mark smiled. "My granddad used the same forecast system. He'd always tell me, 'Gather what you can in good weather, boy, so you'll be prepared for whatever the future brings.'"

"I would've liked your grandfather. He was a very wise man."

CHAPTER 10

★

"Ten minutes," Bart said when he walked into Harley's office. "That's what they'll give you—ten minutes and not a second more."

"You told them I'd take it, right?"

"They were emphatic, Harley. Ten minutes."

"Got it. Ten minutes. Book it!"

Bart had already booked it, but he wasn't going to give Harley the satisfaction of knowing that. It gave Bart a certain sense of satisfaction to annoy Harley in this manner. (The Put Upon take what they can get.)

Harley seemed to be satisfied with the ten minutes, and Bart didn't want to wait around for him to start looking for wiggle room, trying to push the allotted time to eleven minutes, or twelve, or whatever he could add on. As Bart walked out of Harley's office, though, he could have sworn he heard his father-in-law mutter, "Once I'm onstage, they won't have the guts to kick me off."

Bart headed down the hall to the campaign manager's office. Stacy Creighton was in the middle of finalizing a string of a dozen or so whistle-stops on the upcoming Harley campaign train when Bart walked into his office.

"Well, I told him," Bart said.

Stacy looked up from his paperwork. "You said ten minutes, right?"

"Ten minutes and not one second or syllable more."

"And?"

"He said to take it," Bart said with a shrug, surprised at Harley's acquiescence and suspicious of it at the same time.

"I still think it's a mistake," Stacy said.

"The whole campaign is a mistake," Bart replied, glancing up and noticing the latest Harley for President poster on the wall. In this one, Harley's smile looked even wider and brighter than before, sincere even. Ah, the wonders of Photoshop.

"So tell me again why we're backing someone you and I both know would make a lousy president?" Bart asked.

"Because he's paying me to manage this campaign, and you're his son-in-law," Stacy said.

"Well, at least we've got good reasons," Bart said with a sigh, disappointed—mostly in himself.

———

THE TOW-TRUCK DRIVER BROUGHT THE CAR BACK AROUND eleven o'clock that morning. Mark took a much-needed break from baling hay to test out the car. It seemed to be working fine, so he paid the driver and returned to his work. He was exhausted, but it felt good to be out in the sun, working up a sweat. And working off some of that peach cobbler from the previous night's supper.

By midafternoon, the flatbed wagon was piled high with bales of hay. Josiah steered the horses and the wagon back to the barn, where the men loaded the bales onto a conveyor belt that took the hay up to the top of the barn. Once their work was done, Josiah and Mark sat down on a couple of old tree stumps and caught their breath.

"I don't know which was more work—fixing your car or baling my hay," Josiah said. "I think I might owe you."

"I'm all for calling it even."

Josiah nodded in agreement. "Stay for supper?"

"Thanks, but I should probably change and get on my way before my wife decides to drive down and fetch me herself."

"Spend time with her, Mark," Josiah said. "Live your convictions. It's a *gut* thing that you both still care about each other after … How many years you been married?"

"Well, let's see, twenty — oh no!" Mark stopped short.

"What's wrong?"

"The gift! I need to buy my wife an anniversary gift. You see, I've been so distracted, I'd somehow forgotten the date, but I didn't tell her that. Then I told her that I'd already gotten her something. So I …"

"Lied?"

"Well, technically, yeah, I guess. Sort of. But it's one of those lies that doesn't really count."

"They all count, Mark."

"You think I should've admitted I'd forgotten our anniversary? How would that have made her feel?"

"Upset that you forgot one of the most important dates of your life. But she'll know she can trust you to always tell her the truth. No gift can buy that."

Mark wondered if Josiah was right. But before he could agree or disagree with him, Josiah asked, "Does your wife like quilts?"

"Sure. Why?"

"Elizabeth makes beautiful quilts."

"Oh, Cindy would love that! How much do you want for one?"

"It would be our gift to you both."

"No, no. A quilt has too much work in it for you to give it to us," Mark said.

"I'm a farmer and Elizabeth is a quilter. We're specialists." Josiah laughed. "It's either the quilt or a bale of hay. Take your pick."

"The quilt, then," Mark said. "If you're sure."

"*Jah*, I'm sure. And we send it along with our prayer that God continues to bless your marriage."

"We're not talking about 'quivers' again, are we?" Mark asked. "'Cause I've got all the kids I can handle right now."

"God knows what kind of blessings you need, Mark," Josiah said. "Let him surprise you."

Mark selected an impeccably crafted quilt from Elizabeth's collection and then, after a quick change of clothes, loaded his belongings into the car.

"I can't thank you enough for all your help. Are you sure I can't pay you anything?"

"Kindness doesn't have a price tag."

Mark raised an eyebrow. "Have you ever been to D.C.?" He laughed.

"You can make it better, Mark," Josiah said.

Mark was tempted to reiterate how he's tried and how it was someone else's problem now, but he needed to get back on the road. "Thanks again," he said as got into the car.

"Keep her on the road. She'll operate better that way." Josiah laughed.

"No more Dashboard Lady, that's for sure," Mark said, waving a paper in his hand. "Got directions from the tow-truck driver. And I'll tell Cindy the truth about the gift."

Josiah smiled, pleased. "Enjoy," he said. "Both the quilt and the clear conscience. They'll both help you sleep better at night."

With one last wave good-bye to his friends, Mark was finally on his way home.

MARK MADE HIS WAY THROUGH THE COUNTRY ROADS, WATCHING the pastoral setting change into landscape punctuated with billboards and telephone poles. Eventually he merged onto the highway, heading in the direction of Wisconsin.

It wasn't long before Mark glanced down at his fuel gauge and realized it was getting uncomfortably close to empty. He pulled off the highway and into the first filling station he came to. He grimaced at the price of the gas as he took the cap off his fuel tank and began pumping the $5.40 a gallon liquid gold into the car. Other customers stared at him. Mark suspected that they had recognized him and were wondering if they were seeing who they thought they were seeing.

Mark turned to the curious gawkers and said, "Yeah, we have to pay these prices too."

When he was done, he got back into his car and headed down the highway. After settling into a lane, he checked his iPhone, thrilled to see three bars of reception. He decided to place some calls with his hands-free device.

After checking in with Cindy and Carl, it was Sam Lynch's turn. Mark dreaded the call. He knew what Sam wanted—Mark's endorsement for Harley Phillips. But Mark wasn't ready to toss that Harley's way—not yet anyway.

"Where have you been?" Sam barked when he picked up the phone.

"Sorry. Had a car wreck and ..."

"We've been trying to reach you for two days! We need that endorsement."

"I'm fine, thanks," Mark said.

"Car wreck? What are you doing, Stedman? Can't you stay out of the news for one week?" Sam said. Then, realizing his insensitivity, he added, "You okay?"

"Yeah, I'm fine. Tell Harley I'll have to get back to him on the endorsement, though. Still haven't made up my mind."

"We've got an election to win here, Mark. We could use a little cooperation. I thought you were a team player."

"I'm fully aware of the election, Sam," Mark said. "I just need to be sure before I—"

"Listen to me, Stedman! We're running against the clock here. New York and Pennsylvania are just around the corner. Harley needs that endorsement to carry those states."

"My endorsement's going to matter? I only had 10 percent, remember?"

"It could help carry Pennsylvania. You polled well there."

Now he notices?

"And some of the other states that are too close to call," Sam added.

As if on cue, Mark drove past a Harley Phillips for President billboard featuring a broadly smiling, bigger-than-life photo of Harley. It read, "Get America back on the right road! Elect Harley Phillips!"

Mark spoke aloud to the billboard, "Yeah, and let you drive us all right into the ditch?"

"What?" Sam asked, still waiting on the line for Mark's answer.

"Uh, nothing," Mark said, realizing Sam had heard him venting. "I was just talking to an idiot."

"Crazy drivers, huh? Look, Mark, we need a decision, and we need it now."

Okay, if that's the way they want to play.

"Sam, I can't in good conscience endorse Phillips. But I will endorse someone soon. I promise."

"Who's talking about conscience, Mark? I'm talking about not sabotaging the party! Now I'm asking you for the last time, give Harley your votes!"

With that Sam slammed down his phone. Apparently the conversation was over.

"Jerk!" Mark said, confident that this time Sam wasn't on the other end of the line listening. But even if Sam had been listening, the description was a fair one, at least in Mark's opinion. Being pushed into endorsing a candidate he didn't believe in went against everything Mark stood for.

For the remainder of the drive home, Mark tried to put Washington politics behind him. He would drive as far as he could, get a room for the night, and then finish the drive the following day. He would soon be home with his family. Even with all their walls up, Mark never doubted their loyalty. Who needed wafflers? Who needed people who were behind him one day, but who hardly remembered his name the next?

Mark had been instrumental in giving Sam his first official position in the party. Had Sam forgotten that? Of course he had. Just like all the other people Mark had helped over the years. An epidemic of short memory spans was sweeping across Washington and infecting almost everyone in Mark Stedman's political life. The silence of friends and coworkers who had come to his defense following the debate snub had been deafening.

Mark didn't have to wonder where he stood with Cindy and the kids, though. He didn't have to wake up in the morning and wonder if he'd lost their love and support because of some decision he had made on behalf of the family. Or some unfounded rumor they'd heard. They loved him enough to trust his good sense and fair judgment. Even his teenagers.

He wished politics could operate the same way. Even though most of the politicians he knew were good people at the core, these days a politician was only as good as his or her last decision. And sometimes politicians didn't even get credit for that.

But Washington wasn't Mark's problem to fix anymore.

If it could be fixed.

———

As soon as Cindy heard Mark's car pull into the driveway, she ran out to meet him. The thought of Mark running the vehicle off the road had stirred a fear inside her that only seeing her husband in person would settle.

"Are you sure you're okay?" she asked, wrapping her arms around him the moment he stepped out of the car. He returned the embrace.

"I'm fine, really," Mark said. "Oh, I've missed you."

They exchanged a tender kiss.

"I can't believe it's over," Cindy said.

"Seems surreal, doesn't it?"

"You miss it yet?"

"Haven't been out of it long enough to miss it. But I will tell you this ..."

"What's that, Congressman?" she said, snuggling closer, savoring the moment.

"I've missed you. It feels good to have you in my arms again," Mark said. "And to finally be home."

Later that evening, Cindy watched as Mark sat at his bedroom desk working. It was good to have him home with her. During his many years in politics, she had never liked being away from him. She knew he was a family man at heart and would do anything for her or the kids, yet politics was a career that didn't lend itself easily to an abundance of family time. His chosen profession had cost them all something. She knew what it had cost Mark personally, but she was certain he had no clue what it had cost her and the kids.

Cindy finished brushing her hair and then walked over and began massaging Mark's neck.

"That feels good," Mark said, leaning back in the chair.

"I'm sorry about the campaign, Mark, but I'll admit I'm happy I won't have to share you anymore."

"Maybe things will get back to normal now, huh?" Mark said.

Cindy gave a slight nod and waited a few moments before asking what she really wanted to know. When the moment felt right, she cautiously broached the subject.

"Is that really where you were, Mark? An Amish farm?"

"I'm not that creative, Cindy," Mark said. "I couldn't make up something like that."

Mark had never given Cindy any reason to doubt his faithfulness. But with all the time he spent on the road and with the media all too often breaking stories about politicians caught in the scandal of a double life, she couldn't keep her mind from wandering there.

"So we're okay?" she asked.

"Better than okay."

Mark stood and took Cindy in his arms again, holding her close. "You know, sweetheart, I learned a lot these last few days," he said.

"On the Amish farm?"

Mark nodded. "Things I thought I knew about myself but didn't really."

"Like?"

"Like how far off the mark I am."

Mark took the quilt out of his suitcase and handed it to her.

"Happy anniversary," he said.

Cindy was delighted and excitedly unfolded the handmade quilt, marveling at the intricate detail.

"Oh, my. It's beautiful!" she said. "I guess you *were* on an Amish farm. They don't sell these at the mall."

"You like it?"

"Oh, sweetheart, I love it!"

"I have a confession to make."

"Okay," Cindy said, haltingly.

"When I told you I'd bought your gift, I hadn't yet."

"I know," Cindy said with relief.

"You knew?"

"You've had a lot on your mind. It's okay."

"You're not mad at me?"

"Well, the quilt helps." Cindy smiled. "I really do love it."

"I'll have to take you there to meet them sometime — that Amish family. You'd like them. Especially Josiah."

"He really impressed you, huh?" Cindy said.

"Impressed? A man like that should be running this country," Mark said. "Not Harley Phillips! Or any of the others. Not even me."

"An Amish president?" Cindy laughed at the thought.

"Oh, I'm not saying him, per se. I know that's impossible. The

Amish don't get involved in national politics. But someone like him," Mark said. "Someone with that kind of common sense and Lincoln-like wisdom."

"You're like that." Cindy smiled.

"Not even close."

———

"WHAT'RE YOU THINKING ABOUT?" ELIZABETH ASKED JOSIAH as they sat on their porch swing drinking a glass of sweet tea.

"The barn raising this weekend."

"Too bad Mark couldn't have stayed for that. He probably would've liked watching it."

"Watching it? I would've put him to work." Josiah laughed.

"You really enjoyed his company, *jah*?"

"He was an interesting fellow. Hope he made it home all right. So are you still wanting to go over to Sister Burkholder's?"

"*Jah*. I made some fried pies for her today."

"You made extra, right?"

"I made extra." Elizabeth smiled.

"Apple?"

"Of course."

"You're a *gut* wife, Elizabeth."

"All I did was make some fried pies."

"I know. But you planted the apple tree too."

Together Elizabeth and Josiah loaded the children into their buggy to make their special delivery. Mrs. Burkholder, the Amish widow who lived about a mile down the road, had been ill, and Elizabeth, being Elizabeth, had promised her some of her locally famous fried pies.

They were the only buggy on the road that clear, cool evening. Not even an automobile passed by. As DayBreak clip-clopped by the ditch where Mark had driven off the road, Josiah glanced in that direction, remembering the politician who had been a part of their family for a few days and wondering what the purpose had been for that unplanned detour in both of their lives.

———

THE NEXT MORNING, CARL WILSON WAS FEELING DOWN AND had no desire to report to Stedman's Wisconsin campaign headquarters, but he figured he might as well go ahead and finish packing up the campaign paraphernalia. He had to stand on a chair to reach an Elect Stedman poster that was just out of his reach, much as the election had been for the congressman — so close and yet so far away.

Carl had been a faithful campaign manager for Mark, but after Mark's premature withdrawal from the election, there was nothing left to manage. It was time to pack up the past and look to the future. Maybe the congressman would run again someday. He was still young enough to attempt a presidential run plenty more times in his political life. That is, if he wanted to.

Carl freed three corners of the poster and was right in the middle of removing the final tack when his cell phone started ringing. He held the loosened poster with his left hand and took the phone out of his pocket with his right. Then he looked down at the caller ID. It was Mark.

"You back?" Carl said, nearly losing his balance.

"Yeah. It's good to be home."

"Sam's been calling every couple of hours, you know."

"I've already talked to him."

"Well?"

"To tell you the truth, I don't like any of 'em enough to endorse them, Carl. Least of all Harley."

"I know. But Sam's right — it'll be worse if the other side ends up winning in November."

"Would it?" Mark said.

CHAPTER 11

MARK CONTINUED THE CONVERSATION WITH CARL THE FOL-
lowing day at a café around the corner from Mark's Wisconsin office.

"Come on, Mark. Just give Sam what he wants, and he'll help
you win it the next go-round."

"Like he helped me this time? Besides, I might not ever run
again. Then what?"

"Then you'll still know you took the higher ground."

"And sold my country down the river? For what? So a candidate I don't believe in can get elected?"

"Which candidate *do* you believe in, Mark?"

"I told you, none of them."

"Exactly. So what point are you trying to prove here? Someone's got to serve in the office."

"I just wish there was a candidate I could get excited about.
Someone with good old-fashioned common sense. Someone who's
not afraid to roll up his sleeves and get his hands dirty. Someone
like ... well, like that Amish man I met this week."

"The one who pulled you out of the ditch?"

"Yeah."

"You want us to elect an Amish man for president? I take it
there was a head injury involved in that accident of yours?"

"I'm not saying to elect him. The Amish don't run for national
offices. I'm just saying someone with his sensibilities."

"Well, it's probably too late in the game for anyone new to step in and seal the primary nomination. So it's either Harley or Kurtzfield."

"What if it goes to a brokered convention? What if none of the candidates gets enough delegates?"

"Okay, then what? What are you saying?"

"Then the votes are released. An outsider could be nominated at that point, right?"

"Well, sure, but that's not going to happen. Harley's pulling ahead. That's why he's so desperate for your endorsement to seal the deal."

"What if I endorsed someone outside the party?"

Mark could see the disbelief on Carl's face.

"What are you saying, Mark? That you're leaving the party?"

"Just weighing all the options. I wouldn't be the first politician to switch horses midstream."

"You're not thinking about running as an Independent, are you?"

"The thought's crossed my mind."

"Mark, as your campaign manager, I'd strongly advise against it. For a number of reasons."

"Burning my bridges?"

"That. And reality. Look, Mark, you know I'm loyal. In fact, I think you'd make a great president. But you were barely getting 10 percent with the party backing you. Strike out on your own, and you'll just be a spoiler. Besides, talk about sabotaging yourself. Every ounce of clout you've earned over the span of your career would evaporate overnight. Are you willing to let all that go just to make sure Harley Phillips doesn't win?"

"I just said the thought had crossed my mind. Didn't say I was doing it. But I might be endorsing someone else."

"Who?"

"They haven't announced their candidacy yet."

"Well, they'd better hurry. It's getting late in the game, you know."

"Deadline for a write-in-candidate in most states is just weeks out from the general election."

"Okay, you *did* hit your head in that car wreck."

"I assure you my head's fine. In fact, my thinking is the clearest it's ever been."

"Mark, do you know how many write-in candidates have ever won the presidency? None! Not a single one. You'd be throwing away your vote, your endorsement, and your party. That's your brilliant plan?"

"Like I said, I'm weighing my options."

"Mark, think about what you're doing here. Even if you don't switch allegiance, just flirting with the idea is going to cost you something. You realize that?"

"I just want to get the best person in the White House. And that's *not* Harley Phillips."

Mark knew that Sam was chomping at the bit for his endorsement for Harley, and he also figured if Carl delivered it to Sam today, it could translate into a choice party position for Mark should he ever want to call in that card. Reciprocal back-scratching. In Washington, it never hurt to have people owe you favors.

"Think about what you're doing, Mark," Carl was saying. "You've already withdrawn from the race. Let it go. Give it to Harley this go-round, and when he makes a mess of things after four years, you can swoop in again and save the nation."

"I'd rather save the nation now!" Mark couldn't wait to call Sam himself and tell him that he wouldn't be endorsing Harley Phillips or any of the other candidates. He would only endorse someone with old-fashioned values and common sense, qualities none of the current field of candidates possessed in any great amount.

I'm not compromising, Mark thought. *The stakes are too high.*

Mark had intended to let Carl break the news to Sam, but instead, when he opened his mouth, he found himself saying, "I'll announce my decision tonight. Tell Sam to watch the ten o'clock news."

"Just tell me it's Harley, and you'll make Sam's day," Carl said. "It's how the game is played. You know that. We'll do it next time."

"Just watch the news, Carl."

———

WORD SPREAD QUICKLY THAT CONGRESSMAN MARK STEDMAN was going to make an important announcement at a press conference that evening. No one knew what he was going to say, not even Mark himself, but reporters gathered at the Elect Stedman headquarters, hoping to score a scoop. Mark's supporters were also on hand, hoping that their beloved native son would announce that he was being courted as a vice-presidential candidate by one of the remaining contenders. Having their man on half the ticket was better than nothing. But Mark had no such announcement planned.

"My fellow citizens," Mark began when he stepped up to the microphone in front of his campaign headquarters that evening. "Those of you who are gathered here today, and those who are watching this via satellite feed. I am prepared to announce the name of the candidate I will be endorsing for president of the United States ..."

Mark was more or less winging it at this point. He had narrowed his choices down to a couple of names but hadn't yet made up his mind between them. They were both good choices. One was the governor of Oregon, Wendy Horton, and the other was war hero Trent Davidson, who had won a purple heart in Afghanistan. Both were exceptional people. Neither was a clear choice for Mark, but he was reasonably certain he could sleep at night knowing he had put his stamp of approval on one of them, whether or not the write-in campaign caught any traction.

It was difficult, though, to fake an impassioned endorsement when he wasn't really clear on whom or what he was supposed to be impassioned about. So he hesitated. He wanted to endorse one of those people, to tell everyone watching why either of them would make an exceptional president. But he couldn't manage to get the words out. He may have been winging it, but his wing wasn't helping him much, and now he sounded like one more politician just flying in circles.

"Congressman Stedman, who are you endorsing?" a reporter pressed.

"Well, I'm going to tell you," Mark said, "right now. The person I believe will make the best president and whom I will be endorsing is ..."

Mark took a deep breath. His mind was racing with names. Wendy Horton? Trent Davidson? Or should he be a party loyalist and give Harley or Kurtzfield the endorsement they both so desperately wanted?

And then it happened. To his surprise, a name tumbled out of his mouth before he could stop it. He hadn't seriously considered putting forth this name, but there it was. "Josiah," Mark announced clearly and confidently. There was the passion he had been waiting for. But it was also a ridiculous notion. Mark knew it immediately. It was an "Aha" and "Uh-oh" moment all rolled into one. But the name had fallen from his lips in front of the entire nation, and there was no taking it back now.

"Josiah?" repeated a reporter, looking unsure that he had heard the congressman correctly.

No matter how hard Mark tried to stop his tongue from continuing, it went on full speed ahead. "His name won't be on the ballot, of course, but he can be elected by write-in votes."

A puzzled look came over all the reporters' faces, and frenzied whispers began spreading throughout the crowd.

"Josiah who?" several reporters asked at the same time.

"That's all I'm prepared to say at this time," Mark said.

"I take it he's from outside the Washington establishment?"

"He's as outside as you can get," Mark said with a smile. Then ignoring the wisdom of the saying, "When you find yourself in a hole, stop digging," he added, "He's Amish."

The gasp from the crowd almost sucked the air out of the entire state of Wisconsin.

"Congressman, you're joking, right?" a reporter asked.

"I just want to verify that I'm quoting you correctly," another one said. "You're saying you are endorsing an Amish man for president? Is that correct, sir?"

"That is correct," Mark said, mentally slapping himself on the back of the head for not shutting his mouth sooner. He realized the words he had just spoken would have to be eaten, and eaten quickly, if he were to ever salvage his lifetime reputation of being a stable and reasonable man. He also realized that the late-night talk shows would have a field day with such an outlandish endorsement. Still, the questions kept coming.

"Sir, realizing this is one of the most important elections in our nation's history, do you honestly believe a write-in candidate would even have a chance?"

"Don't most Amish refrain from participating in national elections?"

"A write-in Amish candidate? Is this for real?"

"You're throwing your support to an Amish man named Josiah? Did we hear you correctly, sir?" the first reporter asked, trying to offer the congressman one last out.

Mark considered the out. Now was the time for him to retract his statement before it went any further. He could say he had put the idea out there simply to see if anyone was paying attention. He could laugh it off as his humorous opener and then present the name of one of the other two candidates he was considering endorsing. But Mark had never been very good at midspeech U-turns or post-blooper retractions, so he did what he was good at, especially as of late—he dug that hole even deeper. Besides, he was starting to like the idea the longer he thought about it.

"Yes," Mark said. "That is *exactly* what I am doing."

What am I doing? An Amish man for president? Have I lost my mind?

It was Harley's fault, of course. And Sam's. And the media's. They had all been badgering Mark for an endorsement ever since he left the campaign, and he felt obligated to give them one even though he wasn't ready to make an official announcement. But now that Josiah's name had tumbled out of Mark's mouth, he had no choice but to leave it dangling there for a day or two while he gathered his thoughts. Otherwise, he'd look like a man who couldn't stand by his decisions. No politician wanted to be known as a flip-flopper. Mark would figure out some way to explain away the Josiah gaffe and buy himself more time to make up his mind between Horton and Davidson. It wasn't his Plan A or even his Plan B. It was a lot farther down the alphabet than that. But at least it was a plan.

Immediately after the press conference, Mark's cell phone rang. He looked at the caller ID. It was Sam.

"Right on time," Mark said without the preliminary hello.

"You're crazy, you know that? Bonafide. Certifiable!" The adjectives were coming fast and furious, even for Sam. "A write-in Amish presidential candidate? Why don't you just tell the people to drop their ballots into a shredder?"

"Then how would my candidate get elected?" Mark said, fully aware that he was playing on Sam's last nerve.

"Harley Phillips needs those votes, Mark! I don't think you realize the seriousness of this situation!"

"Oh, I realize it, Sam. Why do you think I'm pledging to do everything in my power to make sure Josiah gets elected?"

"Stop the games, Mark. Do you hate Harley that much?"

"No, just everything he stands for."

Mark ended the call with a sigh, wondering what Josiah was doing at that moment and what the Amish man might think of his ridiculous notion. But unless the press had somehow gotten to him, Josiah was still blissfully unaware that his name had been put forth as a presidential candidate. He was living contentedly in his peaceful Amish community, letting the outside world go about its business while he went about his own. He had crops to harvest, farm animals to feed, and a family to care for. Washington politics were the furthest thing from his mind. Other than the few conversations he'd had with his new friend, as well as any tidbits he'd read in the Amish newspaper or discussed with tourists who came through Lancaster, Josiah hardly thought about national politics at all.

That wasn't the story everywhere else in America. Telephone lines at news stations were lighting up so quickly, it seemed as if some titillating scandal had just broken. Mark knew that in the middle of a lackluster political race, the "Amish candidate" was a gift from heaven for most reporters. Mark would let them enjoy the feeding frenzy for a few days and then retract his statement. He'd say that the reporters and the country had taken him out of context or that he was joking. But until then, this news item was pure gold.

———

"No one's taking you seriously. You know that, don't you?" Carl said to Mark when they met for coffee the following morning.

"It just came out of my mouth," Mark said, surprised at his own verbal faux pas. "I'll make another announcement in a few days and clear it up."

"A write-in ballot for an Amish president?" Carl laughed. "Oh, the comedy writers are going to love this!"

And they obviously did. The topic was unbelievably rich with comic possibilities, and TV comedians took full advantage of the situation. Most of their comedy was done good-humoredly and with respect for the Amish, but there were some edgier bits on a few shows that offended Mark enough for him to write to the shows' staffs. Overall, though, the concept of an Amish candidate was handled with a "Hey, why not?" attitude, and the laughter and excitement it generated seemed to lift the country's mood. Mark welcomed the good-natured ribbing and was thankful to be feeling hopeful again.

Josiah, the mystery candidate, was the opening-monologue topic of every late-night show on the air. One host even had a graphic that superimposed an Amish man's head on Mount Rushmore. It was a humorous bit, and the wide-brimmed hat on the new head surely would have provided ample shade for Lincoln's head had it been real.

Another comedian did a Broadway-style production number on his show, featuring Abraham Lincoln, Ulysses S. Grant, Benjamin Harrison, and Rutherford B. Hayes. The presidential look-alikes sang an Emmy-worthy, choreographed number called "Bring Back the Beards!" It sent ratings through the roof.

The nation's columnists and commentators were picking up on the unusual campaign too.

"Listen to this," Mark said over lunch with Cindy, while reading from a well-known national newspaper. "'Congressman Stedman tosses Amish hat into ring ... Congressman Mark Stedman stunned the nation on Monday when he announced that he would be endorsing an Amish man named Josiah for president. The congressman provided no last name, however our researchers are looking into it and will have more on this story as it develops. Some have speculated that the congressman is suffering from campaign fatigue and a possible head injury that he may have sustained in a recent automobile accident.'"

Mark had to laugh. Since he'd crashed a government vehicle, he'd had to report the accident to officials, and apparently some in the news media were using that to explain away his "irrational behavior."

Irrational or not, people were having a field day with the idea of an Amish president, but to everyone's surprise, most of all Mark's, this outlandish idea began to gain traction. It seemed to appeal to both parties in a nostalgic, fantastical kind of way. What if an Amish family really did move into the White House? What would that mean for America? Could an Amish man get the country back on track? Back to basics? It didn't seem to be as ridiculous a notion as anyone originally thought. Could good old-fashioned common sense really be making a comeback?

Mark began to wonder if he should issue a retraction at all. Josiah was the only candidate who could receive Mark's total and enthusiastic support, so why shouldn't he stick with this endorsement and wait to see what happened? Josiah might not have any chance of actually being elected, but it was worth a try, wasn't it?

———

STORMCLOUD44/BLOG

Has the whole country gone mad? Followers of this blog know I am not a fan of any of the candidates. I am sick and tired of having these people shoved down our throats when we've already told them we want someone new. I'm no fan of Stedman either, but I'll give him this—an Amish man for president. Now *that's* original.

———

"So when do you want me to schedule the press conference?" Carl asked. "It's been a few days. I'd say it's time. You don't want this getting too out of hand."

"I've changed my mind. I'm not going to make a retraction," Mark said emphatically. There would be no further discussion on the matter. "Josiah's my pick."

"Tell me you're not serious."

"I know what you're going to say, Carl, but I've made up my mind."

"You're endorsing an Amish man for president?"

"Yes, I am very proudly endorsing an Amish man for president. There will be no retraction."

"You do realize that when the novelty of this wears off, they'll say you've lost your mind?"

"They're saying that now."

"Mark, the American people will forgive a slipup, a mistake, but buffoonery? Taking them for a ride? If I may speak plainly, sir, you're playing with fire."

"Carl, a wise man once told me that it doesn't matter if people listen or believe you; it only matters that you say what you believe. And I'm saying it—I believe Josiah is *exactly* who we need to lead our country right now."

———

"I AGREE WITH CARL," CINDY SAID WHEN MARK SHARED HIS plan with her. "Retract it, Mark, before you can't pull it back."

"Why would I do that? All the major networks and cable news shows are calling me for interviews about this. *Meet the Press* even asked me to appear as a guest this Sunday. Why stop now?"

"They're saying you've had a break from reality. That's why they want to interview you."

"The reality that there's no one on the ballot exciting enough to vote for? Yeah, I've had a break from that."

"Look, whether you decide you want to get out of politics or run again in four years, either way, I'm here for you. Just don't destroy everything you've worked so hard for."

"What would you say if I told you that I'm thinking about leaving the party?"

"I'd say you'd better think it through. Once you close that gate behind you, it will probably lock you out permanently."

"I know."

As if on cue, Sam called again. Mark thought about ignoring the call but decided against it and answered on the fourth ring.

"Does your Amish friend even know he's running?" Sam asked as soon as Mark came on the line.

"I'm going to tell him ... eventually."

"And I'm going to suggest to Congress that they censure you!"

"They can't. I'm not a member anymore, remember? Look,

Sam, why don't we just let the election run its course? Let the best man or woman win—you know, the way elections are supposed to run." Mark knew he was sealing his fate regarding any future political aspirations, but he wasn't going to back down.

"All right, what's the angle, Mark?" Sam said. "Is this some ploy you've cooked up to get yourself back in the limelight?"

"It's no ploy, Sam. And I've never cared that much for the limelight. I'm convinced that a man like Josiah could be our next great president."

"And I'm convinced you're delusional!"

"The voters are ready for someone like this, Sam. You've seen the polls. Harley's in the lead, but it's no landslide by any stretch of the imagination. Could even turn into a brokered convention. There's no enthusiasm for *any* of the candidates right now. From either party. You know that."

"Sour grapes? Is that what this is?"

"Just honest conviction."

"Well, don't count on any support from us!"

"It doesn't matter. He'll be running as an Independent."

"An Independent! Mark, have you lost your ever-loving mind? What's the matter with you? You'll be dividing our party and giving the other side an unfair advantage."

"Seriously, Sam? After the debate debacle, you're going to talk to me about fairness? *Loyalty?* Don't even go there."

"Think about what you're doing, Mark."

"I *have* been thinking about it, Sam. I don't want to leave the party, but if it's the only way to do this, then so be it."

The two men continued arguing for a few more minutes, but neither side gave in. Sam was convinced this was nothing more than payback for Mark's exclusion from the debate. And Mark was beyond convinced that he had come up with the solution for all of America's woes—the perfect presidential candidate. If Mark Stedman couldn't be president himself, then Josiah was the next best man for the job. Maybe even the better man, as far as Mark was concerned.

———

Bishop Miller paid a visit to the Stoltzfus home. Like Josiah, he knew nothing about Mark Stedman's endorsement of one of his community as a presidential candidate. He simply wanted to invite Josiah and Elizabeth and their children to a barbecue at his house the following Friday afternoon. But even though their buggy was there, no one answered the door. The children would be at their one-room schoolhouse down the road, Bishop Miller figured, but Josiah and Elizabeth should be home.

He tried the stable and found the couple cleaning up the area.

"Brother Josiah and Sister Elizabeth," he said as he walked in. "So here's where you are."

Elizabeth wiped her hands on her apron and reached out to shake the bishop's hand.

"So nice to see you, Bishop Miller," she said.

"I just wanted to stop by and personally invite you folks to the barbecue." The bishop knew how much Josiah loved good fellowship, so there'd be no need to ask him twice.

"I heard about that," Josiah said. "We'll be there. Friday, *jah?*"

Bishop Miller nodded.

"What would you like me to bring?" Elizabeth asked.

"Anything you make will be a delight, Elizabeth," the bishop said. The bishop had sampled Elizabeth's cooking on many past occasions, and he was amply convinced of her culinary talents.

Everyone in the bishop's district loved their community get-togethers. The get-togethers were always great fun, filled with good food (including hand-cranked ice cream) and approved music. Much like a Fourth of July picnic among the English, there was even a little baseball.

"Saw you had some company recently," Bishop Miller said, more curious than anything.

"*Jah,*" answered Josiah. "An English fella drove his automobile into the ditch down the road. My horses pulled it out, and then we had to hammer out some of the kinks to get it back on the road. Bent his axle pretty bad. Cracked his radiator too."

"You're a man of all trades, Josiah." The bishop laughed, impressed with Josiah's ingenuity.

"I did what I could. Sent him over to Jake's for the rest. He was a *gut* man, this fella. A politician, he said."

"Really, now?"

"Says he ran for president. Mark Stedman's his name. You heard of him?"

"Sounds a little familiar. What year did he run?"

"This one. He just dropped out of the race."

"Well, well," the bishop said. "He must have been interesting to talk to. Not many politicians spend a lot of time in these parts."

"That's what I told him."

"So we'll see you on Friday, then?"

"We'll be there."

CINDY STEPPED INTO THE BEDROOM AND LEANED AGAINST THE doorway. She looked beautiful. Mark preferred seeing her like this—without makeup, her auburn hair hanging loosely past her shoulders instead of pulled back into whatever style was the latest trend. But tonight even Cindy's natural beauty couldn't get Mark to change his focus.

He held up a mock-up poster that featured an artist's drawing of Josiah in full Amish attire standing in front of the American flag. The caption read "Josiah for President."

"Whaddya think?"

"So this is him?" Cindy said, holding back her true opinion on the whole matter. "Your Amish friend?"

"And the next president of the United States, if I have anything to say about it. The sketch looks remarkably like him."

"Does he even know about this yet?"

"I'm going to drive back out to Lancaster County and tell him."

"When?"

Mark hedged. "Soon."

"He needs to know, don't you think?"

"I'll tell him. After he's showing some promise in the polls. Why bother him if it doesn't happen?"

"So you spent three days with this man, and you're convinced he's our next great leader? Three days. That's all the time you think you needed to vet him?"

"That's more than a lot of people spend getting to know the candidates they vote for. The system will vet him. Believe me, before this campaign is over, we'll know everything there is to know about Josiah. But trust me, you're going to love him."

"What's his last name? Do you even know that?"

"Stoltzfus."

"Stoltz-what?"

"Stoltzfus. But I'm not releasing that yet. He doesn't need the media coming down on him before he's had a chance to digest it all."

"Stoltzfus, huh? You do realize if it's a write-in campaign, no one will spell it right."

"Hey, they managed Dukakis."

"He lost, remember? And he *was* on the ballot! Anyway, has a write-in candidate ever won a presidential election before?"

Mark gave a slight shrug with his shoulders and grinned. "Maybe it's time."

CHAPTER 12

Nate DeMont, one of Mark's campaign volunteers, was at his desk tying up the last loose ends of Mark's campaign when Mark walked in carrying a box.

"Set it over there on top of the others," Nate said, pointing to the boxes of now outdated Elect Stedman paraphernalia.

Mark plopped the box down on the desk instead and opened it.

"Look here," Mark said as he eagerly reached into the box and pulled out a stack of Josiah for President posters and held them up. "Here's our guy. What do you think?" he said.

"Well, he certainly looks Amish, all right."

"Would you vote for him?"

"If you say he's a good man, sir, he's got my vote."

Mark reached into the box again and pulled out an Amish hat. He handed it to Nate.

"You're serious?" Nate asked.

"Go on. Try it on."

Being a sport, Nate pressed the hat down over his mop of brown hair, clearly wondering what wild new idea his boss was going to come up with next. "Aren't you long overdue for a decent night's sleep?"

"It's a *gut* fit, *jah*?" Mark said, ignoring the question as he tried his best to mimic an Amish accent.

Nate looked at his reflection in a glass window. "*Jah*, sure, I like it," he played along.

"Good!" Mark said. "Got me one too. Really keeps the sun out of my eyes. Maybe I should get some for the staff."

Nate looked around the room. "The staff? I don't know if you've noticed, sir, but there's only me and you left."

"And Carl. And Cindy."

"She called, by the way. Told me to try to talk you out of this 'harebrained'—her word—idea. And she said to tell you she still loves you anyway."

"Talk me out of it? Are you kidding? I haven't been this passionate about something since ... shoot ... since I don't know when. No, my friend, it's full speed ahead."

Nate opened his cell phone, pressed a button, then handed the phone to Mark.

"Then tell her I tried."

———

EMILY WATSON WAS A NATIONAL NEWSCASTER WHO OFTEN DID stories of interest on location. It was only natural that she would be the one sent out on the Josiah assignment. This was her kind of story.

She selected the "Welcome to Lancaster, Pennsylvania" sign at the edge of town for her opening image. It would be a good establishing shot, and she could start out off camera and then walk into frame to begin her report.

The cameraman got into position, and the director moved a few strands of hair away from Emily's face, then signaled that the recording was beginning. With the camera focused on the sign, the news pro took a few steps into the shot, smiled, and began.

"For years politicians have been accused of putting their cart before the horse. Well, now we have a presidential candidate who might have good reason for doing just that. His name is Josiah and he's Amish. That's all anyone really knows about him. We don't even know his last name. But I promise you, all that will change very soon."

It was an attention-grabbing opening. Never mind the fact that the Amish never put their carts before a horse — they were superb horsemen. Emily was sure she had stirred the interest of her television audience.

———

AT AN ELECTRONICS STORE IN RENO, NEVADA, CURIOUS AND FAS-cinated customers stood in front of a wall of television screens and watched Emily's broadcast. All of the televisions were pro-grammed to the news show that carried her report, and everyone within earshot stopped their shopping and watched with keen interest. The same scene was being played out in stores and homes all across America — Indiana, California, Florida, New York — people everywhere were fascinated with America's new mystery candidate.

———

EMILY CONTINUED HER REPORT. "THIS NEW CAMPAIGN IS THE brainchild of former presidential candidate Mark Stedman, who is speaking to us today from his Wisconsin campaign headquarters, where he is officially launching the 'Draft Josiah' movement," she said.

Mark's image appeared on the screen.

"Congressman Stedman, you're serious about this, aren't you?"

"I certainly am, Emily."

"Well, then, sir, what exactly are you hoping to accomplish by this most unusual campaign?"

"I'm hoping to elect a great president."

"And you believe this Josiah can be that president?"

"I *know* he can."

———

IN A SMALL TOWN IN NEBRASKA, MAGGIE BENTON, AN EIGHTY-year-old grandmother, sat with her husband in front of their television, watching the news report. She turned to him and said, "Well, we've had Quakers, Catholics, evangelicals, and who knows what else? We might as well have an Amish president!"

———

THE NEWS MEDIA ONLY HAD THE ARTIST'S SKETCH OF THE NEW candidate to work with, the same artist's rendering that was featured prominently on the posters. Ever since Mark had made the announcement about Josiah, people had had to take his word that there even was such a man. Mark had promised he would provide additional information at an upcoming press conference — information such as a last name, candidacy papers, proof of citizenship, back story, and so on — but until then, he was determined to hold the press at bay. Emily's journalistic patience, however, seemed to be wearing thin.

"Congressman, I, or anyone else, could go into this Amish community and find Josiah right now," she said to Mark on the air. "Is there a reason you're still protecting his identity?"

They were live, of course. Mark hated it when news reporters did on camera the very thing he asked them not to do before the interview. Some reporters had a well-known habit of turning on politicians like that — gaining their trust in the preinterview and then pulling the rug out from under them once the interview was underway.

"I'll talk about anything but the recent passing of my mother," a politician might say off camera to such a reporter prior to an interview. The reporter would agree, but once the camera's red light came on, indicating the official interview had begun, the lead question would inevitably be about the politician's mother.

Mark had distinctly requested that the press hold off any interviews until Josiah was ready to officially announce his candidacy. There would be plenty of time for that later. For Josiah to be a write-in candidate, he would need to file a Declaration of Intent in all but two states — Hawaii and South Dakota — that still didn't allow it. The deadline for these filings was still a good bit away, but the papers still had to be filed.

The veil of secrecy concerning Josiah's last name and other details was only temporary. Until the official announcement, however, Mark had requested that the press honor Josiah's privacy and the privacy of those in the Amish community. But now that request was being questioned ... and it was being questioned in front of approximately a million viewers.

The reason Mark had granted Emily this interview was because she had proven worthy of his trust in the past—and because she was persistent. So he'd given in. But now she was threatening to override their previously established guidelines. Mark was disappointed to see it happen with someone he'd thought he could trust, had thought of as a friend, but what could he do? The camera was rolling.

"You can go into Lancaster and ask around if you want," Mark said. "But it won't be as easy as you think."

"The name Josiah kind of narrows it down, doesn't it?" Emily said confidently, apparently determined to be the first national reporter to land this scoop.

"Josiah is a common name among the Amish," Mark said. "Like Mose. There are probably hundreds of them in Lancaster County alone. But feel free to start looking."

Emily hesitated. Mark hoped she was reconsidering his earlier request. After all, even if she did find Josiah, she wouldn't be able to film him, because of his Amish beliefs. Apparently deciding to stick by her word and drop the inquisition for the moment, she smoothly changed the direction of the interview. Mark appreciated it.

When they were off camera and off the record, though, she asked the congressman.

"I don't know why I'm giving you a pass on this, Stedman."

"Because you want the same things for our country I do."

"Same things? Politically, we're polar opposites. You do know that, right?"

"Oh, I think we have more in common than either one of us wants to admit."

Whether or not Mark's assessment of Emily was right, she gave a slight nod. "Promise me his first interview?"

"You have my word."

"A man's word? What does that mean anymore?" Emily asked.

Mark smiled. "It means something there in Lancaster County."

"I've got you on record, Congressman. His first interview." Emily thanked the former candidate for his time and then nodded at the cameraman to start shutting down the shoot. "This is certainly an unusual election year," she said. "Without the incumbent in the mix, it's anybody game."

"Well, something's gotta give," the cameraman said. "Unemployment hit 12 percent last week, and the economy's been in the tank ever since Holt took office. No wonder we're all looking for someone who'll take us in a new direction."

"Moving farther to the right or farther to the left?"

"Maybe neither," he said.

Emily gave him a puzzled look. "The center?"

The cameraman shook his head. "Maybe it's back ... to what really matters."

———

HARLEY PHILLIPS TOOK FULL ADVANTAGE OF MARK STEDMAN'S controversial endorsement of the Amish man by jumping on the publicity bandwagon and attempting to woo the congressman's supporters over to his camp.

"Do you want a president who can lead or who can bale hay?" Harley said on one prominent evening news program. He didn't leave it there, either.

"The nation should be thankful that someone with judgment as bad as Mark Stedman's has dropped out of the presidential race," he commented on a morning talk show. "He did us all a favor. What would he have done as president? Outlaw electricity?"

From television to radio to print, Harley Phillips made the rounds, distancing himself from Mark's "preposterous idea" and courting Stedman's floundering loyalists. Harley knew they were wondering what they should do when they stepped into the voting booth come November. If they couldn't vote for their man, then who should they vote for?

Harley Phillips, of course.

Harley was salivating at this recent turn of events. If he couldn't have Mark's official endorsement, then painting his former opponent as incompetent was the next best thing. Congressman Stedman, in Harley's opinion, had shot himself in the foot and had managed to cast serious doubts on his mental stability. And he had done it all himself. That was the beauty of the situation. Harley hadn't had to go digging around in Mark's past to destroy him. The congressman had handed Harley the votes himself.

Stedman had also proven that he knew nothing about Amish culture, since it was widely known that the Amish traditionally didn't run for national office. Their line between church and state was a well-established historic fact, and they intended to keep it that way — Harley was certain of it.

———

MEANWHILE, MARK WAS MAKING THE PUBLICITY ROUNDS HIMself, ultimately landing the most sought-after spot of all — *The Sunday Morning News* with Mitchell Maxwell.

"I'll jump right in, Congressman Stedman, with the question everyone's asking," Maxwell said at the beginning of the program. "How can someone such as this man Josiah, a virtual unknown, be elected president if he isn't doing television interviews and isn't even on the ballot?"

"First of all, he's Amish," Mark said. "The Amish don't approve of being photographed or having their image recorded. As far as an interview goes, it's against Amish teaching to seek the limelight. They are a humble people."

"Case in point, Congressman. A presidential candidate who doesn't seek the limelight would hardly stand a chance of getting elected."

"Oh, I don't know. Folks might think it's a refreshing change."

"Don't get me wrong," Maxwell said. "I realize humility and politics don't often go hand in hand, but seriously, Congressman, aren't you simply wasting everyone's time and, quite possibly, their vote?"

"Wasting their time or trying to save the country?"

"With all due respect, sir, has the man even agreed to run? Other than some local elections, the Amish don't typically get involved in politics, do they?"

"If the people draft him, it is my sincere belief that he will serve."

"He's told you that?"

"Not in those exact words."

"In what exact words, Congressman?"

Carl watched Mark from the side of the stage. He wanted to be loyal to the congressman he had believed in for so many years, but now he had serious doubts about Stedman's new political direction. And though he didn't want to doubt Mark's judgment, he was also beginning to have serious doubts about the stability of that too.

"Well, that went well," Mark said sarcastically when he and Carl stepped out of the studio following the interview.

"You held your own," Carl reassured him. His assessment was an honest one, even though he wasn't convinced his boss was doing the right thing. Mark had answered some very difficult interview questions, and that needed to be acknowledged. At times during the interview, Stedman may have sounded as though he'd lost his grip on reality, but he hadn't lost his charm.

"So when *are* you going to tell Josiah?" Carl asked.

"Have you seen the latest polls?"

"Yeah. Your man's running sixth."

"Not bad for someone who's not even on the ballot, huh? Unbelievable!"

"You're not going to tell him for a while yet, are you, sir?"

Mark smiled. "I've been thinking about it. Maybe I'll wait until he's in third or fourth place. Why spoil the surprise?"

———

HARLEY SURPRISED EVEN HIMSELF WHEN HE APPEARED AT THE much-anticipated Montgomery/Stead/Ross Foundation Dinner and kept his remarks to nine minutes, forty-seven seconds. It bothered him a little that he'd had thirteen seconds to spare, but he managed to let it go. He had stayed under the ten-minute requirement, and that, he figured, should make the powers that be happy enough to invite him back sometime in the future.

More importantly, according to his own analysis, he'd hit a home run. He'd gotten a standing ovation at the end of his talk. He'd been the final speaker, and the group was being dismissed at the same time, but still, Harley would certainly spin it as a standing ovation for himself in his next press release.

Harley now concentrated his campaign efforts on the upcoming New York and Pennsylvania primaries, passing on Delaware and Connecticut with their smaller pool of delegates up for grabs. It was late April, and since no single candidate had yet been declared the runaway front-runner for either party, fundraising efforts were challenging, to say the least. Campaigning had to be selective. Sure, Harley was leading in the polls for his own party primary, but that could change overnight in this fickle environment.

———

MARK SAT AT HIS OFFICE DESK, READING THE MORNING PAPER.

"Son of a gun!" he exclaimed.

"What?" Nate said, opening another box of Josiah for President posters and taking a bite of a granola bar. The bar wasn't tasty, but he figured it would cancel out the two glazed donuts he'd eaten an hour earlier.

"We've moved up. Says here we're *fourth* in the polls now. Seems the more Harley campaigns, the better we do."

Mark shoved the newspaper article across the desk to Nate, who was rightfully impressed by the showing, especially considering Josiah wasn't doing any campaigning himself and still didn't even know he was running. Still, Nate remained cautious.

"Look, all we've got are enough votes to potentially hurt both parties but not to win it ourselves. Gotta do better than this, Mark," Nate said.

"*Fourth!*" Mark repeated. "Did you catch that? A write-in Independent candidate polling in the number-four spot? This is unheard of!"

"I won't argue with you there, sir."

"Harley Phillips, eat our buggy dust!"

"So what do we do now, sir?"

"Now we tell him!"

———

MARK TURNED OFF THE HIGHWAY AND RETRACED HIS JOURNEY through Amish country.

He passed by the ditch where he'd gone off the road and then turned down one street, followed by another, before finally driving up Josiah's driveway. Elizabeth and the kids were in the garden and didn't immediately recognize Mark in his personal car, even though he gave them a friendly wave.

"You said I could come back," Mark said as he got out of his silver Lexus.

"Yes, and we meant it," Elizabeth said, smiling that shy, sweet smile of hers when she finally recognized him. "Your family didn't come with you?" she asked, clearly disappointed.

"Not this trip. Josiah around?"

"He's out working in the field. You want me to send one of the kids out there to get him?"

"No, I'll walk on over there. Thank you. Good to see you again, Elizabeth."

Mark looked across the field and spotted Josiah plowing. He walked toward him and waved, but Josiah didn't see him until he turned the plow to start up the next row. When Josiah did spot Mark waving at him, he immediately stopped his work and walked toward Mark.

"Mark, good to see you, my brother!" Josiah said when he got close enough. "You're not stuck in a ditch again, are you?"

"No." Mark laughed. "But I told you I'd be back."

"That's right, you sure did. But lots of folks say that, and you never see 'em again. Glad you're not one of 'em." Josiah removed his hat and wiped the sweat from his brow.

"Josiah ..." Mark said with a sheepish grin and a slight raise of his eyebrow.

"Jah?"

"We need to talk."

CHAPTER 13

★

"*Y*OU WHAT?" JOSIAH SAID, TRYING TO MAINTAIN A CERTAIN degree of composure, but finding it a bit difficult given the nature of Mark's revelation.

"I know it sounds crazy," Mark said, "but just hear me out. What good does it do to have all your wisdom and not share it with the rest of the country? Especially now."

"I'm Amish, Mark. Are you trying to get me excommunicated?"

"No, just elected. You're running fourth in the polls right now."

"How? I'm not even in the election!"

"I know. But *fourth*! Did you hear me? No one's ever done that as a write-in candidate. Fourth!"

"A write-in candidate? Don't I get a say in this? Folks can just write your name down on a ballot, and the next thing you know you're president? They can't do that, can they? I have rights, don't I? I've got a farm to manage here. I'm happy here. Mark, what have you done, my friend?"

"We can't elect you without your consent, of course. These are just polls. Sort of a what-if scenario."

"So I pulled you out of a ditch, and now you're trying to drag me into one?"

Mark laughed but continued to press Josiah. "You're exactly who we need, Josiah. And there's still plenty of time to fill out all the necessary paperwork for your candidacy in the states that allow a write-in candidate."

"I can't do it, Mark. This goes against our Amish ways, you know that. You're going to have to clear this up, my friend. Tell everyone it was a joke, a mistake, delirium, whatever you want to say. But you're going to have to let them know there will be no Amish candidate. I can't believe you've done such a thing."

"Desperate times call for desperate measures."

"I'm not your desperate measure. You're going to have to look elsewhere, my friend."

Josiah wasn't sure if he agreed with Mark about his assessment either. To him, desperate times called for simple solutions—good old-fashioned common sense, hard work, and an ample dose of prayer. Not that those things weren't in Washington already. They were. Especially hard work. Congressman Stedman could no doubt attest to that. Politics was hard work. But whatever desperate times America found herself in, it wasn't up to an Amish man from Lancaster County to fix it. He would continue to live his life, love his family, and obey whatever laws were put in place, but that was all that could be expected of him, friendship or not.

"Thanks for the compliment, but I'm not interested," Josiah said emphatically.

"Will you at least think about it?"

"I just did. Still not interested."

"Well, then, can I ask you to at least, you know, pray about it?"

"I'm praying right now. Praying that this whole notion of yours is a nightmare that I shall awake from soon. Besides, if it were in God's will, the bishop would tell me and I would feel a stirring in my soul. But this goes against our *Ordnung*."

"*Ordnung?*"

"Our rules for living. They vary from district to district, but ours are very clear—we don't run in national elections."

"You're the perfect candidate, Josiah. You're as outside the system as one can get. Besides, you said yourself that it doesn't matter if anyone listens. What matters is that you say what you believe. Say it, Josiah! Tell us the truth! We've been lied to long enough

... by too many candidates on both sides. Say what needs to be said, and we'll listen! I'll listen! Who knows? Maybe the whole country'll listen! You pulled me out of a ditch once. Now pull us all out."

"You're right, Mark. I did pull you out of a ditch. But you're making me wonder now if I should've left you there."

"How do you know you wouldn't enjoy being president?"

"You're not hearing me, my friend. My answer is no. I cannot break the rules of the *Ordnung*."

"Is that no as in *no*, or no as in 'Let me think about it'?"

"It's no, Mark. Two letters — *n-o*. I can say it in Pennsylvania Dutch if you'd like, but it's still no."

"That's your last word on the matter?"

"It has to be, Mark. You've got to put a stop to this foolishness right now!" Josiah said with more forcefulness than usual. He wasn't accustomed to raising his voice, but Mark hadn't been listening to what he had been saying. He had to make sure the politician had heard him — his answer was no. Undeniably, indisputably, unwaveringly no.

"All right, I won't say another word about it," Mark said as he turned and started walking back toward his car. But then he stopped and turned around. "Not another word except to say that I would be happy to speak with your bishop about it. I've been told I have a knack for swaying others to my way of thinking."

"Then you should use it for *gut*, Mark, and leave nonsense such as this alone. President? What were you thinking, brother?"

"So it's still a no?"

Josiah looked at Mark and wondered what it was about politics that caused such a severe hearing loss in some of those who entered it.

"It's a no today, tomorrow, and every day after that," he said as emphatically as he could without coming across as rude.

"Then I guess I'll just have to accept that. It's been good to see you, Josiah."

"And you as well, Mark. Come back anytime."

Mark nodded, then got into his car. Josiah watched him drive away. Up until that moment, he had never seen Mark as someone who might disrupt his life and his home with outside temptations. He thought the former congressman respected the lifestyle he and Elizabeth had chosen. But now the stranger had stepped over their boundaries, and it troubled him.

———

THAT EVENING, AS ELIZABETH PREPARED FOR BED, SHE ADMITTED to Josiah that she had seen the two of them engaged in what appeared to be a serious discussion.

"What were you talking about?" she asked.

"I'll tell you what it was about, Elizabeth. Mark wanted to know if I would be interested in running for president."

"Of what?"

"The United States! I don't know where he would get such a notion."

"And what did you tell him?"

"Well, I thought he was joking at first. But when I realized he was serious, I told him the only thing I could tell him—no, of course. The bishop would never approve. I'd be risking a shunning for sure. And I wouldn't blame the bishop either. Anyway, who'd take me seriously as a candidate? I'm just a farmer. I didn't go to some fancy law school, and I've never been elected to any political office in my life, not even local ones. The only experience I have is running our farm and raising a family."

"You told him no, so that should put an end to it, *jah*?"

"I hope so. I certainly can't allow it to go on. Why, do you know he said I'm already running fourth in the polls?"

"How could that be? You're not even a candidate."

"Apparently he's told a lot of people about me."

"They'd vote for someone who's not even running? And they call us a peculiar people."

"It seems our friend Mark is quite the salesman. The English sure get some wild ideas sometimes, *jah*?"

They both laughed and shook their heads over this crazy notion of their former houseguest. But the matter would soon resolve itself, they were certain of it. Mark would withdraw Josiah's name from the campaign, and then it would be over. No real harm done.

Elizabeth got into bed and scooted closer to Josiah. "The vet comes tomorrow for the horses," she said.

"Ah, *gut*. What time?"

"He said around two."

"Fine, fine."

Josiah took his wife into his arms. It was a cold night for spring, and the warmth of her body next to his felt good.

"President . . ." He laughed.

"You'd make a *gut* one," she said.

"Elizabeth, my love, I've got everything I need and want right here."

———

JOSIAH WAS SITTING AT THE KITCHEN TABLE, DRINKING A CUP OF coffee and staring out the window, when Elizabeth entered the room. It was much too early for either of them to be up.

"*Guder mariye*. You're up early," she said.

"Couldn't sleep. Sorry. Did I wake you?"

"Your absence always does."

Josiah smiled, then reached out and took her hand.

"I guess I can't get it out of my head," he said. "Why would Mark even think of such a thing?"

"No *gut* deed goes unpunished, *jah*?"

Josiah nodded.

"Well, it's over, so put it out of your mind," she said.

"You're right. Got too much to do around here to waste any more time on such foolishness."

At the first sign of daylight, Josiah donned his hat and went outside to let the horses out of the barn and into the pasture. A now-familiar car made its way up his driveway. It was Mark, of course.

"I had a feeling you'd be up," Mark said as he exited the vehicle.

"*Gut* to see you again, my friend, but it's still no," Josiah said.

"That's fine, fine. I understand. I decided to stay the night in Lancaster, learn a little more about the place. I'm on my way home now, but figured I'd stop in one last time and check. But that's okay. A no is a no. It is a no, right?"

"You must've been something else over there in Washington." Josiah laughed.

"I do tend to be determined when I want something."

"That's a *gut* quality, my friend, as long as you want the right things."

"This is the right thing. My instincts say it is," Mark said.

"You trust your instincts; I'll trust my heart."

"Don't let our country go into the ditch, Josiah. You've got answers for us."

"What was it your GPS lady said? Recalculate? That's your answer, Mark. Not me. The country just needs to recalculate and get back on the right path. You don't need an Amish president for that. You can do it yourselves."

"If it was that easy, we would've done it already."

"You won't change my mind, Mark."

"Well, I also wanted to thank you again for all the hospitality you and Elizabeth have shown to me."

"You're most welcome. But it's still no."

"I understand. I'll be back again someday. I'm getting to like this town."

"Just get me out of the news, Mark. Respect my family's privacy."

"I will," Mark promised. Then he waved good-bye and returned to his car.

Josiah stepped into the barn to do some cleaning up before the vet arrived. After a while, when too many questions began to fill his mind, he knelt down by a bale of hay and decided to pray about the matter. Not that he hadn't been praying about it already, but now he knew he needed direction, or some kind of validation, on whether he was doing the right thing. He was convinced that Mark's accident hadn't been a random occurrence, that it had been a part of God's plan. But for what? Surely not for Mark's outlandish proposal. Or was it?

———

"So did you hear the Bender family had their baby last night?" Elizabeth asked Josiah over dinner that day.

"What did she have?"

"Another boy. They named him Samuel."

"*Gut* strong name. Is he doing *gut*?"

"*Jah*, very *gut*."

"And the mother?"

"Oh, she's doing fine."

Josiah nodded, pleased at the good news, then returned to the topic that still weighed heavily on his mind.

"So do you think it would ever be God's will for one of us to do something like that?"

"Have another baby? Well, Josiah, first of all, it would be *me* having it" — Elizabeth laughed — "and secondly, when it's God's will, it will just happen like all the times before, *jah*?"

Josiah loved Elizabeth's easy sense of humor. But he also wanted her validation that he had done the right thing.

"I meant run the country."

"Oh, that. I thought you already told Mark no."

"I did. But there's something inside me that … well, to be honest, I keep wondering if this is something I'm supposed to do. Maybe the country does need someone like one of us right now."

"Josiah, what are you saying? You know it's out of the question. It goes against the *Ordnung.*"

"Well, I'd want the bishop's blessing first, of course."

"And he would never give it. He can't give it."

"I know."

"Then why are you even thinking about it?"

"Just thinking, that's all."

"You should leave it alone, Josiah. The bishop would have been the one to tell you if God wanted you to do such a thing. And he hasn't. And he won't. Think about it, Josiah. If it's troubling your soul this much, it can't be from God."

"What if it's stirring my soul instead?"

Elizabeth had no answer.

Josiah didn't speak about it to Elizabeth for the rest of the day, but it remained on his mind. He thought about it during the vet's visit. He thought about it while he was out working in the field. He thought about it while he was playing with his children before supper. He thought about it in bed that night while he stared out the window at the stars.

What if he really *was* the one to help the nation during this difficult period in history? What if the concept of getting back to basics *was* the answer for the country? Who better to represent a back-to-basics philosophy than one of the Plain people? What if Josiah was someone who, as the Good Book said, was created "for such a time as this"?

Josiah's answer was still no, but he was beginning to be less adamant in his refusal. Maybe it was time to talk with the bishop about the matter. Just to get his perspective, even though Josiah was quite certain what that would be.

CHAPTER 14

★

"*You what?*" Bishop Miller said when Josiah stopped in at his house the following day to talk over his predicament. "I'm sorry, but I don't think I heard you correctly. Did you say you are considering running for *president?*"

"Just asking questions, that's all. It wasn't my idea, Bishop Miller."

"Then where'd it come from? You eat some bad sausage?"

"Remember that fella who drove his car into the ditch here a while back?"

"The congressman?"

Josiah nodded.

"Well, for some reason, unbeknownst to me, the fella got it in his head that what the country needs is a president with our Amish sensibilities."

"But we don't get involved in national politics."

"That's what I told him. But now I understand he's gone and caused quite a stir around the country."

"An Amish president *would* cause quite a stir. In both our worlds."

"Well, the congressman went ahead and put my name out there, and now he says I'm running fourth in the polls."

"What do you mean 'running'? You're not on the ballot, right?"

"Of course not, no. He's just been talking about me to the people and reporters."

"You know, I heard about something like this from a tourist a week or so ago, but I told him it couldn't happen. We don't do that. I had no idea it was you."

"Well, neither did I."

"You told him to put an end to this, *jah*?"

"Why, yes, of course."

"*Gut.*"

"I didn't take him seriously at first. But when he told me I was in fourth place, well, I started wondering if maybe God was trying to tell me something."

"As your bishop, I would have been the first to hear from God, my brother. And I can assure you, I have not heard any such thing on the matter."

"With all due respect, Bishop Miller, I can't help but—"

The bishop cut him off. "The fact that you would even consider such a decision is blatant disrespect of the authoritative order of this district, Josiah. As your bishop, I must implore you to examine your heart, my brother. We do not run in national elections, my brother."

"Yes, I am fully aware of that, Bishop Miller. And I do respect and honor your position in our community."

"And that is why you told him no, *jah*?"

"Several times. But listening is not the man's gift."

"But you said it?"

"*Jah.*"

"*Gut.* Sooner or later, he will have to hear it."

Josiah started to leave, then hesitated. The bishop, however, didn't give him any room for further debate: "Josiah, I could never give my blessing on something like this."

"Of course. That's why I came to you. I need your advice on what to do if he doesn't stop his campaign."

"He must stop it. There is no other choice, Josiah."

"I know. But ..."

"But what, my brother? Surely, you wouldn't ..."

"No. It's just … Well, I have to admit, I do find this whole matter a little amusing, don't you?"

"The White House is no place for joking around, brother."

"They say Abraham Lincoln had a keen sense of humor."

"*Jah*, but he presided over a bleak time in America's history. We needed the healing power of laughter back then."

"Perhaps we do again, sir," Josiah said.

———

ELIZABETH WONDERED WHAT WAS TAKING JOSIAH SO LONG AT the bishop's house. She knew her husband had the gift of persuasion, but surely he hadn't managed to talk the bishop into letting him run for president, had he? Such a notion deserved to be tossed out immediately. There were more important matters to tend to — such as their family, their farm, their church, and all the community events that needed planning. Their lives were full enough already without adding the complication of the outrageous plans of an Englisher!

Elizabeth liked Mark well enough. But like Josiah, she possessed that one quality that refused to be ignored — common sense. When an idea came along that went against the grain of common sense, it wouldn't leave either of them alone until they changed their course. Common sense was Elizabeth and Josiah's compass. Running for president went against that compass. Josiah knew this, and the bishop would agree. Elizabeth was certain of it.

But what was taking so long?

Elizabeth sat down on the sofa and picked up some quilting squares from the basket next to her. She began to sew. Sewing always calmed her nerves. Maybe it was seeing all the separate patchwork pieces coming together and taking shape. There was an inherent beauty to that — two or more seemingly unrelated items suddenly taking the form of something unexpectedly lovely.

Whatever it was about sewing that was helping take Elizabeth's mind off her husband's visit with the bishop, it was working.

Almost. Elizabeth stitched and watched the door, and then stitched some more and watched the door some more.

"Josiah will be home any minute now," she said to herself. "Any minute."

———

JOSIAH'S MEETING WITH THE BISHOP LASTED LONGER THAN another minute. There was much to discuss, and it seemed neither of the men was in any hurry.

"Don't we sometimes have to make a stand for what we believe in, Bishop Miller?" Josiah asked.

"*Jah*, but all within the guidelines of the church. This is clearly outside of those guidelines."

"But haven't some Amish entered politics?"

"Local offices. Run for any local office you want, brother. But serving as president of the United States—assuming an unknown Amish man from Lancaster County could even win such a position —would require you to make decisions and live in such a way that would be in opposition to our beliefs."

"Like sending troops to war?"

"For starters. We're peaceful, or have you forgotten that?"

"I would make sure everyone knows my position on war."

"And what about everything else? The president doesn't exactly live a Plain life. It's hard to maintain humility in such a setting. The temptation to become prideful would be overwhelming."

"I don't have a clue about being president or living in the White House, so I don't know what would be required of me. But if I were called upon to do it—and I'm not saying that such a thing would even happen, but hypothetically speaking, if it were to happen—I would tell Mark and the American people that I would bring my Amish faith and Plain ways to the White House. Everyone would know where I stood from the very beginning."

"Until the first compromise ... hypothetically speaking."

"I wouldn't compromise, sir."

"Maybe not at first, but then a second temptation would come along and ..."

"No compromise."

"And a third and a fourth ... They'd keep coming at you until you'd finally give in. You'd change a little here, a little there, and before you'd know it, you would bring shame to our community and dilute your faith, my friend. Can you not see that?"

Josiah wanted to answer, to tell the bishop that there was no way he'd ever fail the test, that he would stand up to every temptation that could possibly come his way, that he would be a shining example of what it meant to be Amish. But even he knew he couldn't make such a vow. He was human, and humans failed. And when a human failed in the office of president, it was magnified beyond the imaginable. Josiah's actions wouldn't affect only him; they would affect his friends and family back home too. Josiah wasn't about to let anything hurt his family.

No, should Mark not do as he promised and end the speculation of an Amish man running for president, then Josiah would have to clear up the matter himself. Josiah Stoltzfus wasn't going to be running for any office, most assuredly not the office of president of the United States!

Still, one question haunted him, and he had to ask Bishop Miller.

"But what if that politician is right? What if the people do need me to serve them in this way?"

"We must please God first, Josiah. That is where our allegiance lies."

"And what if this is what pleases him?"

"What pleases God is obedience, Josiah," Bishop Miller continued.

"And that's what I want to do—be obedient to what he may be calling me to do."

"And you think it's to run for president?"

"I'm not sure what I think. Before that politician came here, the thought never would have crossed my mind. But now … I don't know."

"Have you heard from God on the matter?"

"You said yourself that sometimes God doesn't answer us right away."

"*Jah*, often we do have to wait. Are you waiting, my friend?"

Josiah didn't answer. When it came to helping others, waiting never came easy for him.

———

ELIZABETH CONTINUED WITH HER SEWING, TRYING TO KEEP HER mind off her husband's meeting with the bishop and what might be taking place there, but no matter how hard she tried, her thoughts drifted back to the two men.

Ever since the fatal buggy accident that took the life of their eldest child, Elizabeth had secretly held a fear in her heart about Josiah's well-being whenever he drove their buggy after dark. The idea of an unaware automobile driver coming upon the buggy in the blackness of night left her unsettled. The idea of any of her family being outside of her watchful and caring eyes was always difficult for her. Elizabeth wanted to trust God with their safety, but deep down inside, she wanted to help him a little with it too.

So she continued watching and waiting. And she worried. That's what many a wife and mother did best—worry.

———

WHEN JOSIAH RETURNED HOME, HE FOUND ELIZABETH SITTING on the sofa sewing. She looked lovely in the candlelight, every bit as beautiful as she had looked on their wedding night. She also looked relieved to see Josiah standing in the doorway.

"You coming to bed?" Elizabeth asked, putting down her sewing and greeting Josiah with a gentle kiss.

"In a little bit," Josiah said.

"What did the bishop say?"

"What I figured he'd say."

"Are you going to write Mark and tell him what the bishop said?"

"*Jah.* I will take care of that first thing in the morning."

It was what was best for both of them and for their family. Even if Josiah wanted to run for president, going against the church in such a manner could hold disastrous consequences. Perhaps even a shunning. Yes, Josiah had made the right decision.

Elizabeth walked toward their bedroom, but before she reached the door, she turned back to Josiah and looked at him. Josiah knew she knew him well enough to realize that something was bothering him. She didn't speak for a moment, but then said, "You've decided to run, haven't you?"

Josiah didn't answer verbally, but he knew she could see the answer in his eyes.

"Is this really what you want to do?" she asked.

"No. But I believe in my heart it's what I must do," Josiah said.

Elizabeth leaned into Josiah's arms. "I'm afraid, Josiah."

"That I'll lose?" he asked.

"No," she said.

———

MARK, CARL, AND A FEW VOLUNTEER STAFFERS HAD STAYED LATE at the Josiah for President headquarters, this time taking down the Josiah for President posters and boxing them up.

"Well," Carl said, "it was a good idea while it lasted."

"I can't force him to run," Mark said, wishing it weren't true.

"I know. Still no news from him? No change of heart?"

"Nothing. And he's starting to slip in the polls. Guess the novelty's wearing off."

"Can't elect a candidate the people have never seen. Voters want to know who they're sending to the White House. They're funny that way."

Mark nodded. "I was probably an idiot for even thinking this would work."

"I'm not touching that one," Carl said, smiling. "By the way, Sam's been calling."

"Of course. But I still can't endorse someone I don't believe in."

"You may not have a choice at this point."

Mark's mind wandered to Josiah again, wondering how he could have handled the matter differently. "Maybe I should have kept it from him until after he was elected."

"Oh, that would've worked," Carl said sarcastically. "'Surprise! You're the president of the United States! Oh, and by the way, I think I just got you excommunicated from your church too.' Yeah, that would've worked all right."

"So what are you saying? That it's time to face reality?"

"I'm saying you'd better get used to saying 'President Harley Phillips.'"

"Well, it's easier to say than Ledbetter," Mark said. "Where do they get these names?" he pondered aloud. "'Ledbetter, a go-getter.' What a slogan."

"You think Stoltzfus was better? Voters never would've learned to spell it."

"Sure, they would've. We would've written a jingle."

Carl couldn't resist. "Who can you trust? Stoltzfus! When you've had enough? Stoltzfus! *S–T–O–L–T–Z*–fus! Stooooolllllltzfus!"

Mark chuckled at Carl's improv, but right now, the team needed more than a jingle. They needed their candidate. Mark was beyond disappointed that his plan to draft the Amish man hadn't worked. He was convinced that Josiah was the man of the hour, exactly what the country needed. But Mark had one small problem—he hadn't been able to convince his candidate of that idea. Frankly, he hadn't been able to raise enough money to keep the campaign alive either. Carl was right. It was time to turn out the lights and call it a day. The Josiah presidential campaign was dead on arrival.

"You're probably right," Mark said as he sealed up another box of posters. "They never would've learned to spell Stoltzfus anyway."

"Oh, I don't know. I've been spelling it correctly since I was five," a voice from behind them said.

Mark's eyes widened, and a broad smile broke across his face when he heard the distinctive voice. Both he and Carl turned at the same time to see Josiah standing there, in the flesh, holding a suitcase at his side.

"Josiah!" Mark exclaimed in both shock and excitement. "Are you kidding me? *Are you kidding me?* How'd you get here?"

"Bus," Josiah said. "But I wouldn't recommend it when your likeness is painted all over the side of it."

The men laughed, and Mark threw his arms around the bearded man. "Josiah, am I glad to see you! I hope this means what I think it means."

"Elizabeth and I talked it over," Josiah said, "and we've decided that ... well, we're going to leave it in God's hands."

"Oh, that's great! *That's great!*" Mark exclaimed, bounding around the room with a few fist pumps. Then he stopped in his tracks. "Wait a minute—that does mean you're running, right?"

"It means you're welcome to throw my hat into the air—or however you English say it. If I am meant to serve, then I will win. If not and I lose, then Elizabeth and I will face the consequences of our misjudgment. But if this is indeed what we are supposed to do, then we know in our hearts that we have to take that first step of faith."

"Elizabeth feels that way too?"

"She has turned her fears and doubts over to God. Well, most of them. None of us is perfect, *jah?*"

Mark let loose his excitement once again.

"I can't believe this! Carl, unpack those posters!"

"You do realize I probably won't win," Josiah said.

"You're gonna win if I have anything to say about it!" Mark vowed.

"I believe you, Mark. But this may not even be about winning. Maybe I'm only supposed to be in this campaign to help point people back to common sense and simpler ways."

"Look, if it comes down to you or Harley, I'm going to do everything I can to get you into office. But what about your bishop?" Mark asked. "Did he give you his blessing?"

Josiah hesitated. "Tell me what you need me to do."

"What I need you to do? *What I need you to do?*" Mark was overjoyed and grabbed Josiah in another bear hug. *"I need you to win an election!"*

"Will that make you let go of me?" Josiah said.

Mark apologized and released the gentle Amish man who wasn't accustomed to such exuberant displays of emotion.

Carl had been watching all of this — watching the candidate for whom he had been campaigning and whom he was just now getting to meet for the first time. He extended his hand toward Josiah.

"Carl Wilson," he said, introducing himself.

"Josiah Stoltzfus," Josiah said with a friendly smile. "Apparently I'm the fella on the posters."

"Kinda thought so," Carl said. "Welcome to your campaign, sir."

Josiah laughed. "I do have one condition for you, Mark," he said, turning back to the congressman.

"Name it," Mark said.

"I get to pick my own running mate, right?"

"Sure, sure. A double Amish ticket? That's even better!" Mark said, thrilled beyond measure.

"I want you to be my vice president."

"Me?" Mark laughed. "Oh no. You don't want me on the ticket. I couldn't even win my own election."

"But you know Washington. I don't."

"Yes, and I also haven't been making a lot of friends there lately."

"Then it'll be two outsiders on the ticket. It's the only way I'll agree to run."

Mark had already done a good bit of soul-searching over his own failed candidacy. Even though the idea of getting back into the ring—and possibly even whupping Harley Phillips in the general election as an independent—felt good to his wounded ego, he also knew that his name could be a drag on the ticket. The phones at his now-irrelevant campaign headquarters hadn't exactly been slammed with calls from party officials—or even voters, for that matter—begging him to stay in the race. That was one reality he had to take into consideration. If he truly wanted to see Josiah elected president, it would be an absolute necessity to have the right man or woman on the ticket with him. Maybe that person was him. But there was also a good possibility that it wasn't.

"I'll need to think about it," he told Josiah. "I'm not turning you down—don't get me wrong. I just want to make sure I'm the right man for the job."

"You believed in me, Mark. Now I believe in you."

"Well, let me sleep on it. In the meantime, let's go to my house. Cindy and I will show you some Stedman family hospitality. Return the favor, so to speak."

"I'd enjoy meeting your family, Mark."

Mark quickly sent a text to Cindy forewarning her that company was coming. He didn't tell her who it was, just that it was someone she would enjoy meeting.

———

CINDY AND JOSIAH HIT IT OFF RIGHT FROM THE START. LIKE Mark, she was entertained by Josiah's quick wit and intrigued by his wisdom. She easily saw what her husband had found so engaging about the ruggedly handsome Amish man. He reminded her of what Abraham Lincoln might have looked like, even though by many accounts, Lincoln wasn't all that good looking. His character was what had a strong appeal.

Cindy knew she probably couldn't compete with homemade Amish cooking, so she didn't even try. She ordered a meal from one of their favorite take-out restaurants in town and, after accepting Josiah's compliments graciously, confessed her secret—that she hadn't cooked a morsel of it.

"Well, then, you are a very *gut* orderer," Josiah said, which caused everyone to laugh.

Cindy didn't know if this man had any chance at all of becoming president, but she sure liked him. And as the evening progressed, she was growing more and more convinced that, as Mark had said, Josiah was exactly who America needed living at 1600 Pennsylvania Avenue.

Later that night, Mark and Cindy discussed the matter of Josiah's vice-presidential candidate at length in the privacy of their bedroom. Political pillow talk—not very romantic. But Mark wanted her input.

"So what do you think?"

"About Josiah? I like him. I like him a lot."

"I knew you would. And what about my being on the ticket with him? Think I should do it?"

"Honest answer? Even if you don't like it?"

"Honest answer."

"Well, my biggest concern is whether you'll be able to take a backseat and allow him to lead."

"No question about it—absolutely."

"It might not be as easy as you think. You wanted the number-one position, remember? Could you play second fiddle?"

"I could with him. Not with any of the others, though. But I still don't know if I'm the best pick for the ticket."

"Well, you'd get my vote, Congressman." She smiled and rubbed the back of her hand gently across his cheek.

"I would, huh?"

"Uh-huh," she said, snuggling a bit closer. "What was your name again?" she teased.

"Madam, you've forgotten my name already? Maybe I am vice-president material after all."

They both laughed and then settled down to rest in each other's arms.

———

"ALL RIGHT, I'LL DO IT," MARK SAID WHEN JOSIAH CAME DOWN-stairs for breakfast in the morning.

The two men shook hands, sealing the deal for a Stoltzfus-Stedman ticket.

"You do know this could end up costing us both more than we realize?" Mark said, trying to gauge Josiah's commitment to both the election and his running mate one final time. "Your standing with your church and community; my reputation as a rational and sane individual, which has already suffered for endorsing your candidacy in the first place. And your privacy. Everywhere you go from now on, you'll have Secret Service with you. Are you prepared to pay the price if we do this?"

"What if there's a bigger price to pay if we don't?"

———

THE FOLLOWING WEEK, MORE VOLUNTEERS THAN MARK HAD seen in his own campaign began showing up at the newly reopened Elect Josiah headquarters, thanks to the wonders of social networking sites such as Facebook, YouTube promos, and the novelty of the Josiah for President campaign. It seemed there was a good bit of enthusiasm for this newcomer to politics, and it had gone viral. People had obviously been waiting for a candidate to come along about whom they could get excited. Apparently, Josiah fit the bill. The volunteers for this grass-roots movement began arriving en masse, and they were eager to be put to work.

Carl handed out assignments one by one, and before long,

phones were ringing, interviews were being scheduled, and strategic mailings were being discussed. The Josiah for President campaign was underway.

———

"WHAT GAME'S HE PLAYING NOW?" HARLEY PHILLIPS BARKED AT his son-in-law, who had just walked into his office. Bart knew exactly to whom Harley was referring, but he asked anyway.

"Who's that, sir?"

"Stedman! Who else? Get him on the phone!"

"We've tried, sir. He's not returning our calls."

"Well, did you leave a message telling him it's important?"

"Yes, I did, sir."

Bart had always resented this kind of questioning from Harley. It was condescending beyond measure, as though Harley thought Bart didn't have the intelligence to leave a message on Mark's voice mail. Bart knew his job and, according to everyone around him except Harley, was performing his duties exceptionally well. But this wasn't the time to try to adjust Harley's attitude or to stand up and demand the respect he deserved. There would be time for that later. Someday. Ah, some glorious day!

"Well, keep calling!" Harley demanded. "And leave a long message. Fill up his voice mail. He'll tire of the games soon enough."

Harley was pacing now, red-faced and irritated. Bart, always looking for the silver lining in the storm clouds of life, couldn't help but comment, "Well, at least Stedman's gotten you up out of your chair, sir. You know what the doctor said about you exercising."

Harley shot Bart a look that indicated he wasn't amused.

"We've got to rein him in," Harley said, walking over to the window and looking out. "He's gonna cost us the election. There's gotta be something we can do."

Harley wasn't demanding anymore. He wasn't barking or snapping. He was almost begging. Pleading. Tears may have even formed in his eyes, but Bart couldn't be sure. Bart had picked up Harley's new contact-lens prescription the previous week, so maybe it was the contacts that were causing Harley's eyes to water. Still, Bart felt a twinge of father-in-law loyalty. He tried to be sympathetic to Harley's cause.

"I'm sure there's a way, sir," Bart said.

"No matter what we do, they keep climbing in the polls."

"A temporary bump. That's all it is, sir. When it comes to Election Day, who's going to want to waste their vote on someone who only has common sense to offer?"

"Exactly," Harley said, nodding.

"Well, then, I'm over it," Harley said. "Josiah may be a good man, but he's Amish. The country isn't going to elect an Amish president. They'll forget all about this crazy idea of Stedman's soon and realize they've got a president to elect. They'll come back to me. I'm not wasting any more of my time on this foolishness."

It was a bluff, of course. Deep down, Bart knew Harley was a long way from being "over it." He only said things like that to pump up his own self-confidence. Bart couldn't believe someone like Harley Phillips would need his self-confidence pumped up any more than it already was. The Rotunda could barely hold Harley's ego now.

In a moment of weakness and after too many celebratory drinks, Harley had once admitted to Bart that he couldn't shake the belief that the only reason he had achieved anything in life wasn't because he had stood "on the shoulders of giants," as Isaac Newton had once said, but because he had tripped those giants when they weren't looking and then climbed up on their backs while keeping them in a choke hold. Bart knew that people always feared losing success that was either unwarranted or stolen from someone else, and that in his heart, Harley Phillips believed he hadn't honestly earned any of his success, so he was in constant fear of losing it. But when sober, that painful truth was protected behind well-constructed walls of bravado.

In spite of that, Harley did have the ability to compartmentalize — that talent for putting a matter off to the side and saving it to ponder or solve later. Or simply ignore.

"We've already wasted too much of my precious campaign time on Stedman's antics," Harley fretted. "And over something that's never going to happen. American voters aren't going to waste their vote on someone with no experience and no chance of winning. These are the final days of the primary now, and we need to stay focused on one thing and one thing only — winning."

"You're doing the right thing, sir!" Bart said. "Let it go."

"Exactly."

"Stay above the fray."

"That's right."

"We'll get Mark's voters on our own once they realize this Josiah fellow isn't an actual candidate," Bart said.

"... if there ever even was a Josiah in the first place," Harley added.

"We'll have the last laugh, sir."

"Yes, we will."

"We'll nail the nomination and then sweep the general election!"

"You know, I'm glad my daughter married you," Harley said, placing his arm on Bart's shoulder. "You're a very astute young man."

"President Harley Phillips, that's who'll be taking the oath come January!"

Harley was almost radiant as Bart spoke those words. "President Harley Phillips," he echoed, beaming.

Bart was certain his own radiance was taking on more of a greenish tint at the thought of Harley actually winning the election, yet he still went along. "President Harley Phillips! That's the spirit, sir."

A cell phone began beeping in Bart's pocket, but Bart paid it no mind. He knew Harley didn't like people answering their cell phones in his presence. Harley had told Bart that on many occasions, saying he considered it the epitome of rudeness, even though he often did it himself. Harley didn't have double standards. He had triple and quadruple ones. So Bart dutifully ignored the call.

But after a few more beeps, Harley said, "You're beeping, Bart."

"I know that, sir."

"Well, answer it."

"I don't want to interrupt you, sir."

"It could be Stedman. Answer it!"

"But, sir, I thought you just said you were over it. That you no longer needed his votes."

"Answer the call, Bart!"

Bart nodded and then reached into his pocket and pulled out his phone. He glanced at the caller ID and then back at Harley while the phone continued to beep.

"Well ...?"

"It's Mark, sir," Bart said.

"Well, answer your blasted phone!"

"You want me to answer it, sir? But are you changing your mind about wanting his endorsement then?"

"I'm a politician. Do you know what that means, Bart?"

"You talk out of both sides of your mouth, sir?" The words left Bart's lips before he could stop them.

"No, Bart. It means we adapt. If Plan A doesn't work, we move on to Plan B."

"But Plan A didn't work, sir, and you did move on to Plan B. That didn't work either. And now it appears you're making a U-turn and going back to Plan A."

"Answer your dadgum phone, Bart!"

"All right. But just to be sure, you *do* want Stedman's endorsement if he offers it?"

"Of course, I want it!"

Harley loosened his tie and attempted to massage the bulging veins of his temples. Bart wondered if it was the stress that was getting to his father-in-law or simply years of ignoring his doctor's orders and not passing on the salt, butter, and redeye gravy he loved so much. Whichever it was, Harley's neck veins appeared ready to burst.

Bart finally answered his phone.

"Hello," he said.

"Bart, this is Mark Stedman. Harley around?"

"He's right here. Would you like to speak with him?"

"Yes, I would. Thanks."

Bart switched the phone to speaker and handed it to Harley.

"It's Mark," he said.

Harley seemed almost giddy with anticipation, practically salivating over the possibility of locking in Stedman's endorsement.

"Mark," Harley said, "have you finally come to your senses and decided to endorse my candidacy?"

"Well, that's what I'm calling you about, Harley."

Harley raised his eyebrows and nodded to Bart, signaling, Bart assumed, forthcoming good news.

"I just wanted to let you know that we're moving full speed ahead with our campaign."

"The Amish man? Come on, Mark. You're not serious about that, are you? About your Josiah for President charade?"

"Quite the contrary, Harley. We're more determined than ever. Oh, and FYI—it will be the Stoltzfus-Stedman ticket."

"Oh, this is precious," Harley said, almost laughing. "You're running with him now, are you?"

"I thought I would, yes."

"I won't forget this, Stedman. When I'm elected—and I will be—I won't forget this. You're burning your bridges. You know that, right?"

"See you at the debates."

Bart watched Harley as he ended the call. It looked like he needed something to steady his nerves.

"Eat yet?" Harley asked Bart.

"No, sir."

"Get the car. We're going to Nadine's Diner, that place just outside the beltway. Her blue-plate special is just what I need."

———

As he left the office with Bart, Harley brought along the proposed budget legislation he needed to peruse and sign before morning. He'd been putting off reading it for weeks now, but the final deadline was here. He figured he'd have some time during the stimulating lunchtime conversation he'd surely share with Bart to glance through its thirteen hundred typed pages. If he couldn't finish reading it, he'd go ahead and sign it, then read it later, as he often did with lengthy bills.

But to be honest, he wouldn't read the budget later either. Harley liked to promise things to himself like that. He enjoyed trying to see if he could pull the wool over his own eyes.

"What's the special today?" Harley asked the waitress, who set two glasses of water on the table and retrieved her order pad from her pocket. She was new to Nadine's and didn't seem to recognize Harley at all. Not recognizing Harley cut her tip in half right out of the gate.

"What day is it?" the waitress asked, not-so-discreetly scooting her gum over to one side of her mouth.

"Tuesday," Bart said.

"Then it's meat loaf."

"That was yesterday's special, wasn't it?" Harley said.

"I know."

"So what's on special tomorrow?"

"Meat loaf," she said.

"Is meat loaf the special every day?" Harley couldn't believe he'd never noticed this before.

"On Thursdays, it's chicken."

"So Thursday's the only day chicken's on special? Why's that?"

"That's when we run out of meat loaf. You fellas gonna order or not?"

Harley was too hungry to go anywhere else, so he ordered. "All right. We'll take two meat-loaf specials," he said, not allowing Bart the option of choosing his own meal. "What all is in it, anyway?" he asked the waitress.

"Trust me, it goes down a lot easier when you don't know what's in it," she said. "I apologize for the menu, though. It's about as exciting as the election, huh?"

The waitress didn't realize what she had just said and to whom she had just said it, but Harley figured the barb was mostly aimed at the other candidates, so he let it slide.

"But that Amish fella looks kinda interesting," the waitress said before closing her order book and gathering up the menus. "I tell ya, we need some fresh meat in the White House. No more of that same ole dried-out, hard-to-swallow, something-don't-smell-right stuff they've been dishing up for us lately! So two meat-loaf specials, then?"

Harley grimaced. "Maybe I'll just have the salad."

The waitress changed Harley's order, then walked toward the kitchen. Harley reached into his briefcase and took out the budget, turned to the signature page, signed it, then put the document back.

"You're not even going to read it, sir?" Bart asked.

"It goes down a lot easier when you don't know what's in it," Harley said.

———

"WE'LL LEAVE FOR LOS ANGELES FIRST THING IN THE MORNING," Mark said to Josiah after making a few more quick calls to notify key personnel and the media that the campaign was on and that he would be Josiah's running mate.

"I've never been to Los Angeles," Josiah said.

"No, I don't suppose there are a lot of Amish living in LA."

The truth of that statement struck Josiah as quite humorous, and he began to chuckle.

"Hang on to your hat, Josiah," Mark said. "By this time tomorrow, you'll have seen things you never thought you'd see."

But first they had to get there.

———

MARK AND JOSIAH MOVED THROUGH THE AIRPORT SECURITY line, which seemed unusually long, considering it wasn't a holiday. Finally it was Josiah's turn. He stepped up to the TSA agent and showed the man his identification card. The agent checked it out.

"Step into the body scanner, sir."

Josiah looked at a man in front of him whose hands were raised in the air as he stood in the scanner and was given a full-body X-ray. Josiah turned to the agent.

"No, thank you," he said.

"You want the pat-down, then, sir?" the agent asked.

"No, I don't believe I do."

"You have to choose one, sir, or you can't fly."

"Okay," Josiah said but continued standing there without another word or step toward the machine.

"You do want to fly, correct, sir?"

"Yes."

"Then which security measure would you like us to use?"

"The one you were doing twenty years ago when I flew to Florida."

"We weren't doing either of these, sir. In fact, we weren't doing much of anything twenty years ago."

"I'll take that," Josiah said. He looked back at Mark, who was busy putting his own carry-on luggage through the scanner.

When Mark looked up, Josiah caught his eye and shrugged his shoulders. Mark glanced down at his watch before walking over to Josiah.

"Josiah, our flight to LA leaves in thirty minutes. Just do what he says," Mark pleaded.

Reluctantly Josiah agreed to the pat-down. The TSA agent escorted him to the examination area and asked him to spread his legs and hold his arms out to his side.

To Josiah's dismay, the agent then ran his gloved hands along the outside frame of his body and along his inner thighs. Josiah couldn't understand why anyone, much less himself, would consent to be subjected to such an uncomfortable and embarrassing violation of his privacy, but he kept his opinion to himself. Security for air travel post-9/11 was a valid issue, he figured, so he went along with it.

Mark, who'd chosen to walk through the scanner, was also giving Josiah "Hurry up" hand signals, indicating that Josiah needed to comply with the agent so they could get to their gate in time.

Once the TSA agent completed his task, Josiah gathered up his things, and then he and Mark left the security area and started making their way toward their gate. As they walked, Mark turned to Josiah. "You didn't leave anything behind back there, did you?"

"Only my dignity," Josiah said.

The two men continued down the corridor toward the plane that would take them to California.

Boarding the plane with about ten minutes to spare, Josiah and Mark settled into their seats for the four-and-a-half-hour flight. Josiah leafed through a magazine he found in the seat pocket in front of him and then decided his time was better spent in prayer.

It was a pleasantly smooth flight, and when the plane landed at Los Angeles International Airport, Josiah stepped onto California soil for the first time in his life. Walking through the airport, he got an eyeful of West Coast culture when a punk rocker walked by with a girl Josiah assumed was his girlfriend. The rocker sported a Mohawk and various body piercings, and his girlfriend had psychedelic pink hair and metal chains hanging from various parts of her clothing. Josiah couldn't help but do a double take.

"Are we still on our planet?" he asked.

"I'm afraid so," Mark replied.

"I don't have to dress like that to win this state, do I?"

"Why? You don't think pink hair is the right color for you?" Mark laughed.

Josiah gave him a look that answered that question, then said, "To each his own."

"Believe it or not, there are a lot of good people in this state who agree with your message," Mark said. "You're doing well in the polls here. And look," Mark said as they walked by the airport magazine racks, "your look seems to be catching on."

It had been well over a month since Mark had first introduced his Amish candidate to the nation, and if the airport magazine racks were any indication, the fashion-conscious trendsetters of California had apparently welcomed the offbeat addition to the election process with open arms.

"Are they mocking us?" Josiah said, as he glanced over the various magazine covers featuring Amish fashion and buggy images.

"Mocking you? Are you kidding? They love you! Why, celebrities would sell their souls for this type of media coverage."

"If that's true, then they put too low a price on their souls."

"Well, not all of them. But your look has caught on here," Mark explained. "Californians are usually the first ones to jump on any new trend — fashion or otherwise. And it would appear they've jumped!"

From the valleys to the shops along Hollywood and Vine to Rodeo Drive, Amish fever was apparently spreading like a Southern California wildfire. Local newspapers heralded Amish-themed headlines, such as "Amish Is In!" "Aprons Are Hot!" and "Buggy Sales Surge!"

Something was definitely happening.

True to form, the late-night talk-show hosts had also been

cashing in on the Josiah craze. One popular host even walked onto the stage wearing suspendered pants and a wide-brimmed hat in honor of Josiah's visit to the Golden State. And a well-known pop star's newest recording, "Amish Love," immediately began climbing the Billboard charts after its hurried release.

Apparently, California not only knew about the mystery Amish man long before Josiah ever stepped off the plane; they had embraced him and his fresh and most unusual candidacy. Democrats, Republicans, the rich, the middle class, the poor, and the famous—people from all walks of life in California seemed to be fascinated with the Plain man who would be president. His candidacy was a novelty, to be sure, but it had caught on and was gaining steam in the western state. Who knew how long it would last? For now, Josiah had viral momentum.

Mark seemed to be basking in it. Josiah just felt overwhelmed. And he missed Elizabeth.

STORMCLOUD44/BLOG

Speak before you are silenced. Hold fast to the ideas that unite us before they are lost forever in their Sea of Babble. The waves of their aggression have not drawn back to the sea. They roll over our souls and leave us to wither on the hot sand of time. Are you with me? Or have you already been silenced? Have you already allowed the shutting down of your minds? Have you resigned yourselves to the lesser good and wired your future to their oppressive motherboard? Am I the only one who cares about our future? Who will stand with me, shoulder to shoulder, and say, "We will take it no more"?

AS MARK AND JOSIAH MADE THEIR WAY THROUGH LAX TO THE baggage-claim area, people started recognizing Josiah. They began cheering him, high-fiving him, and even pledging to give him their votes.

Josiah looked uncomfortable with all the attention he was getting. Mark knew he was used to his quiet life back on his farm, where, Mark assumed, no one had ever high-fived him before.

The campaign was now moving very fast. And this was only the beginning. Officially, anyway. Josiah might be new to his own campaign, but thanks to Mark's efforts, it had already been in motion for weeks before he even knew about it.

Mark led Josiah to the airport limo that took them to their hotel. On the way, Josiah wondered aloud, "I sure hope I'm half the man they think I am."

Mark looked out the limo's window at all the car taillights as they pulled onto the 405 freeway and basically came to a dead standstill. California freeways had always frustrated him. Why did the state waste money on speed-limit signs when they were so seldom applicable? Either there was too much traffic to go anywhere near the speed limit, or there was no traffic at all, and everyone used the speed limit as the minimum speed they should drive.

Stressing over the traffic wasn't helping, though, so he turned his attention back to Josiah. "What was it you said?" he asked.

"I said I hope I'm half the man they think I am," Josiah repeated.

"You are. No doubt in my mind."

"I hope so."

It was the first time Mark had stopped to wonder if Josiah had anything in his past that could come up to bite them. Mark had simply assumed that he'd found the perfect candidate and that vetting him would simply be a matter of protocol rather than a necessity. Still, he did need to know.

"Well, I realize this is a stupid question, but once we start gaining momentum, it's an open invitation for our opponents to rev up their attacks. So I need to ask ... is there anything I should know about? Anything in your closet?"

A puzzled look came across Josiah's face. He looked down at his Amish clothing. "Just more of these," he said, "but they all look alike."

"I'm talking about skeletons, secrets, that sort of thing. Anything I need to know about?"

"Well, I did have *rumspringa* in my youth."

"*Rumspringa?*"

"It's an Amish tradition. It's where we leave the Amish community and live in the outside world for a while before deciding whether to join the church."

"Right, right. You told me about that."

"But your world didn't hold anything for me."

"And Elizabeth?"

"She didn't even take a *rumspringa*. Stayed home on the family farm. She's not the adventurous kind."

Mark was nearly satisfied. "Anything else?"

"Not that I can think of," Josiah assured him. "Why so many questions?"

"In politics, we've been known to eat our own. Once the feeding frenzy starts, the media jumps on board, and, well, I wouldn't want someone exposing anything that could hurt you or Elizabeth."

"Who would want to hurt us?"

"Your enemies."

"But I have no enemies."

"You will now."

CHAPTER 15

★

"WE'RE BACK IN THE GAME!" CARL SAID WHEN HE CALLED Mark the following day. "Our numbers are climbing again. We must be doing something right."

Carl's assessment was correct. They were doing something right. Mark only wished he knew what that something was, so he could repeat it.

"Maybe people are listening to Josiah's message," Mark said to Carl.

Josiah's message was simple, but it seemed to be resonating with the masses. Turning to Josiah, Mark added, "They trust you, Josiah, and what you represent — simplicity, truth, and honor. You're the perfect candidate."

"No one is perfect, Mark," Josiah reminded him.

"Well, you're a lot closer than most."

"If I believed that, my friend," Josiah said, "I would be the least perfect of all."

———

BECAUSE THEY WOULD BE CAMPAIGNING TOGETHER, MARK wanted his children to meet Josiah's children and, of course, for the wives to meet as well. So he planned a family vacation to Lancaster County during one of Josiah's trips home.

Cindy and Elizabeth hit it off right from the start. Cindy loved

Elizabeth and her kind and welcoming ways, and she was especially intrigued by the Amish woman's time-management skills.

"I thought *my* day was busy," Mark heard Cindy say after she watched Elizabeth go through her morning routine. "How do you keep up with all you have to do?"

"I rise early and go to bed early," Elizabeth explained.

"I rise early and go to bed late, and I still can't get everything that's on my plate done."

"Maybe you're taking too big of scoops, *jah?*" Elizabeth said, smiling.

Cindy didn't take offense to Elizabeth's advice, because Elizabeth hadn't meant to intrude on Cindy's life. The Amish woman was simply passing along something she'd learned herself about life and all-you-can-eat Amish buffets: "Only take what you can finish."

Mark's kids helped Josiah's children with their chores but admitted to finding farm life too much work for their video-game-softened bodies. They did, however, thoroughly enjoy a game of tag in the corn maze Josiah had made.

All in all, the two families seemed to get along well, despite their different backgrounds. So well, in fact, that when it was time to hit the campaign trail again, groans of disappointment actually came out of Carrie and Seth's mouths. Mark was both shocked and pleased to hear them.

THE PRIMARIES WENT AS EXPECTED. AT LEAST THAT'S WHAT MARK told Josiah as they tracked the returns from the campaign headquarters in Wisconsin. It was all still a confusing blur to Josiah.

Harley Phillips took his party's nomination by a substantial margin and less than a week later asked his former opponent, Anne Kurtzfield, to be his vice-presidential candidate. She accepted.

As for the opposing party, the incumbent had endorsed Governor Karen Ledbetter, and the governor had easily taken her party's nomination. She chose Los Angeles mayor, Taylor Harper, as her running mate.

The race was on. Phillips-Kurtzfield, Ledbetter-Harper, and Stoltzfus-Stedman—although the latter would, more often than not, be referred to as the Josiah-Stedman ticket. Now it was up to one of those teams to win the general election.

Josiah's first national interview had gone to Emily Watson. Mark had explained to Josiah that he was trying to be a man of his word, and he had made a promise to this reporter. Mark had also explained that Emily was a fair and responsible reporter, and in the end, she did a fine job of making Josiah feel comfortable talking about himself, his hopes and dreams for the country, and his difficult decision to run for national office. To her credit, she also honored his request of only filming him in the shadows.

Josiah and Elizabeth had come to a decision early on regarding photographs. They would allow photographs from the side or back or from the shadows but preferred not to be photographed close up or straight on. They hoped most people would respect their Amish beliefs, as they generally did in Amish tourist areas. There would, of course, be some who wouldn't realize the boundaries or care about them. Josiah and Elizabeth had no control over that. But Emily had decided to use artists' renderings to enhance her report, and Josiah was pleased that the camera was focused on the reporter for much of the interview.

Other reporters weren't as accommodating as Emily. They would promise to keep Josiah out of the camera shot and then let the cameras roll as though Josiah were any other presidential candidate.

According to Mark, news commentator Stanley Kingston fell somewhere in the middle. Every election year, and for the year leading up to an election, Stanley tried to interview as many of the candidates from both parties, as well as Independents, as he could. This Sunday, Stanley's guest was Josiah Stoltzfus. Stanley's show was live, but Sunday was the Sabbath according to Amish faith, so a live interview was a no-go for Josiah. His interview was pre-taped Saturday afternoon.

Mark had assured Josiah that Stanley had a reputation for respecting those he was interviewing. Sure, like any reporter, he tried to scoop the best story possible, but he always tried to be fair. Well known to the public and respected among media peers and politicians alike, Stanley didn't seem to be packing his own bias every time he interviewed someone, which had been his duty every Sunday morning at nine o'clock for the past twenty years. *Sunday World with Stanley Kingston* was his program's name, and on it, Stanley had done a one-on-one with many notable people — world leaders, policy makers, and everyday people who suddenly found themselves thrust into the spotlight for a variety of reasons.

For the entire week before the interview, Mark prepped Josiah for whatever questions he might face. Stanley was known to be a tough but fair reporter, and Mark told Josiah there was far too much riding on this interview to go into it unprepared.

"The first question he's going to ask you is how your Amish faith will affect your governing should you be elected. How will you respond?"

"Yes."

"Yes?"

"Yes, it will affect it."

"You can't say it like that."

"But it's the truth, Mark. My faith is what motivates me to lead an honest, fair, and disciplined life. I don't recall any of the presidents in our nation's history being asked to leave those qualities behind when they moved into the White House, although a few may have forgotten they'd packed them once they got settled in."

"All right, then I guess yes *is* a good answer."

"The truth is always a good answer."

"Next question — as a non-resistor, how would you handle mounting tension with foreign enemies?"

"I would pray for them."

"Uh ... Josiah, listen, you're really going to need to be, well, a little more politically correct."

"But that's what I'd do."

"I know, but the voters want to know what else you would do if our national security were at risk."

"Well, while it's true I would always seek peaceful solutions to any tensions with foreign countries, I would trust the judgment of Congress in these situations."

"Good, good. Now you're catching on."

From early morning until late into the evening, Mark prepped Josiah. They stopped only briefly to eat the lunch and dinner Mark ordered from a delivery service. It was intense, but Josiah knew it had to be. Mark had pointed out that this was a national television show with millions of viewers. That translated into millions of votes. And Josiah needed every one of them.

———

ACCORDING TO THE NEWS DIRECTOR, JOSIAH NEEDED SOME-thing else on the morning of taping the interview.

"Makeup!"

A pretty twenty-year-old makeup artist had suddenly appeared.

"What's that?" Josiah asked as she opened her makeup kit and pulled out a few essentials.

"Just a little pancake foundation for the cameras," she said.

"But they told me I wouldn't be on camera."

"You won't be."

"Then why are you wanting to put pancake mix on me?"

"Your side view will show."

"I have a beard."

"I know. But I'm only going to put it on your cheekbones and around your eyes."

"Why would you want to do that?"

"The studio lights make everyone look washed out, so we apply a little color to help."

Mark, who had accompanied Josiah to the interview, stepped in. "Trust the professionals, Josiah," he said. "They know about this sort of thing."

"No offense," Josiah said. "But I've gotten this far in life without wearing any makeup or pancake mix. I figure I can go the rest of my life without any too."

The makeup artist laughed as she put away her makeup kit. "Well, I think you're charming even without foundation," she said before walking away.

The cameramen got into position as one of the show staff led Josiah to his seat across the desk from Stanley. Josiah was more fascinated with his surroundings than he was nervous about the interview. He was dressed in his church clothes — dark trousers with suspenders, a dark, lapel-less jacket with hooks instead of buttons, and a broad-brimmed black felt hat.

"Here we go," the director said. "Five, four, three, two, and ..."

The director motioned toward Stanley, and Stanley began talking.

"My next guest has turned conventional wisdom on its head," the commentator spoke into the camera. "He only began his campaign a few months ago, and he is running neck and neck with the two lead candidates in every poll. What's even more incredible — his name isn't even on the ballot!

"He's breaking all kinds of political records, and due to his surging popularity, he will be included in next Thursday's debate. Out of respect for his Amish ways, we have agreed to film this guest only from the side. Welcome, candidate Josiah Stoltzfus."

Josiah nodded a friendly greeting toward Stanley.

"Josiah, sir, I'll get right to the point. Some people are labeling you a spoiler, saying your campaign will simply take votes away from both parties, or worse, that your candidacy is some kind of practical joke that someone is playing on the country. What say you?"

"Well, sometimes a spoiler is a *gut* thing, *jah*? Shaking things up a bit, making people think," Josiah said. "But I can assure you, sir. I have sacrificed much to run for this office. My campaign is no joke."

"Sir, people are wondering that if by some miracle—and I'm sure you would agree it is a long shot—you become the first presidential write-in candidate to ever win the White House in the history of our nation, will you be bringing your Amish ways to 1600 Pennsylvania Avenue?"

"Let me put an end to that speculation right now," Josiah answered. "The Amish ways are what I know. And even though I am going against accepted Amish practices by running for national office, I still, and always will, consider myself Amish in my heart. My answer, then, would be yes. I will be bringing my Amish ways with me."

"So are you planning to, say, go without electricity in the White House?"

"It's how the White House was originally built, *jah*?"

"Well, yes, I suppose it is."

"Imagine what that alone will save the country after four years!"

"So in other words, you are the ultimate green candidate?" Stanley said with a slight grin.

"Green?"

"It means that you're interested in preserving the earth."

"I'm a farmer. I take very good care of the earth."

"I noticed, too, sir, that you said four years. If elected, you'd only serve one term? You wouldn't run for reelection?"

"I would serve my term and then go back home. Wouldn't want to wear out my welcome."

"Josiah," Stanley continued, "on issues of national security, it's a known fact, is it not, that the Amish are pacifists?"

"We are nonresisters," Josiah explained. "Our goal is to live in peace with all people."

"But what if someone doesn't want to live in peace with us?

Do we sit back and do nothing, knowing that weakness will only embolden our enemies? Or worse, the terrorists?"

"While it's true we Amish are peace-loving, we do not tolerate evil. And though I would never declare war, I would not stand in the way of Congress if they felt it was the only way to handle a situation that threatened our national security."

"And what are your thoughts on capital punishment, sir?"

"The Amish believe that God is the ultimate judge. Personally, I could not in good conscience take another person's life for any reason. But I also realize our legal system is in place for a reason. The people and the lawmakers have the right to vote their conscience on such matters."

"But what about 'an eye for an eye'?"

"It's what's inside a person that must be healed."

"So you would forgive someone who has killed, say, one of your own children? Hypothetically speaking, of course."

Josiah didn't blink. "I already have, sir," he said.

Josiah realized that he was a candidate unlike any other presidential candidate the nation had ever seen before, and he hoped his beliefs were becoming quite clear to Stanley Kingston and his viewers. Josiah had no agenda, no spin, and no desperation. He was simply answering each question as honestly and clearly as he could, whether it was a popular answer or not.

After the interview, Mark and Josiah stopped by an outdoor café to grab a bite to eat.

"A home run!" Mark said ecstatically. "You hit it out of the park, my friend!"

"You think so?" Josiah said.

"Are you kidding me? You were great! Sincere and honest, passionate about your vision for our country. I think that's what's resonating with the people. They know you're more than a bumper sticker."

"You don't see a lot of bumper stickers on buggies."

"Well, whatever it is you're doing, keep it up! We're surpassing everyone's expectations in the polls. We just might win this election after all!"

Josiah still wasn't sure what he'd gotten himself into, but Mark seemed to be satisfied with the way things were going so far.

"We're reaping what you've sown, Josiah. Your good choices, as well as your restraint," Mark said.

"Never thought I was sowing seed to run for president one day," Josiah said. "But then, I never saw your car wreck in my future either."

———

AFTER THE KINGSTON INTERVIEW, THE PHONES AT CAMPAIGN headquarters exploded with requests for interviews and appointments, as well as speaking invitations. But with the debate just days away, Mark and Josiah concentrated all their time and attention on preparing for the event.

"Hang on to your hat!" Mark told Josiah when they both looked at the latest poll, which showed the Amish farmer closing in on the front-runner.

"I always have." Josiah laughed.

———

THE FIRST DEBATE BETWEEN THE TOP THREE CONTENDERS — Harley Phillips and Karen Ledbetter, each representing their own political party, and Josiah Stoltzfus as the leading Independent candidate — was taking place at Radio City Music Hall in New York City. It was a much-anticipated event, because for the first time, America would see and hear the Amish candidate debate. The press, as well as party officials, played up the fact that Congressman Stedman had "abandoned his party," but Mark assured Josiah that he was focused on the bigger picture — winning the election.

This was also Josiah's first trip to the Big Apple. Never before had the Plain man seen so many people heading to so many different places in such a hurry. At least in California, most folks were laid back. In New York, however, there was a different energy. The city was crowded, but everyone still moved quickly. Taxis darted in and out of traffic, walls of pedestrians seemed to move together toward oncoming walls of pedestrians, somehow integrating at the last possible second and then moving on in their respective directions.

"Where's the Statue of Liberty?" Josiah asked Mark as the limo passed through Manhattan.

"It's not far from the hotel. Would you like to see it?"

"I would, yes. I surely would. My grandparents used to tell me about her, about how beautiful she was when they first saw her in the harbor on their way to Ellis Island. Wouldn't mind seeing her for myself."

Mark asked their limo driver to take them down to the harbor, where Josiah could get a look at France's gift. The driver nodded and maneuvered his way through the streets, turning into the parking area of Battery Park.

"There she is," the driver said, pointing across the water.

Josiah turned and saw her, Lady Liberty, standing as tall and inviting as he had always imagined her — her torch held high and tight in her hand as she reached toward the heavens.

"That's what this is all about, Josiah," Mark said. "Us not letting her down."

"Whether we win or lose, Mark, she will still be here."

"I hope so."

———

MARK AND SEVERAL OTHER CAMPAIGN STRATEGISTS HAD BEEN prepping Josiah on what he might face once the lights came on and the debate began. Josiah didn't really understand the necessity of all the preparation, nor did he understand the enormous importance of the event.

"Can't I just answer the questions honestly? If what I'm saying is true, why do I have to rehearse it?" he had asked.

"It would be nice if it were that easy," Mark had replied. "But it's not all about honesty or answering from your heart. It's about keying in on what the people want to hear and delivering it to them."

"But what if what the people want to hear isn't what's good for the country?"

"Trust me on this," Mark had assured him. "Give the wrong answer now, and you'll never get the chance to do what's good for the country. You'll be out, and Phillips or Ledbetter will be sworn in. Do you want that?"

"No, I don't suppose so," Josiah had said, though he wasn't convinced.

"In a debate, even an honest answer can be skewered and mis-interpreted," Mark had insisted. "That's why we prep."

The evening of the debate, Josiah looked out at the crowd from where he stood on stage. They looked friendly enough. He wondered whether all that preparation had really been necessary.

Connie Hawkins, the reporter chosen to be the moderator for the Radio City Music Hall debate, began her questioning that evening with the one question that most folks were understandably concerned about: How would an Amish president handle foreign affairs?

When the question came up, Harley couldn't seem to resist "ad-libbing" a strategically placed, well-rehearsed jab: "My opponent thinks foreign affairs is whatever happens outside of Lancaster, Pennsylvania," he said.

There was a small ripple of laughter, but because the audience had been told ahead of time not to respond, most of them honored the rule and remained quiet.

"I would seek a diplomatic answer to most foreign-affairs issues," Josiah said. "But if a peaceful solution could not be reached, I would defer to Congress regarding any escalation in America's response."

"But you personally would be against going to war in any circumstance?" the moderator asked.

"I would be, yes."

"Mr. Stoltzfus," Connie said, "how could our country protect herself if her enemies know ahead of time that we will not fight back?"

"Being fully capable of responding yet restraining your power *is* living peacefully, is it not?"

"With all due respect to my opponent," Harley interjected. "I believe it's called living in denial. Sometimes you have to respond so that a bullying nation cannot rob the rest of us from living in peace. When a nation becomes an aggressor, innocent people suffer. Which is the greater goal then — living in peace with the bully or making the bully live in peace with everyone else?"

"Any response, Mr. Stoltzfus?"

"My opponent makes a good point. And if you've seen his latest campaign ad against me, he could very well be considered America's leading expert on bullying."

Despite the admonition to hold applause and laughter, the room now erupted in both.

———

IT WAS HARD TO KNOW WHO WON THE FIRST DEBATE FOR THE general election. Some news analysts said that Harley had gotten in enough good jabs to be declared the victor, while others leaned toward either Josiah or Governor Ledbetter. The experts, though, declared it was Josiah who had won. But two more debates were to come. The race for president was far from over.

Unfortunately for Governor Karen Ledbetter, an allegation of inappropriate fund-raising had caused enough controversy to leave her sorely trailing in the polls. As hard as she tried, and as innocent as she may have been, she never seemed to be able to recover from the damage. By all estimations, her run for the White House was all but over.

Josiah was the number-two candidate now, but there was still a wide gap between the Stoltzfus-Stedman ticket and the Phillips-Kurtzfield ticket.

But it was narrowing.

CHAPTER 16

★

After the first debate, Mark ramped up the personal appearances. He knew Josiah's appeal was strongest during one-on-one meet and greets and at town-hall meetings. When people saw the Amish man in person, away from the intrusive cameras, spotlights, and entrapping questions, when they heard his unfiltered comments, they loved him.

One of the most intensive events Mark planned, in terms of logistics, was the Josiah for President Whistle-Stop Tour, which stopped at twenty major railroad stations across America in half as many days. The decorated railcars and prearrival publicity drew crowds from all over the country. People traveled for miles to catch a glimpse of the Amish man who just might become the next president of the United States. They knew they were witnessing a once-in-a-lifetime event, and they wanted to be part of it.

While Josiah may have been uncomfortable in the limelight, Mark was used to working a crowd:

"Ladies and gentlemen, it's wonderful to be in the great city of Chicago!"

"Hello, Kansas City!"

"Greetings, Hoosiers!"

"Denver, we're counting on you!"

And on it went. Oklahoma City, Grand Rapids, Provo, and beyond.

At every stop, Mark and Josiah got off the train, signed posters and bumper stickers (even though Josiah didn't understand the attraction of such things), and then took turns stepping up onto a makeshift platform for short, impromptu greetings and some Q and A time.

Unlike Mark, Josiah rarely had a prepared speech. He simply talked off the top of his head and from his heart and then answered people's questions. No monitor or cue cards were needed.

Words came easily to Josiah because he treated everyone he met like a neighbor or friend. To him, it was like standing on his front porch and having a conversation with one of the brethren from the church or with a tourist who happened to be visiting their community to see how and why the Amish lived the way they did. Josiah was already comfortable in his own skin, and now he was beginning to get more comfortable in his campaign too. At least he was getting comfortable with the curiosity and questions, but he was still uncomfortable with the praise. The Amish way was one of humility, and it felt awkward for others to be placing such hope in him. He was only human. And only one human at that.

What did everyone expect of him? It seemed they wanted a miracle.

Josiah valued his heritage and his faith. He knew the Amish lived a different lifestyle from most other Americans, some of whom considered the Amish downright peculiar. Many in the nation spent their money as quickly as they made it on fast cars, fancy clothes, and all the latest electronic gadgets. But all Josiah had ever known was the Plain life, and now it seemed that folks in the outside world wanted some of that simplicity for themselves.

Elizabeth had told Josiah that Bishop Miller had informed the community of Josiah's willful disobedience in going against the *Ordnung* and entering a national election. The bishop had requested their prayers for wisdom and God's direction in handling the matter. Thinking about that, Josiah wondered how Elizabeth and the children were getting along on the farm without him. He wished he could be in two places at once—on the campaign trail and at home with his family. Or better yet, three places, if he added in bed taking a nap. He was exhausted.

Most of the cities and towns that Josiah and Mark visited during the campaign tour looked the same to Josiah. Well, except for Las Vegas. In Vegas, Josiah had a hard time understanding why people would drop their hard-earned money into a machine that made a little noise and then kept it. He also didn't understand why some of the people he saw walking around town dressed the way they dressed, especially the women. Why would they want to wear such skimpy outfits? Was cloth in such short supply in this Nevada town that women were forced to dress this way? He offered to send one lady some of Elizabeth's handmade aprons to help her cover up, but she just looked at him strangely and walked away.

The train tour was draining.

"This is a lot harder than farming," Josiah said to Mark after the whistle-stop in Denver. "As a farmer, at least you know if you plant corn, you're going to reap corn. But harvesting a crop of votes is unpredictable. Even when you sow good seed, you can still reap a gust of wind that blows it right into the next guy's camp."

"By 'gust of wind,' are you referring to Harley Phillips?" Mark said.

Josiah laughed and then shrugged his shoulders, not wanting to personally call Harley a bluster of hot air, even though it fit.

Harley's television attack ads against Josiah continued, and Mark gave Josiah an update on them along the train route.

One of the ads said "Let's make America great again. Not Plain."

Another one played off Josiah's own ad about his name: "Gimme an *S*. Gimme a *T*. Gimme an *O*. Gimme a *T*. Gimme a *Z*. Gimme a break! Elect Harley Phillips! At least you can spell it!"

Josiah couldn't understand why Harley was choosing to run such a negative campaign.

"It's the only way he knows how to play the game," Mark told Josiah over coffee one evening after a campaign stop.

"Why would he even think of it as a game? It's more important than that, *jah*?" Josiah replied.

Life on the road, or rather the train, was getting lonely. Josiah missed Elizabeth and his children something fierce. Elizabeth had taken a bus to Philadelphia when they were campaigning there and had traveled to Washington several times to see him as well. Josiah also tried to go home whenever he was able.

Elizabeth and the children were taking care of the farm in Josiah's absence. Others in the community helped out too. Some were clearly disappointed in Josiah and that he wasn't taking care of matters at home, and they were more than happy to tell Elizabeth how they felt.

Elizabeth related some of their comments to Josiah.

"Josiah's duty is to God first and then to his family," one neighbor had said.

"You can't run this farm by yourself, Elizabeth," said another.

When Josiah asked Elizabeth how she responded, she'd said, "I told them, 'Oh, can't I now? I appreciate your help, but don't mistake it as a sign of my helplessness. The children and I are quite capable of running this farm.'"

Surprisingly, Elizabeth said the bishop helped whenever he could as well. And for the most part, he kept his disappointment with Josiah to himself.

Josiah loved hearing from Elizabeth, no matter how difficult the stories were. He faithfully borrowed Mark's cell phone to place a call to her every evening. As long as it wasn't their own phone, borrowing a cell phone was allowed in some Amish communities. Josiah and Elizabeth had a prearranged time set for her to be at the Mennonite neighbors' house — 10:00 a.m. — and Elizabeth didn't miss a single day.

"I sure miss you," Josiah said on the eve of the last day of the tour.

"I miss you too, Josiah."

"Guess we'll both be glad when this is over, *jah*?"

"But what if you win? I fear this kind of schedule will only get worse."

Josiah sighed at the thought but tried not to let her hear his weariness ... or the doubt and frustration that suddenly and unexpectedly began to gnaw at him. For the first time since joining the campaign, he was beginning to wonder if maybe this had been a bad idea after all. Maybe the bishop had been right: an Amish man had no place in national politics according to the *Ordnung* by which Josiah ordered his life. How prideful of him to think that he could go against it in such a way and yet still hold on to his Amish beliefs.

It was becoming increasingly challenging for Josiah to remain separate from the world. He still managed it, but it was a difficult struggle. Josiah missed the peace and feeling of safety that came from the self-imposed boundaries of the Amish lifestyle. And he missed being home with his beloved Elizabeth, his children, and his community.

The final train stop of the campaign was in Minneapolis, where the crowds were even larger and more enthusiastic than any of the previous stops. The Minnesotans loved Josiah's plain-speaking ways and his stance on energy conservation (his carbon footprint was practically invisible).

Finally it was time to ride the rails back to D.C. Josiah was so drained from the grueling schedule that he fell asleep in the rear car as the train raced down the track in the middle of the night. He was so exhausted he didn't wake up until the train rolled into the D.C. station the following morning. Josiah couldn't remember ever sleeping in that late before. Or being that tired, even during harvest season.

THE TRAIN TOUR GAVE THE STOLTZFUS-STEDMAN TICKET another good bump in the polls. No matter how hard Harley Phillips tried to label their campaign a novelty and a joke, the novelty wasn't wearing off. And no one was laughing.

"Don't look back, Harley. We're gaining on you!" Mark shouted enthusiastically upon their return from the train tour. He then led the roomful of staff and volunteers at their Washington headquarters in a "Josiah! Josiah! Josiah!" chant.

"We're closing the gap," Carl said, handing Mark the latest poll results. "We just might pull this off."

Josiah was pleased but focused on borrowing Mark's phone again to call Elizabeth and the children to tell them that he'd made it back to Washington safely.

"More reporters were in town today asking questions," she said.

"Guess they have to get their stories."

"I don't feel comfortable with all of this," Elizabeth said. "If they have questions, why don't they ask you directly? That's how you get the truth. Why all the secrecy?"

"Maybe the truth isn't what they're after," Josiah said. "Is the bishop taking any interviews?"

"No."

"*Gut*. Not that he's hiding anything. I just wouldn't want them bothering him. He has much to do."

"I wish things were back to normal. We're a tight community that protects our privacy."

"I miss that too," he told her before reluctantly ending the call.

All the mudslinging seemed especially unnecessary in Josiah's eyes.

"If Harley doesn't like a position we've taken, shouldn't he give us a chance to explain? To attack me as a person is taking the low road," he'd often comment to Mark.

Mark agreed with Josiah but explained that Harley Phillips was a politician whose moral GPS was permanently set to take the lowest road possible.

The more dirt Harley tried to throw in the direction of Josiah, however, the more voters the Amish man won over with his witty comebacks and gentle manner.

"Josiah Stoltzfus only has an eighth-grade education," Harley spouted.

"I once read that three of our presidents — Andrew Jackson, Andrew Johnson, and Zachary Taylor — didn't even graduate from grade school, sir," Josiah countered. "The test of the office is more about depth of character and leadership than the number of diplomas, is it not?"

"My opponent hadn't even been to Washington before this campaign, and now he wants to move into the White House?"

"It's a big place, but I'm sure I can find my way around the rooms."

Some news reporters compared Josiah's quick and easy wit to Lincoln's. Indeed, his appearance was Lincoln-like, as was his courage and heart. He didn't have to fake sincerity with a furrowed brow or down-turned lips that were choreographed to memorized words. He truly did care about the people. Not that America's former presidents hadn't ever felt the people's anguish, but Josiah's concern was real and without an agenda. And apparently folks could tell. There was something about him that seemed to make them believe he could be trusted. And that trust had turned into campaign donations, which in turn helped buy more radio and television commercials.

The gap between the two front-running candidates continued to close.

The real thrust of Josiah's campaign, though, was happening on the Internet, spontaneously and virtually free. With committed bloggers writing about the campaign, YouTube clips from Josiah's rallies going viral, and Facebook posts being shared all over the country — all over the world, for that matter — this amazing and most unusual campaign was breaking all sorts of political records.

———

JOSIAH'S CAMPAIGN WAS ALSO BREAKING HARLEY'S POOR HEART.

Josiah's continued climb in the polls frustrated Harley beyond measure. As he saw his lead eroding, he began asking Bart to release some YouTube videos featuring Harley. But his videos were obviously self-serving and lacked a certain creative eye as to what was viral-worthy: Harley on a visit to the site of his boyhood home; Harley interviewing his mother; Harley playing Frisbee with his dog. Titillating material all—at least for the less than fifty viewers who had checked them out to date.

The videos that *were* going viral, though, were some of Harley's bloopers and previous debate gaffes.

"What are your feelings on the growing tensions in the Middle East, sir?" one debate moderator had asked Harley.

"Personally, I think everyone should lighten up and just go to Disneyland."

It was Harley's attempt at humor, but it backfired on him and made him look as though he was the one who should be wearing the buffoon label that he was so desperately trying to pin on Josiah. The question had required a serious answer from a would-be president, not an inappropriately timed diversion. Not that Disneyland wouldn't have been a fun diversion for everyone involved in the elections.

Couple this with other clips of when Harley's words raced out of his mouth ahead of his thoughts, when he randomly misquoted the Founding Fathers and the Constitution, and when he tripped stepping up to the microphone at a campaign rally in Louisville, and it was easy to see why his clifflike slide in the polls was becoming a concern.

STORMCLOUD44/BLOG

Are you watching? Are you seeing the clouds as they gather over us? The storm is coming. Who will take the reins and

lead us through the valley of our affliction? Harley Phillips?
Josiah? Ledbetter? Or one who is yet to come?

"Bart!" Harley called from his desk at the Elect Harley headquarters. "Get in here!"

Bart hurried into Harley's office. "What is it, sir?" Bart said as he stood in the doorway.

"You sure you've turned over every rock on this guy?"

Harley was referring to Josiah, of course, and whatever dirty laundry the Amish candidate might have hidden in his past. Harley wanted his hands on that laundry more than anything else in the world, and he was convinced that Bart simply hadn't searched deep enough. Harley would have done the investigating himself, but when did he have the time? He had an election to run, an election that—if he weren't surrounded by nincompoops—he just might win.

Harley couldn't help but feel sorry for himself. He was a good man. By his own estimation, a man worthy enough to be president. It wasn't his fault his daughter had fallen in love with a man so inept and bungling, a man Harley now had to involve in his campaign. There wasn't a thing Harley could do about it except keep reminding his daughter of her husband's shortcomings, an assignment that came rather easily to Harley.

"You're missing something, Bart," he said, getting up from his desk and pacing around the room. "It's there. You're probably looking right at it and just not seeing it!"

"I've looked," Bart said defensively. "There's nothing of any significance. Trust me. He's Amish, Harley. What do you think I'm gonna find? That he forgot to remove his hat one Sunday during church? I'm telling you, there's nothing to go on."

"Well, then, how else can we trip him up?"

"The only thing left is his faith, but you can't go there."

The thought lingered in the air.

"His faith? That's perfect! Bart, you're a genius!" Harley said, clapping his hands together and smiling that poster smile of his. "We make that the issue. Scare people into thinking he'll turn the whole nation Amish. The power companies will go berserk!"

"But he won't turn the country Amish, sir. The Amish don't proselytize."

"The average person wouldn't know that."

"You want me to lie, sir?"

"I want you to get me elected!"

Harley shot Bart a look that he knew would get his point across. It was Bart's duty as Harley's son-in-law and assistant to get Harley elected. Or else.

———

THE THIRD AND FINAL DEBATE WAS SCHEDULED A FEW WEEKS before the election. By most reports, Harley and Josiah had each won a debate now, and the results of the vice-presidential debate was almost a draw, with Stedman edging out his opponents by only a narrow margin.

This debate was crucial. It was much too close of a race to call, and Josiah still had an uphill battle if he wanted to win over the undecided voters. He was looking good in the polls, but polls had been wrong before.

Harley prepared day and night for this last debate. His staff asked him every conceivable question and prepped him with every possible answer. He even had his ad-libs and spontaneous comebacks memorized should anyone manage to get in an accusation that stuck. Harley was ready, willing, and determined to come out on top in this final debate and then slide on through to a win in November.

Governor Ledbetter had followed nearly the same course as Harley — studying and prepping — and had even undergone a somewhat extreme makeover (hair, makeup, and fashion) in an attempt to take ten years off her appearance and also replace the still-swirling accusations in the news.

"Give 'em something else to talk about," she had told her campaign staff.

On the eve of the big debate day, Harley was like a bull trapped in a pen, raring to get out and start the stampede. That same night, in a nearby hotel room, Josiah read his Bible and then turned in early to ensure he got a full night's rest before the debate.

And he ate the mint on his pillow.

———

MARK WAS THRILLED THAT THE DEBATE WAS BEING HELD ON THE campus of Yale University, his alma mater. The stage was set with three lecterns. From his vantage point in the audience, Mark watched Harley Phillips enter and stand behind the lectern on the left side of the stage, then Governor Karen Ledbetter entered and stood behind the lectern on the right, and finally Josiah entered and stood behind the center lectern.

The moderator was popular news anchor Will Wilcox, a former presidential-spokesman-turned-news-reporter. Cameramen were in place to capture every moment and word and broadcast the debate to the millions of people who would surely be watching. Whether the cameramen would honor Josiah's request of being filmed from the side or in the shadows as they had the other two debates was anyone's guess.

When the red light appeared on top of the lead camera, Will began the questioning.

"I want to welcome our viewers to this, the final debate of the presidential race."

The moderator had the candidates introduce themselves, and then he directed the first of his questions to Governor Ledbetter. This was followed by a question to Harley Phillips, and then a follow-up question to each of those candidates. They were well-thought-out questions, and each presidential hopeful handled them impressively.

Then it was Josiah's turn.

"Mr. Stoltzfus, if elected president, what would you do to get this economy growing again, sir?"

Josiah cleared his throat. "Hard times are never happy times. But they do serve a purpose. They teach us and help us grow in our spirits.

"The way I see it, there is plenty of blame to go around. As a farmer, I've planted a lot of trees in my lifetime—apple trees, pear trees, cherry trees. I've yet to plant a money tree. Try as I might, I can't seem to find the seeds for it. That tells me there isn't any such thing. So why do we continue to believe that there is?"

As Josiah continued his answer, he didn't point fingers, but he did spread the fault around. He listed just about everyone, from the banks to the car companies to the politicians to those in the housing market to Wall Street, and finally, to the general public. Mark had prepped him well. By the time Josiah was finished, there wasn't a pedestal left standing.

But Josiah hadn't done it in a condescending or critical way. It was simply a call for each American to take responsibility for his or her own actions, or lack of foresight, and not look around for a scapegoat. He made it clear that the nation had arrived at its current state of affairs because of the actions or inactions of each person. In small ways and in big ways, everyone had played a part.

"Instead of blaming one another, we must pull together. We're going to be okay. We may need to start using our reserve—open up the silos so some folks can eat—but we can and will pull out of this."

"The silos?" Will Wilcox inquired.

Josiah turned and looked at the other two candidates, both of them experienced politicians. "Surely you've prepared for uncertain times such as these, haven't you?"

An uncomfortable silence followed, and then Governor Ledbetter responded, "Well, yes, uh ... no. I mean, yes, I'm sure we have. Haven't we, Harley?"

"Of course we have," Harley stated firmly. "I believe I read that in the budget ... somewhere ... Sir, what is your point?"

"You make hay while the sun shines, not in the middle of a thunderstorm," Josiah said. "I believe I read that in the *Farmer's Almanac*."

The audience couldn't help but laugh and applaud.

Josiah repeated his question, "You did make good use of our times of plenty, didn't you?"

Governor Ledbetter hesitated and then looked over at Harley, who looked at Will Wilcox and then back at Josiah. "Can we get back to you on that?"

"Certainly," Josiah replied. "But it's the people who need to know."

"This question is for you, Josiah," Will said, continuing. "What do you think most concerns the average American today?"

Mark had prepped Josiah for this question, and there was a list of possible answers, but what they'd settled on was an old Amish joke. When he'd first heard the joke, Mark hadn't been sure about where Josiah was going to take it, but in the end, he chose to trust Josiah's judgment.

Josiah smiled at the moderator and, with a twinkle in his eye, said, "Seems an English man was traveling through Amish country one day, when he veered off the road and got his car stuck in a ditch," Josiah glanced over at Mark, who smiled in return.

"Well, an Amish farmer happened by in his buggy and told the English man that his horse, Benny, could pull him out. The farmer hitched Benny up to the bumper of the man's car and yelled, 'Pull, Nellie, pull!' But Benny didn't move.

"Then the farmer yelled, 'Come on, Ranger, pull!' Still, Benny didn't budge.

"Then he yelled, 'Benny, I said, "Pull!"'" And sure enough, ole Benny started pulling, and wouldn't you know it, that car came rolling straight up out of the ditch!

"The English man thanked the Amish man but then asked the farmer why he'd called his horse by the wrong name twice.

"The farmer smiled and said, 'Ole Benny's blind, and if he thought he was the only one pulling, he wouldn't even try.'"

The audience erupted in laughter, and as much as he tried not to, so did the moderator.

"The way I see it," Josiah said, "Benny's like a lot of folks today. They don't mind helping, but they don't want to be the only ones pulling the car out of the ditch."

"And you believe the people have the power to pull the country out of the ditch, so to speak?" Will asked.

"A horse is trained by trust," Josiah said. "The people's trust in their government has been broken. Rebuild that trust, and they'll pull."

Will Wilcox turned to the other candidates, "Any rebuttal?"

Harley was chomping at the bit. "Are all of my opponent's answers going to be about horses?" he said condescendingly.

"I'm Amish," Josiah said. "Horses are what I know. But I could change my stories to be about mules if it would make my opponent feel more comfortable."

Once again the audience erupted in laughter. After a moment, Will managed to bring the debate back into line.

"Moving on to my next question," he said. "How do each of you feel about tax breaks for the wealthy?"

It was obvious that Harley Phillips couldn't wait to voice his opinion. "I believe that everyone should pay their fair share, including the wealthy."

"Mr. Stoltzfus?" Will asked.

"I believe everyone should pay their fair share and live within their means ... including the government."

Governor Ledbetter then jumped into the fray. "With all due respect to my opponent, isn't it true that the Amish don't pay taxes, Mr. Stoltzfus?"

"With all due respect to Governor Ledbetter," Josiah replied, "that is a misconception. When it comes to the government, our stance is 'Pay, pray, and obey.' And we don't ask much of the government either. We take care of our own."

Then came the question Mark knew the political pundits were waiting for.

"Mr. Stoltzfus, since your religious faith is so much a part of your lifestyle, would you be able to maintain an acceptable separation of church and state?"

"Sir," Josiah began, "let me start by saying the Amish are strong believers in the separation of church and state. Religious freedom is what brought us here to America in the first place. We understand the curiosity of others and will answer questions about our faith when asked, but we do not expect the rest of the country to take the vows we have taken."

"But haven't you broken some of those vows by even running?"

"I am following what I feel in my heart I must do."

"So if elected, you would govern from an inclusive viewpoint, realizing you would be the president of all Americans?"

"Yes, all faiths would be invited to the White House barbecues."

The audience laughed again, clearly delighted with Josiah's response.

So far, Mark thought it was a healthy debate. Will didn't shy away from asking tough questions, and most of those were directed toward Josiah. The questions gave Josiah the opportunity to address many of the concerns Mark knew the people had, concerns they'd shared with Josiah in conversations all across America.

———

HARLEY DIDN'T LIKE THAT JOSIAH SEEMED TO HAVE THE AUDIENCE in the palm of his hand. It was evident they loved his simple, clear answers. When Harley had about as much as he could stand, he interrupted. "How much longer is the country going to tolerate this ridiculous campaign?" he said. "We are becoming the laughingstock of the whole world!"

"According to the latest polls, Congressman Phillips," Will Wilcox said, "it appears the global community supports this 'ridiculous campaign' three to one."

Harley snapped back, "The global community does not elect our presidents, sir!"

The line didn't garner the response Harley was hoping for. The audience was clearly in Josiah's court and didn't appreciate Harley's tone with the gentle Amish man. But it had been a long campaign, and Harley knew all he needed to cinch the election was one good sound bite. That's all, just one quotable quote that all the major news outlets could pick up and run with. He hadn't said anything all that interesting or noteworthy so far in the debate. No new revelations had been uncovered about his opponents, and he hadn't been able to convince the American public that Josiah's campaign wasn't a serious choice.

To Harley's vexation, it was Josiah who got the most supportive applause and bursts of spontaneous laughter during his speeches. And now here he was, standing right next to Harley, center stage —an Amish presidential candidate who was being treated with the respect and validity that Harley felt he himself deserved. Had the whole country gone mad?

If Harley was going to score a home run, he had to play dirty politics, and he had to play them now.

"While it pains me to have to take the path of other politicians who have attacked a candidate for his or her faith, I believe that since we are talking about the presidency here, it is of great concern that my opponent is a member of a religion that is considered by some—not me but some—to be archaic, narrow-minded, and cultlike," Harley said.

An uncomfortable hush immediately fell over the audience, but Josiah didn't flinch. The remark had obviously backfired on Harley. Those in the audience now appeared to feel extremely sympathetic toward the Amish man.

"Is that the best you've got, my friend?" Josiah said. "My faith?

Are you going to point out the size of my nose and how my chin tilts slightly to one side, as well?"

"The people have a right to know whether your beliefs will interfere with your presidential duties should you, by some miracle, be elected," Harley said, desperately trying to defend his comment.

"Sir, I have answered that question in every debate and every interview I have given since I first tossed my hat into this election. I have already answered it this evening. Yet I will answer it once again—I make no apologies for my faith now, nor will I in the future."

If not for the rules, Mark was certain the entire audience would have been on their feet applauding. Even so, about half of the audience, Mark among them, ignored the rules and gave Josiah a standing ovation. It was near the end of the debate, and some things just couldn't be controlled.

———

ACROSS THE COUNTRY, PEOPLE WERE WATCHING THE DEBATE IN their homes, offices, and public meeting places, and most were impressed by what they saw from this unconventional presidential candidate. His appearance automatically made him stand out among the other candidates, but it was his answers—clear, concise, and passionate—that won over the masses.

In Las Vegas, Nevada, a young married couple who were sitting at their dining-room table going through a stack of overdue credit-card and mortgage bills watched the debate.

"Maybe he'll turn things around for us," the wife said, almost afraid to give herself the luxury of hope.

In New Orleans, Louisiana, a middle-aged musician watched the debate along with customers in his club.

"I believe he'll do what he says. If you can't trust the Amish, who can you trust?" he said.

All across America people had tuned in, and they liked what they were seeing.

———

"ANOTHER HOME RUN, MY FRIEND!" MARK SAID AS THE LIMO carrying Josiah, Cindy, and Mark maneuvered its way through the cheering crowd following the debate. "Harley couldn't do a thing but watch you score!"

"There were some tough questions," Josiah said, still uncomfortable with how this whole political game was played.

"Yes, but you knocked 'em right back. Didn't miss a single pitch. Handed ole Harley Phillips his ego on a platter, that's what you did! It was beautiful! Just beautiful!"

"It is a sinful thing to gloat," Josiah said, "but there were a couple of times tonight when I think I might've sinned."

Giving someone their long overdue comeuppance did feel good, Josiah realized, even though he knew it was wrong. But as he'd suspected a long time ago, the campaign was changing him. Perhaps not a lot, but in small ways. Ways not noticeable to anyone but himself, Elizabeth, and of course, God.

"We're on the home stretch!" Mark said as he prepared a toast from the beverage center in the limousine. Josiah raised his bottle of water.

"To the next president of the United States!" Mark cheered.

"And to his vice president!" Cindy added.

The three of them clinked their beverages against each other and took a celebratory sip. Then they all sat back to watch the post-debate coverage.

Most of the political analysts concurred that Josiah had indeed hit a home run at that night's debate. The majority of those analysts also maintained that Josiah didn't stand a chance of actually being elected, even though Mark had told Josiah that campaign donations were increasingly pouring in, volunteer campaign workers were joining his campaign by the droves, and he and Harley were running neck and neck in the polls. Even the analysts had to concur that the campaign was doing quite well for "a novelty campaign that could never end in an actual win."

———

THE FOLLOWING MORNING, JOSIAH FOUND MARK SITTING IN THE hotel coffee shop.

"How did you sleep, my friend?" Josiah said.

"Great!" Mark replied, "But I still had to order a strong cup of coffee to keep me awake while I read through this mountain of Internet messages and blogs.

"May I?" Josiah asked, pointing to Mark's phone. It was ten o'clock. Elizabeth and the children would be waiting for his phone call at the neighbors' house.

"Of course," Mark said. "Call her and tell her the good news."

Josiah smiled as he took the phone from Mark, then moved to an out-of-the-way table that would offer some privacy.

"I miss you," Elizabeth said, when she answered the phone.

"I wish you were here with me. But I understand with the kids and the farm and all you have to do ..."

"I know. This will all be over soon. So how did it go last night?"

"Well. They tell me it went well."

"*Gut.* You sound tired."

"I am."

"Do you still believe we're doing the right thing?"

"*Jah* ... I think."

"I didn't realize how much the campaign was going to take from us."

"*Jah.* But I still believe this is what we must do."

———

IN THE DAYS THAT FOLLOWED, PEOPLE ACROSS THE COUNTRY continued to add their opinions to the mix. Most news reports and blogs were in favor of Josiah, but some, written anonymously of course, were dead-set against him.

One blogger, STORMCLOUD44, wrote a string of especially negative and rambling pieces, taking exception to Josiah's continued candidacy for a number of reasons, none of which were credible complaints. The writing was angry and at times incoherent (as were many posts by this particular writer). Thankfully, the scathing remarks against Josiah were immediately and fervently challenged by a dozen or so of the blog's forty-six faithful followers. It was unclear why any of them bothered to follow a blogger with whom they so vehemently disagreed, but apparently some folks rather enjoyed the rush from adrenaline-charged spikes in their blood pressure.

The rebuttals didn't give STORMCLOUD44 any pause, however. If anything, they simply fortified the blogger's position and passion, however misplaced or confused. The rambling blog posts continued making outrageous demands, accusations, and manifesto-like statements for the liberation of some faction that no one in the mainstream had ever heard of.

Just another day in politics.

———

BISHOP MILLER HEARD A TIDBIT HERE AND A TIDBIT THERE OF how the election was going. It was mainly through word of mouth from the tourists or through comments made in *The Budget*, the newspaper of America's Amish communities.

The bishop also heard about the Josiah Stoltzfus situation in letters from various members of the Amish leadership who were commenting on what should be done regarding the unprecedented rebellious and very public actions of one of their own. They acknowledged Bishop Miller's authority over his own community but didn't approve of Josiah's run for president, and they felt official action, such as a shunning or other behavior-modifying punishment, was long overdue.

For Bishop Miller, who had gone on record as disapproving of the campaign, the punishment wasn't as clear-cut. He knew Josiah's heart and his intentions. True, Josiah was going against the church's teaching and rules and would need to be disciplined in some way, but Josiah and Elizabeth were his friends. It would hurt him to cast out this good man and woman.

Yet Josiah had clearly gone against the church. He was no longer considered a practicing Amish by many in the community, even though he steadfastly maintained his Amish beliefs on his own accord—most of them, anyway, the national-election rule notwithstanding. It was a problem Bishop Miller hadn't encountered in all his years of leadership. Most folks who adamantly went against an Amish rule in the *Ordnung* usually departed the community of their own accord to take up a different lifestyle. But Josiah was emphatic that he was still Amish. He loved the Amish faith and his Amish community. He was simply following what he felt in his heart he needed to do, what he felt God was calling him to do. Elizabeth, too, believed in her husband and had vowed to stand by him even though she was still living in their Amish community and considered herself Amish as well.

But the countdown to some kind of disciplinary action against them both had begun.

Bishop Miller knew he was in over his head. He had tried to convince Josiah to give up this outrageous notion, but his counsel had been to no avail. It pained him to take matters to the next level, but Josiah's actions had pushed the leadership into a corner. Bishop Miller had had no choice but to call a meeting with other church officials to seek further direction.

"Thank you for coming, brethren," Bishop Miller said to Ezekiel Yoder and Mose Rediger, who represented other church leadership beyond Bishop Miller's own district borders. "As you are aware, the situation with one of the members from my district continues, and I am in need of your counsel."

"This has gotten too far out of hand," Ezekiel said. "Something must be done."

"You cannot overlook such blatant disregard for the *Ordnung*," Mose agreed.

"I realize it's a concern," Bishop Miller said. "I've been hoping the matter would take care of itself. But now it appears he very well might win the presidency."

"One of our own can't be president!" Mose said. "You should've stopped this months ago."

"I know, but what I struggle with is whether God has indeed led Josiah in this decision."

"God wouldn't lead one of our members to break the rules," Ezekiel stated emphatically.

"But what if God's plan is greater than our rules?" Bishop Miller said.

"Think about what you're saying, brother!" Mose said. "Did God speak to you about this? Did God tell you that this was his plan for Josiah?"

"I have heard nothing from God. Only a feeling that ... well ... my spirit is troubled over the whole matter, my brother. What if Josiah truly is who our country needs at this time? What if the answer to our nation's woes is indeed one of our own?"

Ezekiel bristled. "We can't pick and choose which rules we choose to follow, Bishop Miller! After his *rumspringa*, Josiah joined the church and agreed to abide by its rules, did he not?"

"Of course."

"Then he is breaking that vow!"

"Yes, I know, and I've told Josiah that very thing," Bishop Miller said.

"And his response?" asked Ezekiel.

Bishop Miller hesitated, so Mose filled in the silence. "I think we're seeing it."

"Well, God wouldn't ask an Amish man to lead a nation!" Ezekiel said firmly.

"Like he wouldn't ask a shepherd boy to slay a giant? Or a babe in a basket, floating down a river, to one day stand before Pharaoh and free his people? You yourself were named after a man God used in unexpected ways, Ezekiel. I could go on if you like, gentlemen," said Bishop Miller.

Ezekiel shook his head. "Keep those in your charge in line, Bishop, or we will be forced to step in and do it for you. We simply cannot cast aside our centuries-old rules for one man."

"What is more important, brethren—our rules or the plan of God?" Bishop Miller asked.

"Our rules do not stand in the way of God's plan," Mose said.

"Do you have any idea of the precedent you'd be setting to allow this to continue to the end? What if he were to win? Someone from the Plain community serving in the White House?" Ezekiel scoffed. "It will not be!"

"Take care of the matter before such a thing happens, brother," echoed Mose. "For the good of all our districts."

That was the heartfelt opinion on the matter. The men turned and walked out the door. The meeting was over.

There were no easy answers. Bishop Miller couldn't allow such disregard for the church's rules to continue unaddressed. If he didn't handle the Josiah matter, it was clear that others would step in and do it for him. The other church officials had made that abundantly clear. But Bishop Miller also didn't want to stand in the way if Josiah had truly heard from God, which the bishop, for the most part, doubted, since he himself hadn't heard anything from God about the situation. He wished he had too—clearly, audibly, leaving nothing to chance. Or faith. But God hadn't talked to the bishop through a burning bush as he had Moses. The bishop could only trust. And schedule a face-to-face meeting with his old friend as soon as possible.

———

BISHOP MILLER HAD WRITTEN A LETTER TO JOSIAH IN CARE OF his campaign headquarters, requesting they discuss the matter at Josiah's earliest convenience. Josiah had intended to write back right away to tell Bishop Miller that he was more than willing to meet with him — it was important to keep the lines of communication open between himself and the bishop. But he'd found that time had a way of slipping away from him these days.

Now, however, with the polls increasingly leaning in his favor, Josiah knew the impossible might actually become reality come Election Day, so he figured he'd best have that talk with the bishop.

Josiah hired a driver to take him home to Pennsylvania. He would spend most of his time with Elizabeth and his children, of course, but he also needed to meet with the bishop while he was there.

The reunion with his beloved Elizabeth couldn't have been more wonderful. When she was in his arms, it mattered little whether or not Josiah had the votes of anyone else in the country. What mattered was that she believed in him. That alone was worth waking up for each morning.

Josiah's children were thrilled to have their father home again as well. Josiah could tell by the way they rushed their words together in frenzied excitement.

The meeting with the bishop, on the other hand, wasn't quite as wonderful.

"Josiah, the reason I wrote to you requesting a meeting was so I could let you know that if you continue your campaign for president, there will have to be serious consequences. The matter is causing a great deal of concern," the bishop said.

"I realize what I'm doing isn't in keeping with the *Ordnung*," Josiah said, "but Elizabeth and I have prayed about this, and we've left the matter in God's hands."

"Have you, Josiah? Or did your eagerness to be the one to save our country move the matter into your own hands?"

"I didn't seek out this mission, Bishop Miller," Josiah said respectfully. "It sought me out, my brother."

"You don't have to open every door that presents itself."

"But aren't there many reluctant heroes in the Scriptures? People who never intended to be in the forefront but ended up there by God's divine plan?"

"It's not your heart that I question, Josiah, or God's plan. It is your judgment that gives me pause."

"But if I can do good for my neighbor by leading the country at this time, how could that be wrong?"

"There are many good paths we can follow, Josiah. But God's will is the only perfect one for each of us."

"I believe this is that perfect path for me."

"Then what you're saying is that you are leaving the church."

"You mean if I win?"

"I mean if you continue to run."

———

A FEW DAYS LATER, AFTER JOSIAH HAD RETURNED TO WASHING-ton, and after yet one more meet-and-greet luncheon in a seemingly endless lineup of such events, Mark sat down on the edge of the bed in the hotel room. Cindy was already lying on the bed next to him, relaxing on a mountain of pillows. She didn't really want that many pillows, but she was too tired to move them anywhere else. She watched as Mark loosened the shoelaces of his wing-tipped shoes, then kicked off the shoes. This was the kind of pace set by people half their age.

"Maybe the kids can come on the next jaunt," Cindy said.

"That would be nice. Have they noticed yet that I'm not home?" Mark asked, teasing.

"They've noticed."

Mark and Cindy both needed a good night's sleep, but it was only two o'clock in the afternoon. They couldn't even get in a decent nap before they had to start getting ready for the evening's black-tie dinner.

"Sorry I asked you to leave the luncheon early," Cindy said.

"I didn't argue, did I?" Mark smiled. "I was drained too. Besides, Josiah was only going to greet the crowd. His keynote's tonight."

Cindy was growing tired of the organized breakfasts that ran into luncheons that ran into evening banquets. All she wanted was her husband back. She lovingly ran her fingers along the curve of his neck and shoulders.

"I've missed you," she said.

"I've missed me too. But I've missed us more."

"Do you really think we've got a shot at winning?" she asked, almost wishing the possibility away.

"Well, the polls have been wrong before. But you might want to step up your efforts on finding that perfect gown for the Inaugural Ball."

"And if we lose?"

"Keep the tag on it just in case."

Cindy started preparing for the dinner, putting on her makeup and doing her hair. At six o'clock, after donning her gown, she sat down to watch some TV, hoping to take a break from the political scene. Her break didn't last long. A special news bulletin broke across the screen mentioning Josiah by name. Mark must have heard it, too, because he immediately came over to turn up the volume.

"It is being reported that Josiah Stoltzfus, the write-in candidate whose back-to-basics message has been sweeping the nation, allegedly was once arrested for a hit-and-run and driving a stolen vehicle," the newscaster said. "Stay tuned for more on this developing news story."

Mark immediately tried calling Carl. Cindy could hear the busy tone from the bed and listened as the call went to Carl's voice mail.

"What are you going to do?" Cindy asked Mark.

"Find him!" Mark said, walking out the door.

———

MARK QUICKLY MADE HIS WAY DOWN THE HOTEL CORRIDOR toward the conference center, not willing to stop for anyone. The news bulletin had just been reported, so Mark had to get the truth before the story got any bigger, and he wanted to get it straight from Josiah himself.

The hotel was one of those massive complexes with a conference center and a shopping mall attached directly to it. It was so spread out, hotel patrons practically had to use a golf cart just to get around. But Mark didn't have a golf cart. He had to walk at his fastest clip, with Secret Service agents continuing to protectively tail him, while at the same time trying his best not to bring any undue attention to himself or create any cause for alarm.

When he got near the banquet hall, he could hear the cheers of the crowd coming from inside. The people were pumped. This was the third event of the day, and they were still going strong. Josiah was scheduled to make a few opening remarks before the dinner and then return to the stage after dinner for his formal speech.

With only a couple of weeks to go until Election Day, some news analysts were predicting a tight race, while others were telling people to prepare for a virtual landslide ... for somebody. Either the voters would surprise the pollsters, come to their senses, and vote for one of the more traditional candidates, or they would surprise the political establishment and vote for the outsider, Josiah Stoltzfus. After all, voters could always change their minds within the confines of a voting booth when no one was around to tell them they were wasting their vote by casting it for a Plain man from Lancaster County.

Or voters could turn on Josiah, especially in light of a late-breaking news bulletin.

So exactly how the election was going to turn out in the end was anyone's guess, and Mark wasn't wasting a single second. He needed to do damage control. It had all come down to these final weeks of the campaign, and the mud was slinging fast and furious. Governor Ledbetter was still in the race but was limping to the finish line. The real contest was between Harley Phillips and Josiah, and Harley was pulling out all the stops.

Mark made his way to the private side entrance of the banquet hall that would take him to the green room, where he hoped to find Josiah. There wasn't any time to waste. Mark had to speak with Josiah before he addressed the crowd. But Josiah wasn't in the green room. Mark took his cell phone out of his pocket and hit a button on his speed dial.

———

CARL WAS IN THE MIDST OF MAKING SURE EVERYTHING WAS IN place for Josiah's big speech. It fell to him to oversee the lighting, sound, additional security, and other particulars for the night's event. He wasn't in charge of the venue, of course. They had staff for that. But he was in charge of the people who were in charge. So it was understandable that Carl was much too busy to answer his phone when it rang. And when it rang again. And when it continued to ring. Finally he looked at the caller ID and gave in.

"Hello?" he said, trying to listen over the boisterous crowd. "What? I can't hear you."

"It's Mark. I need to speak with Josiah *immediately.*"

"He's about to walk onstage," Carl said.

"Well, stop him!"

"Stop him? Do you hear this crowd? They can't wait for him to take the stage. Why aren't you here yet anyway?"

"I'm on my way. Don't let him take that stage until I get there!"

Carl wasn't sure what was going on, but he knew it had to be something important. He made his way to the area where Josiah stood ready to greet his enthusiastic supporters.

"Josiah," Carl said, grabbing Josiah's arm just as his entrance music began to play. "Mark needs to speak with you."

"Now?" Josiah said. "Is he serious?"

"I've got him," Carl said into the phone, still unsure what all the urgency was about.

"Tell him to wait by the side of the stage," Mark said. "I'm on my way!"

Carl turned to Josiah. "He's coming."

Almost immediately, Mark hustled up.

"What's wrong?" Josiah asked.

"Why didn't you tell me?"

"Tell you what?"

"About your police record!"

Carl moved in a little closer to get a better listen. Eavesdropping was worthless unless done correctly.

"I didn't think it mattered," Josiah said.

"You didn't think it mattered? A hit-and-run?"

Carl couldn't help interjecting. "In a horse and buggy?"

The band continued to play "I'll Take You There," the classic song that had become synonymous with Josiah's campaign, while Josiah explained the situation to Mark.

"It was during my *rumspringa* days."

"So it's true?" Mark asked. "What they're saying is true?"

"I don't know. What are they saying?"

The crowd was now chanting, "We want Josiah! We want Josiah!"

"They're saying you were driving a stolen car and were involved in a hit-and-run," Mark said. "That's what they're saying!"

"Well, they got that part right."

"What?" Mark shrieked. "And no license?"

"I'm Amish."

"Look, you'd better get out there and lead with your explanation ... whatever it is. And it had better be good! I'm sure the crowd's probably tweeting and texting about this already."

"Well, they can twix and teet all they want; I know the truth of what happened."

"Yeah, a hit-and-run in a stolen car, and you were behind the wheel!"

"You only know part of the story, Mark."

"Look, Josiah, good people will forgive past sins, but they don't want to be lied to. I don't either. So you'd better tell it all to me, every last detail, right here and right now."

Carl knew Mark was serious. Mark had had to deal with enough falsehoods and half-truths himself from politicians like Harley — innuendo was Harley's favorite weapon. But that was Harley. Mark didn't want or need the top of the ticket he was running on to not be forthcoming with him.

"I wasn't dishonest with you, Mark," Josiah said in his defense. "You asked if I had any secrets. That incident was never secret. The whole community knew about it. I've never tried to hide it."

"So what's the truth then? What happened that night?"

The band continued to play, trying to make it appear as though all was going according to plan, despite the fact that the plan hadn't been for them to play every verse and six choruses of Josiah's theme song.

"Four of us were in Philadelphia for *rumspringa*," Josiah began. "Most of the stuff we were doing was harmless, except for one night."

The band members looked over in Carl's direction. Carl twirled his arm, the classic "keep going" motion. They shrugged their shoulders and played on.

"Peter Dunkirk, a bit older and more daring than any of the rest of us, showed up at the house where I was staying," Josiah continued. "He was driving a new car, so I asked where he'd gotten it."

"We want Josiah! We want Josiah!" the crowd chanted again, obviously eager to catch a glimpse of their new political hero.

Josiah looked toward the stage.

"Keep going," Mark pressed.

"Peter said the car was his cousin's, so we all went for a drive. Peter got ahold of some beer and started drinking. The next thing I knew, he'd picked up some girls and got to showing off and acting all crazy."

"He was driving?"

Josiah nodded. "And was drunk as all get out. He hit a car, then just took off. He didn't even stop to see if the people in the car he'd hit were hurt. By the time the police tracked him down, he and the others had gotten their story together and lied to the police, saying it was me who was behind the wheel that night."

"Because you were the sober one?"

Josiah nodded. "He wanted me to take the bounce for him, as you English say."

"You mean 'the fall'?"

"See, I can't even talk tough. But the truth came out at the trial ... if anyone had bothered to check."

"The file's been sealed."

"By court order. But I could've opened it."

"Well, in a tight race, in the weeks just before a presidential election, they're going to report first and check it out later."

"They?"

"Everyone who doesn't want to see you get elected."

"So what should I do?" Josiah asked.

"What do you want to do?"

"Tell the voters the truth."

———

Josiah stepped up to the microphone. "Ladies and gentlemen," Josiah began.

An immediate hush fell over the crowd. They didn't want to miss a single word of what Josiah Stoltzfus had to say.

"Some of you may have already heard about an incident that happened in my youth, over thirty-five years ago ..."

Josiah went on to explain the whole story, marveling out loud at how some people didn't bother checking facts before condemning someone. He pointed out that most stories had mitigating circumstances that were edited out of the version that got passed around. That was what made gossip so damaging. And kept it interesting at the same time. It was sad, Josiah said, but sometimes the truth just wasn't exciting enough for some folks.

"Winston Churchill once said, 'A lie gets halfway around the world before the truth has a chance to get its pants on,'" Josiah said. The famous quote got resounding applause.

Josiah ended his explanation with a simple request: "I ask your forgiveness for putting myself in a position that would allow others to cast doubt on my character. I used poor judgment in my actions, my inactions, and my choice of friends. But I never lied to you."

A lady in the crowd answered for everyone. "We love you, Josiah!" she yelled out from the balcony. The people sprang to their feet, cheering and applauding the man they had come to love and trust. Josiah had faced the lies and all the half-truths head on, and the people respected him even more.

Later, Josiah gave his after-dinner speech, speaking as he always did—from his heart. As foreign as the spotlight felt to him, Josiah was in his element. He was a natural-born speaker, and the crowd hung on his every word.

———

By the time Josiah finished his speech, Mark was convinced that a final-inning catastrophe had been avoided. All people wanted was the truth. They were tired of all the mudslinging, political games, and manipulative posturing typical of so many past election years. Good men and women from both sides of politics had been vilified, often for no reason other than someone's sheer jealousy or desire for control. As far as this crowd was concerned, it was high time for that practice to come to an end.

There was another incentive for Josiah's opponents to stop trying to assassinate his reputation. Too much mudslinging from one side had been known to lead to a landslide on the other. And more than anyone else in the running, Josiah had been on the receiving end of the mud. Mark knew that if Harley Phillips didn't want to suffer a severe ego-whipping come election night, he'd best lay off the attacks.

The cheers following Josiah's keynote speech that night were deafening.

"I picked the right man, all right," Mark said to Josiah as he stepped off the stage.

"The truth still matters, *jah*?"

"At least we hope it does," Mark said.

CHAPTER 17

★

WHEN WORD OF THE BOTCHED "LEAK" REACHED HARLEY, HE made a call to Stacy Creighton.

"Stacy," he said, "I need you to take care of a little business for me."

"Of course," Stacy said. "What is it, Harley?"

"Something important I need you to tend to. Out of town."

"But what about everything I have to do here?" Stacy said.

"It'll keep. And don't discuss this with anyone."

"Very well, sir," Stacy said.

"I need you to take a little trip over to Lancaster County," Harley said.

"Amish country, sir? But why?"

"To buy us a little insurance."

The campaign had been long and arduous. But it was almost over. Only a couple of weeks remained before voters would go to the polls and voice their choice for president and vice president of the United States. Only a couple of weeks before Harley would know the direction his future path would take.

Harley had grown weary of Bart's continual failure to uncover anything significant enough to derail Josiah's chances of getting elected. The hit-and-run controversy hadn't caught any traction at all once it was explained, and Josiah's honest handling of that past incident merely endeared Josiah to the public even more. Harley needed something more current—a bad decision, a quotable verbal blunder, a controversy—anything that would bring Josiah's good judgment and character into question. But so far, there had been nothing.

Harley trusted Stacy to do better. Money could make people talk—maybe even the Amish.

This would be a covert operation, of course, known only to Harley and Stacy. Harley's plan was for Stacy to drive to Josiah's community to talk to his friends, neighbors, and perhaps even his bishop to see what he could find out.

Maybe the town could use a new building for their monthly flea markets, a new wing for their library, or perhaps even some new streetlights. Stacy could dangle all sorts of temptations in front of whomever he needed, as far as Harley was concerned.

If I still don't discover anything new about Josiah, he vowed to himself, *then I'll drop the matter altogether and leave the election in the hands of the voters.*

No one would ever need to know about Stacy's visit to Amish country.

But if there was a sliver of a chance that something in Josiah's character or past that the public should know about might turn up, then it would be Harley's duty to "leak" it to the press before the election, would it not?

Harley loved it when he could put a noble spin on some underhanded or manipulative action of his. It made it so much easier to live with himself.

———

STACY FELT AS OUT OF PLACE IN THE AMISH COMMUNITY AS HE was sure Josiah felt in politics. And he looked about as out of place too. Even the suspenders he'd picked up at Yoder's General Store didn't help him blend in. Of course, he hadn't put them on quite right, so they made his pants ride a little high in the saddle, but Stacy couldn't be blamed for trying.

Mrs. Burkholder was the first Amish person Stacy chose to talk to. It took a while for the elderly widow to answer her door, but she finally managed to get to it with the aid of her cane. Stacy introduced himself and then, after placing his cell phone out of sight and pressing Record, got right to the point—or several points, to be more accurate.

"How well do you know Josiah Stoltzfus?"

"Have you ever seen him involved in any suspicious activities?"

"Do he and his wife seem to get along?"

"Has he ever voiced any controversial opinions about anything?"

"What do you know about his *rumspringa* days?"

Stacy could tell that Mrs. Burkholder wasn't sure who the man standing on her front porch was or why he was asking such probing questions about her good neighbors. But her answers to his questions seemed forthright and honest. When it became obvious to Stacy that his visit wasn't yielding anything juicy enough about Josiah, he moved on to questions about Elizabeth.

"What about Mrs. Stoltzfus?" he asked.

"Elizabeth?"

"Yes."

"Oh, my, the woman is an angel," Mrs. Burkholder said. "Why, Elizabeth would do anything for anyone. She's always helping out with church or visiting the sick, and she's a wonderful wife and mother too."

"Sounds like she's almost too good to be true," Stacy said, probing for something, anything. "No one's that perfect, are they?"

"No, but Elizabeth Stoltzfus is as near to perfect as you can get," Mrs. Burkholder said. "Oh, she went through a rough spell a while ago, but she's doing much better. Those days are behind her now."

"Rough spell?"

"A dark period. Depression, I guess. Dr. Willoughby gave her some medication. It seemed to help some. If you ask me, she just needed time to heal, to accept reality."

"Reality?" Stacy's interest was stirred. "Did Mrs. Stoltzfus ever tell you what kind of medication she was taking?"

"That was none of my business, sir," Mrs. Burkholder said, eyeing the stranger with suspicion. "None of yours either, I reckon. I need to go now. I've got chores to tend to."

"Sure, sure," Stacy said, taking a step back so she'd feel more comfortable. "I should be on my way too."

Stacy opened his wallet to take out his business card, which just happened to be sandwiched between a couple of hundred dollar bills.

"You sure that's all you know?" he asked again.

Mrs. Burkholder's expression hardened when she saw the money. It was obvious that she had picked up on the hint.

"Sir, I must ask you to leave now," she said coldly.

Stacy thanked her, shoved his wallet back into his pocket, and made his way back to his car. The lady had given him nothing to go on except perhaps the depression angle. There might be something there. Still, Stacy needed more information before he could take it to the press, or rather, before some "unknown source" could "leak" it to the press. An important difference in Harley's mind.

Stacy drove over to Bishop Miller's home.

"Come in, please," the bishop said, welcoming the stranger into his house. "Can I get you a glass of iced tea and some fresh blueberry muffins my wife just baked?"

Stacy politely said he'd take one muffin, for starters anyway, and began chatting with the bishop. When the time felt right, he brought up the subject of Josiah Stoltzfus.

"What is it you would like to know?"

"Are Josiah and his wife still members of your community?"

"They are, but ..."

"But?"

"Nothing. What is your next question, sir?"

"Are the Amish allowed to run in national elections and still remain in good standing with the church?"

"That is a matter for our own community to deal with."

"Has he ever been disciplined by the church before?" Stacy asked.

"Never," the bishop said. "Josiah Stoltzfus is exemplary. Don't know what's gotten into him of late. This whole election situation is out of character for him."

"Irrational, would you say?"

"Out of character," the bishop repeated.

It was something, but still not enough.

"So who's been helping Elizabeth with the farm during his absence?"

"I've helped her some, and a few of the other men."

Stacy raised an eyebrow. The bishop clearly took offense at the implication. Stacy was offending people all over Lancaster County. His boss had trained him well.

"We believe in helping our neighbors, sir," the bishop said firmly. "And Elizabeth does most of the work of running that farm herself when Josiah's gone. She is a capable, strong woman."

"Yes, of course," Stacy said, then moved his line of questioning to Josiah's *rumspringa* incident.

The bishop verified Josiah's version of the incident and then added, "Sir, there is no finer man than Josiah Stoltzfus. He would, in fact, make a *gut* president, if such a thing were allowed in our community. But it is not. Now if you have no further questions, I must ask you to ..."

"If he is such a '*gut*' man, as you say, why is he disobeying the church's orders?"

The bishop was done with the interview. He showed Stacy to the door, and Stacy still hadn't uncovered anything new about Harley's formidable opponent. Elizabeth's depression, and perhaps the fact that discussions were in progress among the Amish leadership to possibly shun Josiah for his continued disregard of church rules, were the only "secrets" he'd found. Both tidbits could be used to his boss's advantage, perhaps, but considering what Harley was after, it was a total waste of a day.

Well, almost a total waste. Before leaving the Lancaster County area, Stacy stopped at a local restaurant to sample some of the Amish cooking he'd been hearing so much about. And to his pleasure, he discovered these rumors were 100 percent true. And these were "rumors" Stacy wouldn't mind leaking.

THE EVE OF ELECTION DAY ARRIVED, AND CARL CALLED MARK with some disturbing, albeit not surprising, news.

"Someone leaked information about Elizabeth to the press."

"Elizabeth? What information?" Mark asked.

"Her depression."

"Her depression? That's what Harley's going after? That?"

It was a Hail Mary play of the desperate. But Carl knew Harley had a well-earned reputation for using such plays. The story spread quickly across the wire services, and soon every news station in the country was reporting on it.

"How can a president lead our nation during troubled times if he has to care for a depressed wife?" the reporters asked.

Never mind the fact that former presidents and first ladies had battled a variety of similar mental-health issues (Abraham and Mary Todd Lincoln both battled depression) and that in the current climate of a challenging economy and rising joblessness, a good number of Americans were depressed too. Harley must have been banking on the issue costing Josiah a good deal of votes. Prejudice against someone's mental or emotional struggles was callous and narrow-minded, to be sure, but Carl knew Harley was a politician who believed the ends justified the means.

As the news made the rounds, the story of Elizabeth's health issues grew even bigger and took on a life of their own. Elizabeth now had, according to the tongue waggers, "a prescription-drug dependency" and was "suffering from delusions." It wasn't true, of course. Slanderous rumors started by the jealous and desperate seldom were. If the lies were allowed to continue escalating, Elizabeth might have ended up being described as the next Lizzie Borden, according to "anonymous sources."

"If the rumors are true," Harley said during one interview, "Lizzie's about to move into the White House. But we can stop her! Vote for me on Election Day!"

His sound bite didn't go far, but some damage had already been done. Mental-health conditions should be handled with dignity, like any other medical challenge, but that didn't matter to Harley Phillips. He had an election to win.

The voting precincts would open in less than fifteen hours, and Harley wondered if the unsubstantiated rumors about Elizabeth had managed to change the minds of enough of Josiah's supporters to get Harley himself elected. A dirty game, yes, and it wasn't over yet.

Harley placed a call to Stacy.

"Get it out there," he said without so much as a hello.

"Now?"

"No. *After* the election," Harley said sarcastically. "Of course now!"

"The shunning?"

"That's all we've got left. If the people want to elect an Amish man, they'll have to find another one. This one's being kicked out of his community and church."

"But it hasn't happened yet."

"Details. Let the voters figure that out. Leak it!"

"The same source?"

"Anonymous is my middle name."

"YOU NEED TO ISSUE A STATEMENT," CARL TOLD JOSIAH WHEN they heard the breaking news item come over the television at campaign headquarters late that evening. "Voters will be heading to the polls first thing in the morning, so there's no time to waste."

Josiah knew Carl was right. He was tired of all the rumors and lies he'd already had to deal with and was in no mood to go chasing down new ones. But this time they'd attacked the character of his wife and his own standing within his Amish community. He cherished both. Harley likely figured that Josiah would have little fight left in him. He was wrong.

"Get him on the phone," Josiah said, praying for both wisdom and a forgiving heart for a man who apparently possessed neither. Though Harley had declared himself Josiah's enemy, Josiah's faith told him to seek a path of peace.

Carl called Harley, who answered on the first ring, on speakerphone.

"I know what you're going to say, Carl, and it wasn't me. I didn't leak it to the press."

"You don't expect us to believe that, do you, Harley?" Carl said.

"It's the truth, Carl."

"Josiah would like to speak with you."

Carl nodded at Josiah.

"Congressman Phillips . . . ?" Josiah began, giving Harley the respect Harley had seldom shown to him.

"Josiah, before you say another word, I want you to know I feel terrible about this. I assure you if I find out that it was anyone in my camp, they will pay dearly. I give you my word."

Harley's word meant little in the Stoltzfus-Stedman camp. They had banked on it before, but that check had always bounced due to NSF — nonsufficient forthrightness.

"Harley," Josiah said, taking a long, deep breath. "It is the peaceful way of the Amish that keeps me from reacting as others might ... with a well-placed fist to your mouth!"

Those within earshot raised their eyebrows and looked at one another. They'd never heard the peaceful Amish man upset before. Few people had. Josiah was even surprised himself. But he wasn't deterred. He took another long, measured breath and continued.

"We are a gentle and forgiving people," Josiah said. "And your accusations against my wife only prove your serious lack of knowledge about my life, my wife, and our Plain ways, sir. Elizabeth was medically treated for depression after the death of our daughter. Here in America, how one grieves such a loss is still up to that individual, is it not, sir?"

ON THE OTHER END OF THE LINE, HARLEY FELT HIS STOMACH sink to his ankles. He was vaguely aware of Josiah and Elizabeth's loss but hadn't connected the two situations. His actions now made him appear like an uncaring, insensitive, tactless oaf. Indeed, he knew he was an uncaring, insensitive, tactless oaf most of the time, but he didn't want the voting public to know that.

"I'm so sorry," he said with as much sincerity as he could muster. "I truly am sorry."

"And as for the other matter," Josiah continued, "I am not shunned as yet, although it is true they are considering taking that action against me, sir. However, I am, and always will be, Amish in my heart, no matter how the church handles this."

"But you're running on the fact that you're Amish."

"I am Amish. The church may indeed shun me, especially if I win, but should that happen, I will serve, but I will also do everything in my power to ask their forgiveness once my term is up. But you, sir, have no power to take my faith from me."

After the call ended, news of how Josiah had defended his wife and his faith, as well as Harley's gross insensitivity toward

Elizabeth, quickly spread throughout the news outlets. But this time it spread because Harley himself leaked the story—the true story—to the media. For once, Harley did the right thing.

He also did it hoping that publicly taking the high road would win him more votes.

Harley was always thinking.

The decision was now up to the voters.

Election Day was just hours away!

CHAPTER 18

★

BY LATE AFTERNOON OF ELECTION DAY, A CROWD OF SUPPORTers had gathered at the Elect Josiah headquarters in D.C. to await the closing of the precincts and the tallying of the ballots. Included in the crowd was the friendly couple Mark had met while waiting for his car at the Willard Hotel way back before any of this had started — before Mark's car trouble, before meeting Josiah, and before this most historic election night.

"Thanks for letting us share in this moment, Congressman," the man said as he greeted Mark with a sincere handshake.

"Well, I told myself if I ever ran again, I was going to track you two down and put you to work in the campaign," Mark said. "I try to keep my promises, even the ones I make to myself."

"Well, you kept this one, that's for sure. And we've enjoyed every minute of it!" Agnes said. "We hope you win!"

"If we do, it'll be thanks to people like you. There's no way Josiah and I could have done this alone."

The woman reached into her purse and pulled out her camera again.

"Agnes," the man said, shaking his head. Then he turned to Mark and apologized once more.

"It's fine. I don't mind at all," Mark said.

"Well, I have to take it now," Agnes explained to her husband. "Once he becomes vice president, we may never see him again."

Mark laughed. "I'm more than happy to take another picture

233

with you both. But you'll have to forget about that never-seeing-me-again stuff. I owe you!"

"And you know how you can pay us back, don't you?" the man said.

"How's that?"

"Win this thing!"

ELIZABETH HAD WANTED TO BE WITH HER HUSBAND ON ELEC-tion Day — it was the day that would determine their future — so Mark had arranged for Secret Service to pick her and the children up from Lancaster and then drive them to D.C. It was about a 250-mile drive, and when they arrived in the capital city by late afternoon, the children looked out the car window in awe of all the national monuments. This was their first trip to D.C., and they had a lot to take in. Elizabeth had already been to the capital city several times during the campaign, so it was beginning to feel a little more familiar to her. She was able to answer her children's string of questions almost as an authority.

"What's that?"

"The Lincoln Memorial."

"What's that?"

"The Jefferson Memorial."

"What's that?"

"The Capitol Building."

"What's that?"

"A man selling T-shirts."

"But that's Daddy's face on it."

"It would appear to be, yes."

It was only an artist's drawing, and Elizabeth knew there was no way that Josiah could control all the marketing that was going on in his name. It was all part of the process.

All she was really thinking about this day was how much

she longed to see her sweet Josiah and finally put this campaign behind them.

———

AT THE STOLTZFUS-STEDMAN HEADQUARTERS, THE ENERGY WAS electric, hopeful, and exceptionally tense as family, friends, and supporters watched the TV, switching between different news broadcasts. They wanted to see how the coverage was being handled on each of the major news shows. The polls would close soon, and no one wanted to miss a second of the results once they began coming in.

Elizabeth and the children arrived at campaign headquarters by early evening. Josiah was thrilled and relieved to see her. He took her hand and smiled tenderly, then he greeted each of his children. They were in Washington, D.C., more than two hundred miles away from Lancaster, Pennsylvania, but having his family beside him made him feel like he was home.

Mark's family had arrived earlier that morning. None of them could believe that Election Day was finally here. The children wished their fathers luck and meant it.

———

THAT NIGHT, WHEN THE PRECINCTS STARTED CLOSING AND THE results began rolling in, it was obvious that it was going to be a very tight race. The two front-runners, Josiah Stoltzfus and Harley Phillips, ran neck and neck for most of the evening.

But then Harley started nudging ahead just a bit. Then a little more. And a little more. Perhaps his last-ditch evil ploy had worked after all. It wasn't fair. Sometimes nice guys really do finish last though. No one in Josiah's camp wanted to think about a defeat, but it was beginning to look like a clear possibility.

The Ledbetter-Harper ticket wasn't doing as well. Around ten o'clock, the candidates on that ticket conceded, giving eloquent and gracious speeches that were carried live on all the news broadcasts.

It was now a contest between Harley and Josiah, and Harley remained in the lead.

"Have you thought about what you'll do if we lose tonight?" Mark asked Josiah when they finally got a quiet moment to talk.

"Go on with my life," Josiah said.

"It wouldn't bother you to have come this far, be this close, and lose?"

"Never want something so much that you question God's plan, Mark," Josiah said, "even if the thing you want is a *gut* thing, and you want it for all the right reasons."

As expected, Josiah took Pennsylvania. It was the home of Lancaster County, and while the Amish typically didn't vote in national elections, they were a loved people there. Mark had been counting on the state voting for one of their own, and Pennsylvania hadn't let him down.

The Stoltzfus-Stedman ticket also took Wisconsin, Tennessee, North Carolina, Iowa, and Indiana. Harley secured Ohio, New Hampshire, and Maryland. New York and Michigan were up for grabs, with the tallies for the remainder of the states continuing to come in throughout the night.

"We just took Texas!" Carl shouted when the announcement came over the television around midnight. Texas had been waffling between the two candidates, with Harley taking the lead at one point, then Josiah, then Harley, then back to Josiah. But now the race had been called. With 85 percent of the votes now in, Texas fell handily into the Stoltzfus-Stedman camp, and the room erupted in cheers.

But then Harley took New Jersey and Delaware.

Florida came in for Governor Ledbetter, even though she had already conceded the race by then. And on it went.

Idaho went to Harley, but Arizona, Michigan, and Illinois went to Josiah. Mark had been hoping that Josiah's stance on illegal immigration and jobs would help carry those states, and apparently it had. For Michigan and Illinois and their soaring unemployment, Josiah had pushed the idea that most folks would prefer to have the opportunity to work at a decent-paying job rather than simply being given a handout. But he'd also pointed out that sometimes good folks need help. Somehow he'd found an acceptable balance between the two ideas.

Josiah had managed to find the middle ground on Arizona and Texas's border issue as well. His Amish ways gave him a welcoming heart for immigrants; after all, he had come from a long line of immigrants himself. Most Americans had, too, for that matter. But being Amish had also taught him the importance of having healthy boundaries when it came to stopping certain negative outside influences from coming into one's own community, such as the trafficking of people and drugs. Josiah had found common ground between the two factions, and it translated directly into votes.

As the night wore on, Josiah took even more states, edged into the lead in the popular vote, and began to dominate the electoral college as well. He was clearly the front-runner now, and it was beginning to look like there would be no stopping him.

And then came the mother lode.

"We just took New York!" a Josiah campaign volunteer shrieked. The cheers that followed were deafening.

New York! Mark couldn't believe his ears. That had seemed like a virtual impossibility. New York—with its high fashion, Wall Street, and Broadway—had been polling in Harley's pocket for months. It had even been Harley's state for most of the evening. But now Josiah nudged ahead with a narrow majority. New Yorkers had given him their vote of confidence—not a resounding majority, but a majority nonetheless.

On one level Mark could understand it. The Amish sense of community had appealed to the post-9/11 Big Apple. Most New Yorkers knew what it meant to come together in a time of crisis and help out their neighbors, and they liked that Josiah held to those same beliefs. They also resented Harley's overconfidence that he had New York in his back pocket. New Yorkers didn't like to be told how they were going to vote. And maybe that Lizzie Borden comment had also caused them to rethink their stance on Harley. On the news reports, many voters said they had made their decision to vote for Josiah while in the voting booth. Much like the timing of Harley's leak, their change of heart happened at the last minute.

One look at the electoral college tally, and Mark could see the election could very well shape up to be a Stoltzfus-Stedman landslide.

But it wasn't over yet. Many of the western states were yet to be counted, and California, as well as Oregon and Washington, with their abundance of electoral votes, was still up for grabs. Josiah was the front-runner in at least two of those states, but none of them was close to being called.

The atmosphere at the Stoltzfus-Stedman headquarters was ecstatic. People hugged, noisemakers sounded, and confetti rained down. Mark hugged Cindy and each of his children. Tonight there were no walls. They were proud of their dad, and Cindy beamed as the results continued pouring in in their favor. Mark's children posed happily for the news cameras, while Josiah's four children spent most of their time around the refreshment table or playing board games with some of the other children. Elizabeth stayed by her husband's side, while Cindy greeted friends, longtime supporters, and the campaign volunteers who were all on hand for the night's festivities.

When California's absentee ballots had begun to be counted, the two remaining candidates were running nearly even. Ledbetter's paltry showing validated her early concession. But when the regular ballots started coming in from the precincts, Josiah took hold of the lead and didn't give it back.

Could it be? New York, Texas, and California? Could it really be possible? Mark wondered.

It certainly looked that way. The triple crown. This was simply unheard of for an unknown. And a write-in candidate to boot. But then, this was an election year like no other.

Political analysts would say that California, like Michigan and Illinois, had been hard hit by unemployment, and a lot of people were underwater in their home payments due to the economic tsunami that had crashed on shore, burying California's real-estate market. It's no wonder, then, analysts would say, that the state would vote for whoever was going to get the economy moving again. Exit polls further explained the people's thinking:

"I wasn't sure who I was going to vote for when I stepped into the voting booth," said one unidentified lady from the Fresno area. "I liked Josiah and the things he had to say, but I also didn't want to waste my vote by writing in the name of someone who couldn't win. But then I told myself to just make a statement, to vote my conscience, you know? Josiah was who I wanted in the White House, so that's who I voted for!"

The woman had no idea that a good majority of the state would end up doing the exact same thing. In fact, people all over the country were doing it.

By the time all the votes were counted across the nation, Josiah would be declared the winner by a sizable margin. At their Washington campaign headquarters, Mark was in a state of shock. Josiah looked stunned. They had done it. They had really done it!

Josiah Stoltzfus was the president elect of the United States!

"God help us," Josiah said.

Mark grinned. "I think he just did."

———

IMMEDIATELY, MARK'S CELL PHONE BEGAN RINGING WITH CONgratulatory messages, including ones from President Holt and Governor Ledbetter. From his campaign headquarters, Harley Phillips placed a call to Mark too.

"Well done," Harley said when Mark answered the call. "I

don't know how you did it, but I can't argue with a miracle. You two sure pulled it off. I have to congratulate you for it." Harley sounded sincere. Maybe he was simply relieved that the grueling campaign was finally over.

"Thanks, Harley," Mark said. "Let me hand you over to Josiah."

Mark turned up the volume of the phone and then held it out for Josiah, who took it cautiously. They hunched over the phone together.

"Harley?" Josiah said.

"Looking forward to working with you, Mr. President," Harley said.

"Get ready to roll up your sleeves. We've got a lot to do," Josiah answered, forgiving Harley without being asked to. Mark wandered away when it became clear that Harley wasn't going to antagonize Josiah.

Harley's concession speech came a short while later. Carried live on all the major networks, it was four minutes of authentic praise for his worthy opponents. Unfortunately, Mark noticed it was another six minutes of Harley promising to return in four years.

Harley did, however, end his speech with a challenge for his fellow congressmen.

"The people have spoken," he said to the cameras. "They are tired of partisan politics and have sent a true outsider to Washington. It has been a hard-fought race, but I have to accept the will of the voters. Mr. President, I want to offer you my hand of cooperation. I appeal to all of Congress to do the same."

To Mark, Harley's broad smile appeared sincere and the speech seemed perfect ... until the camera lingered on Harley too long.

"Are the cameras still on?" Harley asked. "Can I quit smiling now?"

———

MARK WAS ECSTATIC WHEN HE OPENED HIS HOTEL DOOR THE following morning and found a stack of morning newspapers and a note that had been left there by Carl. The note simply read, "Enjoy!"

He quickly thumbed through them, reading each headline.

"President Stoltzfus—Better Learn to Spell It!"

"An Amish White House? Hang On to Your Bonnet!"

"Hail to the Hat!"

"The Beards Are Back!"

None of the headlines were meant in a mocking way—it was endearment and sheer amazement. Josiah Stoltzfus, an unknown latecomer, a write-in candidate, had won both the popular vote and the electoral college. There would be no counting of chads and no court challenges in this election. The decision was clear and unprecedented—America had elected an Amish president, and the populace was thrilled!

Mark called Josiah's room.

"Well, did you get them?" Mark said.

"The newspapers?"

"Yes, sir. So what d'ya think, Mr. President?"

"I gotta admit, you did it."

"*You* did it, sir. So what's our first order of business, President Stoltzfus?"

"Spending time with my family."

Mark knew that with all the excitement of the evening, Elizabeth and Josiah hadn't been able to have much family time together. Neither had he and Cindy. So he decided to do likewise. He hung up the phone and spent the rest of the morning with Cindy and their kids. All of their lives were about to change in every imaginable way. Maybe they could try enjoying a little normalcy for a short while longer.

INAUGURATION DAY SEEMED TO ARRIVE BEFORE ANYONE IN THE Stedman or Stoltzfus families had time to catch their breath. Elizabeth was both excited and nervous that day. She wasn't used to such attention. Reporters had been speculating for weeks that this presidential inauguration would be a bit unusual, even by Washington's standards, but Elizabeth hadn't taken it as a slight.

Someone from the Plain community being elected president? Unusual indeed. She laughed to herself as she got dressed.

She and Josiah wore their best Amish attire, the clothes they would typically wear to a wedding back in Lancaster County. She knew her husband had told the American people that if elected he would be bringing his Amish ways to the White House, and since the people had elected him knowing that, Elizabeth saw no reason for them not to follow through with the promise.

Not everyone agreed.

"Washington's gone from bailouts to baling hay!" was just one of Harley's sound bites concerning Josiah's win. But Harley's opinion didn't matter much to Elizabeth on that day. The American voters had invalidated his opinion, at least temporarily, and had elected her husband. Harley would have to wait another four years before even attempting another presidential run. In the meantime, President Josiah Stoltzfus was officially on his political honeymoon, and Elizabeth was humbly proud, if there were such an emotion.

At the inauguration ceremony, Elizabeth couldn't help but tear up as her husband stood in front of the chief justice on the steps of the Capitol Building and placed his right hand on the Bible. Then he began to repeat the inaugural oath ...

"I, Josiah Stoltzfus, do solemnly affirm that I will faithfully execute the office of president of the United States, and will, to the best of my ability, preserve, protect, and defend the Constitution of the United States."

At the end, he added, "So help me God."

It was a phrase traditionally added by most presidents, and Elizabeth was both pleased and not surprised that Josiah had followed suit. She knew Josiah would need God's help to lead a country in such desperate straits, and she wanted him to have all the divine guidance he could get.

Until Josiah's inauguration, Franklin Pierce had been the only president to change the word *swear* in the oath to *affirm*. It had been Josiah's personal choice to do the same.

He also chose to follow the action of George Washington and kiss the Bible following the ceremony. Elizabeth knew his intention wasn't to offend anyone; he simply figured if it was good enough for Founding Father George Washington, then it was good enough for Josiah Stoltzfus as well. It was the part of the ceremony that was left up to each individual president being sworn in. The chief justice wasn't involved in these highly personal decisions.

Only a few from the Amish community attended the ceremony. Josiah hadn't been shunned as yet, but the controversy of his running for national office made it risky for members of the community to be too involved with Josiah and his blatant disobedience. A shunning was just a matter of time. Bishop Miller had told Elizabeth that he was hoping to wait until after the inauguration before throwing any disciplinary action from the church into the mix.

The absence of the Amish wasn't all that noticeable, however, because vendors were selling Amish-style hats and bonnets to anyone with the means to buy them. Elizabeth thought it was rather enterprising of the vendors, but then, she thought, the items did make a nice souvenir for such a historic event.

Following the oath, Elizabeth watched as President Josiah Stoltzfus stepped up to the microphone to deliver his inaugural address.

"My fellow Americans," he began, then paused and smiled. *"The beards are back!"*

The crowd went wild. They laughed, they cheered, they whooped and hollered.

"We love you, Josiah!" they yelled. A multitude of "Josiah" signs waved among the crowd, and people chanted, "Josiah! Josiah!" until their throats hurt.

When the enthusiasm died down, which took well over a

minute, Josiah continued, "When Vice President Mark Stedman's path crossed with mine on a road outside of Lancaster, Pennsylvania, I believed it was a God-ordained moment. When I later learned that Mark had entered my name in the race for president and that I was already doing rather well in the polls, well, to be honest with you, I wondered if maybe I should have ridden on by and not stopped to help the congressman out of the ditch that day. I even told him that I had pulled him *out* of a ditch, but he was trying to pull me *into* one!"

The crowd roared with laughter. Elizabeth smiled as Josiah nodded good-naturedly in Mark's direction before continuing.

"But today I am glad I listened to my friend, because as I stand before you now, I have no doubt that this is what I was meant to do. Not everyone has agreed with me, of course, and to those I would ask their patience, understanding, and in some instances, their forgiveness.

"I'm here now, elected by what is nothing short of a miracle. I feel the burden of that miracle and will do my very best to serve as your president—each and every one of you—those who voted for me and those who didn't. We are one now; let us come together as Americans. I know we can do it. We've done it before; we'll do it again. I look forward to working with Congress and putting together a plan that will jump-start our economy, get our people back to work, and get America back on course. We will recalculate and find our way once again!"

The audience gave boisterous approval, and the band, complete with dulcimers, began playing "Hail to the Chief."

———

NEEDLESS TO SAY, THE INAUGURAL PARADE WAS LIKE NO OTHER in recent times. The Secret Service ran alongside "Horse-and-Buggy One," as it was later dubbed by the press.

DayBreak, Josiah's buggy horse from Lancaster, had been

brought in early for the special occasion and seemed quite pleased to be showing off her trotting skills for the crowd of spectators.

Reporter Emily Watson covered the parade from her vantage point. "The president and Mrs. Stoltzfus will ride in their horse and buggy all the way to their new residence at 1600 Pennsylvania Avenue," she announced to the rest of the country, tuned in via TV, radio, or the Internet.

Just then cheers and applause broke out in the background, and Emily knew that the president's buggy had come into sight. Josiah and Elizabeth waved to the hundreds of thousands of well-wishers who lined both sides of the parade route.

"Folks," Emily said, with confetti raining onto her hair, "all I can say is — this is going to be an interesting four years!"

———

AT THE REQUEST OF JOSIAH AND ELIZABETH, ONLY ONE INAUGU-ral ball was scheduled. In the past, incoming presidents had been expected to spend the evening making brief appearances at multiple inaugural balls, but Josiah was emphatic that there would be only one.

"Do a party right, and you only need one," he had told the event planners.

"But, sir, how will we accommodate all the dignitaries and donors if we only have one ball?"

"We're broke," Josiah said. "Most folks don't throw a party to celebrate that."

"I realize that, sir, but it is well-established protocol to have several inaugural balls."

"One'll do just fine," Josiah had replied. "Besides, just think how much money this will save."

Josiah was intent on looking for ways to save America and the American people money, and he was ready and willing to start at his own address first. Whatever ways he could find for the White

House to cut back on its own expenses without sacrificing dignity or historic procedure, he wanted to do it.

"Washington is going to tighten its own belt first, before we ask the public to tighten theirs—or in my case, its own suspenders. Like ole Benny, no one wants to be the only horse pulling. Our recovery will be a team effort, or there will be no recovery," he said to one reporter.

The nation respected the one inaugural ball idea. Josiah was doing what he had promised to do—living simply and by example. In fact, simplicity was the theme of the ball. Simple Elegance.

Elizabeth wore her own blue wedding dress, which she hadn't worn in years, and only a few times since her wedding day. It still fit, and without a shred of Spanx. Despite all the good home cooking for which Elizabeth was so well known back in Lancaster County, she had somehow managed to maintain her youthful figure over the years.

The inaugural partying went well into the night, but the First Couple excused themselves early. They needed to get up before dawn the following day to start the business of running the country. Besides, the moving van would be dropping off their furniture and various other belongings to the White House first thing in the morning.

Josiah and Elizabeth enjoyed a good party as much as anyone, but they were tired, their feet hurt, and the music was way too loud.

The exhausted couple slept soundly that night. Not even the fireworks could wake them. But that was okay. They'd earned their rest.

What a day it had been for both of them. When they had woken up that morning, they'd been Josiah and Elizabeth Stoltzfus. But when they went to bed that night, they were the president and First Lady.

What in the world had this sweet Amish couple from Lancaster County gotten themselves into?

CHAPTER 19

★

JOSIAH HESITATED IN THE DOORWAY, OVERWHELMED BY THE sheer magnificence and magnitude of the Oval Office, which stretched out before him. It was nothing like the space where he conducted his farm business at home. Josiah's home-office desk had been relegated to a corner of the common area in his Lancaster home.

But now Josiah would be sitting where so many great men had previously sat—at this massive desk, which was flanked on one side by the presidential flag and on the other by the flag of the United States. It humbled him.

Josiah appreciated the fact that President Holt hadn't gotten caught up in the fray of the campaign mudslinging. Josiah also knew that since the economy was in such bad shape, most politicians running for office might have figured they'd do better without attaching their name so closely to President Holt's. It wasn't completely fair, of course, that Holt was being blamed for everything that had gone wrong in the country. But even Josiah saw that although Holt had been the one standing at the helm of the ship, he hadn't seen the iceberg approaching.

The incumbent now rose from his chair and welcomed his successor. Josiah nodded a greeting but remained frozen in the doorway, hesitating to step on the immaculate rug with its inset presidential seal. It appeared far too splendid for mere men to set foot upon.

"Welcome to your new home," President Holt said and then motioned toward the presidential chair, offering Josiah his first experience sitting on it. Josiah stepped forward, humbly and haltingly, his shadow overlapping President Holt's shadow as he walked toward the chair and sat down upon it. The chair was bigger than he imagined it would be.

"You grow into it," President Holt said. President Holt's relief at exiting his post was evident on his face. It had been a long four years.

Josiah ran his fingers over the Resolute desk. He loved his own desk back home, the one he had carved with his own hands and sweat, but the Oval Office desk was a mighty fine piece of furniture and history. Its superb craftsmanship didn't escape the Amish man's notice.

"This desk was a gift from Queen Victoria back in 1880," President Holt said. "They made it from wood taken from the HMS *Resolute*."

"Is that so?" Josiah said, admiring the grain of the wood.

Glancing around the room, Josiah could hardly believe all the history the space held. And he could barely wrap his mind around the fact that this day had actually come. America was his charge now, and while he hoped everyone would pull together once they realized how much stake they had in their own futures, he knew much of the responsibility for the outcome still fell to him, the one holding the reins.

And he was a long, long way from Lancaster.

———

It was about 8:00 a.m. when the moving van, pulling a horse trailer behind it, made its way up the delivery drive of the White House.

"Where do you figure they want the horses?" Kenny, the driver, asked.

"Beats me," Hank said, looking over the work order from the passenger seat. "It doesn't say."

"Well, where does the White House usually keep its horses?"

"I don't think they have any."

"Sure, they do. Didn't George Washington ride a horse?"

"Yeah, but that horse has gotta be dead by now," Hank said. "Wait. Here it is on the work order. It says to tie 'em up to the new hitching posts in the Rose Garden."

"The Rose Garden has hitching posts?"

"Guess it does now."

Kenny shrugged his shoulders and then drove as close as he could to the Rose Garden. The two movers began unloading the animals.

White House personnel watched in shock as the creatures were escorted down the driveway toward the Rose Garden. A few gasps could be heard, frenzied whispers, and even some *oohs* and *aahs*. They were beautiful horses. Even the mule was exceptional.

True to his word, Josiah was indeed bringing the Amish influence to the White House. He'd had some of the White House furniture in the living quarters moved into storage so it could be replaced by more sparse and simple furniture.

"Is it true he's living without electricity in the living quarters?" one reporter asked a member of the White House staff.

"It is. But only on that floor," the staff member said.

Due to national security issues, Josiah couldn't very well turn off the electricity in the entire White House. But in those areas where he could, he opted for the Amish style of living and, again, saving the nation money.

"How can he keep up with everything going on in the world and Washington with no television or Internet?" the reporter asked.

The White House staff member didn't hesitate. "Guess they'll all just have to talk to each other. What a concept, huh?"

What a concept, indeed. Unfiltered information, straight from the horse's mouth. Of course, if he needed it, television, Internet, and every kind of technology Josiah would ever need was available on other levels of the White House. But in his personal living quarters, it was the Plain world, the Amish world, Josiah's world.

Some of his own hand-carved furniture and gas lanterns were brought from his house in Lancaster, and he had a clothesline installed on the East Lawn. Josiah stretched the line out between two trees, and when Elizabeth hung their family's Amish clothing from it, it was quite a sight to behold. It was rumored that the first time she did this, the echo of the collective gasps could be heard all the way to the National Mall. Postcards, posters, and T-shirts featuring the charming visual immediately began selling to tourists from all over the world.

Most people thought the changes at the White House were a refreshing difference from the expensive tastes of a few of the former first ladies. This wasn't the time for wasteful spending, and President Josiah and his first lady were leading by example.

But it was the barn raising that caused the biggest stir. The White House staff was involved, as were some members of Congress, along with anyone else who wanted to help. The event attracted a crowd of onlookers, drawn by both curiosity and the sheer novelty of the event.

———

HARLEY TRIED HIS BEST TO CUT THE NEW PRESIDENT SOME slack. If the nation wanted an Amish man in the White House —and apparently they did—then he would have to accept it and try to work with the man. But that didn't stop him from bending the ear of anyone within earshot, complaining about the changes.

"A barn, Senator O'Brien?" Harley said over lunch one afternoon. "The president had a barn raising at the White House? Preposterous!"

"Gerald Ford put in a new outdoor pool," Senator O'Brien said. "Not to mention, the pool Franklin Roosevelt had put in, which was later covered up to house the Press Briefing Room."

"I'm fully aware of the outdoor pool. Every First Family since has benefitted from that. But a pool isn't a barn, Senator."

"Well, what about Nixon? He added a bowling alley."

"One lane," Harley said defensively. "And even he had the good sense to keep his addition *indoors*."

"Clinton added a jogging track. And what about Obama's half basketball court? And don't forget the jungle gym President Holt installed for his kids," the senator said, taking a bite of his ham sandwich. "So the White House has a barn now." He shrugged.

"And that's an improvement?"

"To the mule I suppose it is."

"You mean the First Mule, don't you, Senator O'Brien?" Harley smirked.

———

HARLEY PHILLIPS ASIDE, MOST CONGRESSIONAL MEMBERS FROM both sides of the aisle were willing to give Josiah a chance. Oh, there were a few who, like Harley, didn't want the grounds of the White House being altered in this or any other way. But the barn Josiah raised wasn't a very large barn, and he did need a place for the animals during the cold winter months. Winter in Washington, D.C., could be brutal.

Once the barn was up, Vice President Stedman shook his head in wonder. "Presidents have remodeled this house before," he said, "but I don't think any of them ever did it quite like this, sir."

"A house isn't a home without a good barn!" Josiah said. Then, standing back to admire the hard work of so many, he added, "*Now* it feels like home."

———

TWO WHITE HOUSE STAFF MEMBERS, ADELE AND WINSTON, WHO had been watching the barn raising from a window in the White House, were flabbergasted.

"I've been here thirty-nine years, and I've never seen anything like this!" Adele said. "Have you, Winston?"

"No, ma'am, I haven't," he said. "I surely haven't."

"A barn raising. Horses. Clotheslines. It's starting to feel like *Green Acres* around here!"

Adele and Winston both laughed and went back to their duties of dusting and sweeping and ... wait a minute!

What was that standing in the open doorway?

"Oh, my!" Winston exclaimed. "Looks like we've got us some company."

Adele turned to see what Winston was looking at and then shrieked. It was a goat! The little fella was standing right there on the marble floor just inside the room, staring up at them, almost daring them to try to shoo him away. Joseph, Josiah's boy, appeared on the scene.

"I was just trying to sneak him up to my room, but he wiggled himself loose from me," Joseph said. "Am I in trouble?"

"Not if we can catch him," Winston said.

Within seconds, Secret Service was on the scene trying to contain the farm critter.

"Grab him before he breaks something!" Adele yelled.

Winston lunged toward the goat, but it took off running down the hallway, its little hooves slipping and sliding as it desperately tried to get traction on the marble floor. Adele and Winston, Joseph and the Secret Service all chased after the critter.

Each time it rounded a corner, the goat would barely maintain its footing, but it kept going.

Other White House staffers noticed the pursuit and joined in the adventure. Before long, the White House staff, the Secret Service, the First Kids, and even a few lobbyists and congressmen were chasing after the renegade goat.

Winston finally caught up to it, and when he did, he reached out, barely tagging the goat's hind leg. The goat lost its footing but managed to work loose from Winston's grip before running away again, ultimately slipping and sliding on its bottom down the marble hallway, directly toward an open elevator. There was barely an inch to spare as the critter slid through the closing doors just in the nick of time.

Nathaniel, the elevator operator, quite mellow from far too many hours spent listening to soothing elevator music, didn't even look away from the elevator buttons to see who it was who had just entered the elevator.

"Floor please?" Nathaniel said, lifting his gloved hand toward the buttons in preparation for pushing the correct floor.

"Maaaaa!" the goat answered. Nathaniel slowly turned and looked down at the goat who was innocently looking up at him.

"Only in Washington," Nathaniel said, undaunted.

———

STILL STINGING FROM HIS DEVASTATING LOSS, READING THE DAILY reports of all the happenings at 1600 Pennsylvania Avenue was adding insult to injury for Harley.

"It's not that I have anything against his leadership," Harley said to a group of congressmen when they met over dinner one evening during a break from an exceptionally long session. "There are some matters I would have handled differently, but he's doing as well as any inexperienced outsider could be expected to do."

"His performance ratings are through the roof, Harley," one of them noted.

"Well, yes," Harley said. "But he's still on his honeymoon with the country and the press. It'll wear off."

"Not in the near future, Harley," another congressman interjected. "He did win by a sizable margin. The people like him."

"Well, all I know is there are a lot of folks who are indignant over these little additions to the White House and its grounds."

"Oh, I don't know. I kinda like seeing the horses grazing on the lawn. Very pastoral," another congressman said.

"It's the *White House*," Harley reminded them all.

"I know, but they fenced off an area for the animals, so I don't really see that they're hurting anything."

The Amish were known for their pristine landscaping and housekeeping. Harley knew he couldn't go there. So he stayed on the subject of the animals.

"Horses and goats at the executive mansion? Something has to be done to stop this madness," he said.

It didn't matter that the White House had a long history of being the temporary home to a variety of farm and ranch animals.

"Kennedy owned a horse," said one congressman.

"That's right," concurred another. "And two ponies."

"Calvin Coolidge, he had a donkey, right?" the first congressman said.

"And a pet bobcat named Smokey."

"Woodrow Wilson owned some sheep and a ram," said a third congressman. "And William Taft kept a cow at the White House."

"And don't forget, Benjamin Harrison had a billy goat named Old Whiskers," said the second congressman.

"And your point?" Harley pressed.

"Go back through presidential history, and you'll see farm animals were quite commonplace at the executive mansion, Harley," the first congressman said.

Even Josiah's barn wasn't setting any real precedents. The original White House stables had burned down in a fire during Lincoln's term, and it wasn't until the Taft administration that a second stable was converted into a garage for the most modern mode of presidential transportation that appeared on the scene —the presidential motorcar. If the nation was going to truly get back to basics, most would have said this was an excellent start.

JOSIAH WAS MAKING OTHER CHANGES IN THE COUNTRY TOO. With the Amish man in office, the people felt hopeful about the future, and the economy slowly began to improve. People were spending again, especially in the Amish-themed stores that were popping up all across the country. Hat, bonnet, apron, Amish furniture ... even buggy sales were continuing to soar.

Things were almost too good. And in the world of politics, that usually meant someone was fixing to stir up the pot. Josiah's honeymoon didn't even last the full one hundred days. The media, hungry for fresh headlines, started searching around for something other than the Amish angle to talk about. With vigor, some in the media began to criticize Josiah's decisions, his policies, and anything else it could.

"If President Stoltzfus decides to veto the Riley-Turner bill, his decision will have long-term consequences for the stability of our educational system. But what can we expect from a man with only an eighth-grade education?"

"The infrastructure of our country is in dire need of repair. These projects will put America back to work. President Stoltzfus needs to quit building barns and start building bridges!"

At first Josiah took the criticisms in stride. The constructive ones, anyway. If there was any truth in any of them, he figured the assessments would help him improve his style of governing.

One criticism, however, he ignored completely. And that was the pending veto of the Riley-Turner bill. He was entrenched in his *no*.

"When's the president going to sign the bill?" supporters of the bill asked.

"He's on farm time," Mark said in Josiah's defense. "You don't harvest until it's ready. It's not ready, gentlemen."

Josiah knew he was gaining a reputation for not moving very fast when it came to signing or vetoing a bill. He would read it — every word of it — and then seek advice from his trusted advisers. His advisers consisted of a handful of professionals and political figures. He'd also run some of these matters by Elizabeth. She was his stabilizer in the common-sense department. And he'd pray. But he wouldn't sign any bill while it was still green on the vine. Josiah said that that kind of fruit would just give the nation a bellyache, and he was a better farmer than that.

This "procrastination," as those in the media would label it, annoyed some people. But Josiah figured it was important to know what he signed or didn't sign. And why.

When it became clear, though, that the comments from certain reporters and political pundits were getting heavier on criticism and lighter on constructiveness, the comments began to take their toll on Josiah. The stress began to show on his face, as it had on many presidents before him. He could no longer hide how the office was changing him.

STORMCLOUD44/BLOG

The president has not listened, like those who have gone before him. They do not listen. They see only with their clouded eyes of tyranny. Let them try to rip our destiny from our clenched fists, but we will not relinquish it. Our time to act is now. You will hear us, Mr. President.

"How are you feeling?" Elizabeth asked Josiah one night when he retired to bed looking especially exhausted.

"All right, I guess," he said.

"You look tired."

"It shows?"

"*Jah.* On your face, around your eyes mostly."

"Older?"

"Just as handsome, though."

"There was stress on the farm," Josiah reminded her.

"I know. But this stress is different. It leaves deeper trails."

Elizabeth had put her finger on a simple fact of Washington life. Compare a photograph of any president on his Inauguration

Day to a photo of him by the end of his term, and most observers could see that the office did indeed age its leaders.

"Maybe I'm the smartest president of all then."

"Why's that?"

"I've not posed to have my picture taken."

———

THE FOLLOWING DAY, A LETTER ARRIVED IN THE WHITE HOUSE mail. It was from Bishop Miller.

"Dear President Josiah," it began, respectfully. "It is because of my love for you and Elizabeth and my faith in the goodness of your heart that I have postponed disciplinary action. It pains me to begin the process today. I will keep you informed of any formal decisions I make. I trust you will understand, and while I know it is your desire to continue the Amish lifestyle, you will do so without the benefit of community as long as you serve as president."

Although Josiah had always known this day was coming, it still crushed his spirit.

———

VICE PRESIDENT STEDMAN WAS MORE THAN SATISFIED WITH HIS presidential choice. He firmly believed that Josiah was the man America needed to lead her, and he was proud to be watching his dream being played out in reality.

"See, I told you I could take a backseat to someone like Josiah," he said to Cindy over lunch one day.

"You think you'll run next time?" she asked. "Josiah said he'd only serve one term."

"Let's get through this term first," Mark laughed.

———

HARLEY PHILLIPS WAS PLEASED WHEN HE RECEIVED HIS INVITA-tion to attend a White House dinner given in honor of the Swedish prime minister. It didn't matter which party was in the White House, Harley always enjoyed being a part of the inner circle at these prestigious events. He usually made a good impression on foreign dignitaries and other notable guests. Perhaps they found his loud and blustery ways fascinating, or maybe they enjoyed the jokes he would often share during dinner conversation. Whatever it was, Harley could be good company when he wanted to be.

The invitation had been at Josiah's specific request. In spite of the congressman's vocal criticisms of Josiah, the president continued to graciously extend a hand of friendship toward him. Elizabeth had even assigned Harley the seat directly across the table from the prime minister, which Harley took as a gesture of goodwill.

After a wonderful Amish-style family dinner, Harley flagged down one of the servers and requested some coffee.

"Cream and sugar, sir?" the server asked.

"Cream, please."

Harley didn't like sugar in his coffee, but he did like cream. Three servings of cream, to be exact. Harley viewed his veins the same way he viewed his work in Congress — what's one more clog blocking the flow?

What happened next would be the topic of international curiosity for years to come. Harley took a sip of the coffee, grimaced, and then flagged down the server again.

"I think I got some spoiled milk," he said. The words were garbled as Harley tried to talk around the mouthful of coffee, but the waiter could make them out.

"It's not spoiled, sir," the waiter said. "It's goat milk."

"Goat milk!"

Harley gagged and unintentionally spewed the mouthful of coffee across the table, spraying it all over the Swedish prime minister. Not since President George Bush Sr.'s unfortunate stomach incident in Japan with their prime minister had there been such a surprised and pitiful look on the face of a foreign dignitary. But at least George had been ill and unable to help it.

Harley was mortified. He apologized profusely to the prime minister, who was now dripping in goat's milk, coffee, and a healthy helping of humiliation.

"I am so sorry," Harley repeated to President Stoltzfus and the prime minister.

The prime minister was trying to wipe himself off amid all the camera flashes, but the damage had already been done. The photo was a front-page news story the following day, with Harley passing the blame off on "that blasted goat" and, of course, on Josiah and his most unusual presidency.

———

JOSIAH KNEW THERE WOULD BE MORE EVENTS AND DIGNITARIES to entertain at the White House, and hoped these would go off without a hitch. In fact, one such event was right around the corner.

The media and White House staffers were all aflutter over the news of Queen Elizabeth's upcoming visit to Washington. Even President Josiah and First Lady Elizabeth were looking forward to hosting England's beloved queen in the nation's capital.

"What do you think she'd like to do while she's here?" Elizabeth asked Josiah one evening over dinner.

"I'm not sure. Maybe something she usually doesn't get to do back home?"

"But what could I possibly offer a queen?" Elizabeth said. "The closest we've ever come to meeting royalty was that man who visited Lancaster and claimed he was the king of some island — that island we never were able to find on a map."

"And if I recall, he didn't drop any money into the Good Faith Jar for those three quarts of jelly he took, either."

"This royalty is real, though," Elizabeth said.

"Now Elizabeth, don't forget she's just one of God's children, like me and you."

"I know. And well, maybe we do have something in common."

"What's that?"

"She wears head coverings too."

———

THE NEWS MEDIA DIDN'T MISS THE OPPORTUNITY TO FIND OTHER ways to compare the two Elizabeths. One, a descendant from royalty, lived in castles, basked in opulence, and was the rightful owner of a crown of jewels, no doubt worth millions. The other, a Plain woman, came from a modest house, was willing to do her own housework and cooking, and wore a simple handmade bonnet.

It was soon discovered that Queen Elizabeth and the First Lady did share one more very definite interest.

Nate, the campaign volunteer who had been so helpful and loyal during Josiah and Mark's campaign, had been awarded the position of chief of staff, otherwise known as the White House press secretary. Nate was a terrific multitasker and seemed to have a natural flair for being a liaison between the press and the president. And he was punctual to a fault.

When Nate tried to find the queen for a press photo op in the Rose Garden, he approached Charley Mulligan, a longtime White House staffer.

"Have you seen the queen?" Nate asked.

"She's with the First Lady, sir," Charley told him.

"But I didn't see either one of them in the Rose Garden," Nate said. "The press is waiting."

"Try the Blue Room, sir," Charley said.

Nate walked briskly down the hallway toward the Blue Room, glancing at his watch at regular intervals as he went. He prided himself on having a good relationship with the press, and that included not wasting their time. If he told them 10:00 a.m., he wanted to make sure everything was in place and ready to go at 10:00 a.m. Not 10:02 or 10:15, but 10:00 sharp.

When Nate arrived at the Blue Room and opened the door, he saw — to his astonishment — several members of the White House staff, as well as both Elizabeths, sitting in a circle *quilting*!

"Yes, Nate?" the First Lady asked when she looked up and saw the chief of staff standing there gawking at them.

"Uh, nothing, madam," he said. Were his eyes playing tricks on him? The Queen of England was *quilting*? Could it really be true?

Then, all of a sudden, it hit him. "Stay right where you are!" he said. "I'll bring them in here! *This* is the photo op!"

Nate had learned throughout the campaign how to handle the issue of photographs of the president and First Lady. He was sensitive to their beliefs on the subject, and whenever possible, he made sure they were positioned in such a way as to either get their profile or have the photo taken in shadows. Some photos of them still slipped through, but for the most part, the Amish couple's wishes were honored.

The sewing circle photo, with the First Lady's head turning to the side at just the right moment, was featured on the Internet, television news programs, and print articles. It was an amazingly poignant photo.

As Nate was ushering members of the media out the door, he overheard the two women chatting.

"I never dreamed you were a quilter," the First Lady said, as the two ladies continued their stitching.

"Oh, there's lots of things the world doesn't know about me," the queen said with a smile.

"And me as well," Elizabeth agreed.

"For one thing, I get tired of wearing hats."

"Maybe you should try a bonnet."

"Maybe I shall," the queen said. "And I read Amish romances."

"And I have at times gotten quite frustrated with my children."

"Oh, we shall have to talk." The queen laughed.

Nate chuckled to himself as he closed the door behind him.

———

CONGRESSMAN HARLEY PHILLIPS WALKED DOWN A WHITE
House hallway with Senator Bob Thorton from Florida, venting
his frustrations.

"I like him well enough, Senator, but this is Washington, D.C.,
not Lancaster, Pennsylvania. Isn't there something we can do?"

Just then, the First Kids ran across the hallway in front of them
in a single line, giggling and playing as kids do.

"I'm telling you, Bob," Harley said, "not since Teddy Roosevelt's brood was here have there been such goings on at the White
House."

"They're just being kids, Harley," Bob said in a soothing tone.
"And anyway, at least it was only a goat. Teddy's youngins once
tried to sneak a pony into the elevator."

Harley grunted, then paused at a window and looked out over
the White House grounds. He had a clear view of the barn, the
goat, and the clothesline filled with Amish clothes flapping and
drying in the breeze.

"You're telling me you approve of this, Senator?"

The senator stepped closer to the window and took a look for
himself.

"You have to admit, Congressman," he said, "there is a simplis-
tic beauty about it."

"This is the White House, Senator. *The White House!* Is everyone forgetting that?"

"He's Amish," Senator Thorton said. "He made no secret of
the fact that he was going to bring his Plain ways with him to
Washington. Now you know as well as I do that the country's put
up with worse than a clothesline from its presidents. From both

parties. If you've forgotten some of those escapades, I'd be happy to remind you, Congressman."

Harley didn't have a comeback, so he turned and walked off in a huff. A moment later, Senator Thorton called out after him, "You are coming to the barbecue Saturday, aren't you, Congressman?"

Harley's only reply was a snarl and a dismissive gesture with the back of his hand. Middle-school behavior, to be sure, but it somehow made Harley feel better.

CHAPTER 20

★

THE STOLTZFUS BARBECUES HAD BECOME MUCH-ANTICIPATED events at the White House. If Josiah had had the time, he would have held one every week. But as it was, they came around about every other month or so. Government officials and their families, White House staff and their families, and Amish friends from Lancaster and neighboring communities would all gather on the White House lawn for a good old-fashioned Amish barbecue and fellowship. While Bishop Miller and other leaders of their community continued to oppose Josiah's presidency and the threat of shunning still hung in the air, some of the Amish people, mostly Josiah and Elizabeth's closest friends, were becoming more accepting of having one of their own in the White House. The barbecues were also a prime photo op to see the blending, however reluctant, of the two worlds.

"Did you get enough barbecued chicken, Senator Thorton?" Josiah asked the senator as he walked by.

"Three helpings, and I gotta call it quits." The senator laughed.

President Stoltzfus loved his barbecues. They had become a way for him to get to know the Washington establishment, otherwise known as the "movers and shakers." He had been in office for about six months now, and it was his hope that he could get certain members of the establishment to move and shake a little less and actually get more done, but that was sometimes a challenge. Not that he wanted a bunch of yes-men and yes-women around him. He enjoyed a good debate as much as anyone. He'd told his cabinet from day one that he'd rather have them vote their conscience than what they thought he was expecting.

Other than the food, a highlight of the barbecues was the baseball game Josiah arranged, which always pitted the White House staff and the First Family against members of Congress, their staff, and their families. It was just for fun, and no one really kept score, honoring the Amish tradition of guarding against such vanity. Josiah recognized his inconsistency, realizing that the election would have fallen under the same rule, but he chalked it up to his having authority over his barbecues and not having authority over the way elections were run. Still, the competitiveness of the election process had always troubled him. It seemed to bring out the worst in some folks. He was glad not to feel that same competiveness on the baseball field.

Harley, on the other hand, seemed to thrive on competition. He may have lost to Josiah in the voting booth, but in the batter's box, it was obvious that he wanted his due. He once even made an announcement over the PA system that a certain congressman had just hit a home run with the bases loaded. Harley was that congressman, of course, and his panting was so loud in the microphone, people could barely understand him. But it garnered him a smattering of applause, and that was what Harley had apparently been hoping for.

From what Josiah had observed, Harley's involvement in the events went only as far as one inning of baseball, three trips to the food line, and multiple complaints about the music. Banjos, dulcimers, and harmonicas obviously weren't Harley's style. But then what exactly was Harley's musical style? A funeral dirge?

"Batter up!" Senator Thurman called.

Josiah stepped into the batter's box and took position.

Stacy Creighton was on the pitcher's mound. He tilted his head to one side, and then to the other, stretching out his neck muscles. Then Stacy thrust the ball into his mitt a couple of times and suddenly hurled the sphere right over home plate.

Josiah didn't swing.

"Steeeeeerike!" Senator Thurman said. There was no denying it. It had indeed been a strike.

Josiah got into position again. This time when the ball reached him, he swung and connected with it. Unfortunately, the ball also connected with the trees on the far end of the lawn. Out of bounds.

"Foul ball!" Thurman said.

Yet again, Josiah took position. This time it was a perfect connect — ball against bat, and the bat won. The ball flew high into the air, over the heads of senators, congressmen, and children alike. Josiah took off running and didn't stop until he crossed over home plate. The people cheered. His team whooped and hollered. But Josiah had no sooner touched home plate than he walked over to Senator Thurman, the umpire.

Mark had been just about to step into the batter's box, but he held back when he saw Josiah.

"I don't think I touched second base," Josiah told the umpire.

"We're not even keeping score, Mr. President," Senator Thurman said. "It doesn't matter, does it?"

"It matters to me."

Senator Thurman announced to the crowd that the home run hadn't actually been a home run, just in case anyone in the audience happened to be keeping his or her own personal scorecard. The crowd groaned in disappointment, but Josiah waved to them, indicating that he was fine with the call, then took his seat on the bench.

There was no pecking order there on the White House lawn. No Democrat or Republican. No one was better or less than anyone else. Everyone was just a ballplayer, and they were all having a wonderful time.

As soon as Josiah sat down on the bench, Benjamin, an Amish man, approached him.

"Benjamin!" Josiah called out when he turned and saw his old friend. "Glad you came, brother!"

"Thanks for inviting me, Mr. President," Benjamin said. "I've never been to the White House before. Didn't know they had a baseball field here."

"They didn't." Josiah smiled. "Say, you haven't seen Bishop Miller around, have you?"

It was obvious by Benjamin's expression that he wished he could deliver different news.

"He couldn't come, Josiah."

Josiah was disappointed. "I understand."

"He said he hoped you would and to thank you for the invitation anyway."

"Any word ... you know ... on the ...?"

"Shunning?" Benjamin said, assuming that was what was on Josiah's mind. "There are still discussions going on, but no decision yet. You're in a delicate situation, my brother."

"Tell him I will accept whatever decision he makes. Will you do that, Benjamin?"

"I will."

"Did you get yourself some of those ribs?" Josiah asked, changing the subject.

"Sure did. You haven't lost your touch."

Josiah laughed and thanked him again for coming. "Well, I guess I better get back to the game."

"Sure, sure. Go on."

"Good to see you, Benjamin."

"Good to see you, too, Mr. President."

———

FROM THE BATTER'S BENCH, SENATOR THORTON AND HARLEY watched the president as he stood in the right-field position and caught a beauty of a fly ball, making an out for his team. Onlookers cheered their president.

"You can't fight it, Harley," Senator Thorton said. "His Plain ways have taken the nation by storm. Actually, if you ask me, they're a breath of fresh air."

"Breath of fresh air?" Harley said. "Have you not walked by that barn and taken a whiff? Well, I, for one, am not going to stand by while our nation's dignity is nibbled away one hoedown at a time!"

Harley brushed at the back of his pants. It felt like they had gotten caught on something, and Harley figured it was an over-reaching branch from one of the bushes. When the feeling didn't go away, however, Harley turned around and saw it was that blasted goat nibbling on his pants. Harley tried to swat the critter away, but the determined goat wouldn't let go of his pants.

Senator Thorton, seeing the situation, started laughing.

And eventually, to his own surprise, Harley did too.

———

TOURISTS WATCHED WHAT THEY COULD OF THE FESTIVITIES FROM behind the safety barriers and fencing that protected the White House. Most of them were fascinated to see such an event being held on the White House lawn. The Secret Service stood in strategic locations throughout the grounds. They had adamantly advised President Stoltzfus against such public happenings, but Josiah was equally adamant.

"It's the people's house, is it not?" he had said. "Why not let them watch their elected officials getting along? They've already seen enough of the bickering."

Josiah's barbecues were similar in spirit and popularity to the annual Easter Egg Roll on the White House's South Lawn, which drew thousands of people each spring. The barbecues had a way of making everyone feel closer to the president and their elected leaders, especially if they happened to catch a glimpse of one of the limos arriving or leaving.

On this day, one of the tourists, a man dressed in camouflage, seemed especially interested in the festivities. It wasn't unusual to see a military man in Washington. The men and women of the armed forces regularly visited the capital. The interesting thing about this man, though, was the fact that he had never served. He simply liked the military look, as well as the attention and respect the camouflaged clothing brought to him.

"Thank you, soldier," people would say as they passed by. Some would even offer their hands for a heartfelt handshake. "Thank you for all you've sacrificed for our country."

The expressions were sincere. Most Americans respected those who had given so much of themselves for their country. The man in camouflage smiled and thanked them, even though the only thing he had sacrificed was $75.27 for the outfit and boots from the army surplus store.

The man was that empty.

The White House had a long history of attracting its share of emotionally unstable visitors. But more often than not, they turned out to be of no concern. All Camo Man wanted to do was get close enough to Josiah so he could tell his friends that he had been there, maybe even that he had met or talked to the president.

That's all he wanted.

STORMCLOUD44/BLOG

We are left alone in the Valley of Death. They bid us follow them, but to where? Where are our minds that were once free to choose another way? The president and his minions have taken them captive and have wired us to an eternal oblivion. They will not triumph. We will break free, and they will remember our name.

THE FOLLOWING DAY, MARK MET WITH JOSIAH IN THE OVAL Office.

"So what's on your mind, Mark?" Josiah asked.

"Well, Mr. President," Mark began, "I wanted to talk with you about your recent decision, sir."

"The Murphy-Stotter bill?"

Mark nodded. "You're seriously going to veto it?"

"I am."

"If I may, sir ... I think you're making a terrible mistake."

"Mark, I can't sign that bill. It goes against every principle we ran on."

"With all due respect, sir, it's how Washington works. You do this for that side of the aisle, and the next time you need them, they'll—"

"What?" Josiah cut in before Mark could finish. "Agree to do something I don't want so the other side will someday agree to do something they don't want, and the people will get what they don't want? Is that the way Washington works?"

"You'd rather have gridlock?"

"I'd rather have a congress that voted its convictions. They don't have to agree with me; just be honest and tell me where they stand."

"If you veto this bill, Mr. President, you'll anger a third of the population."

"If I sign it, I'll anger two-thirds! And I'll be going against my own heart. I've never made it a secret where I stood on the issue."

"We ran on ideas, sir. They were good ideas, but we're here now."

"Yes, and I will be voting the way I promised I would vote."

"The people won't hold us to campaign promises, sir. And if they do, we've got three more years before the next election to mend those fences. Sign the bill, Mr. President, or it's political suicide!"

"Mark, my friend," Josiah said, "have you lost your way so soon?"

"I haven't lost my way, Mr. President. I'm just talking about using our heads."

"If your head's leading you in the wrong direction, I'd suggest letting your heart lead instead."

"Is it so wrong to pass a bill that, for the most part, will ultimately be for the people's good?"

"What about the parts that aren't for their good? Isn't that a bit like saying the fox only ate half the chicken?"

"This is how the game is played, sir. We're not breaking any hard-and-fast rules. Washington is about give-and-take."

"I'm just concerned that it'll be the people who are doing the giving, and we'll be the ones doing the taking."

"The people know we can't perform miracles here. They just want us to keep everything running."

"I don't recall being sent to Washington to just 'keep everything running.' What's happened to your vision, Mark? Isn't that why you brought me into this thing? To make a difference?"

"Some differences have to be made slowly."

"Or not at all. Look at your compass, Mark. When in doubt, always check back in with your compass."

JOSIAH'S REFUSAL TO SIGN THAT BILL TOOK COURAGE, BUT AS IT turned out, vetoing it wasn't political suicide. Josiah's approval rating slipped some for several months following the veto, but he remained well liked and, more importantly, an overwhelming majority of Americans trusted him.

Some tried to make his faith and his Amish ways an ongoing issue, but Josiah's quick wit and humble heart deflected most of that. Even Harley was running out of things to complain about. Almost.

With the holiday season approaching, there was growing speculation as to whether President Josiah would take part in the traditional lighting of the national Christmas tree.

"He won't use electricity himself, but he'll turn on electric Christmas tree lights? Smacks of hypocrisy, if you ask me," Harley said on one news program. And another. And another.

Harley loved making the rounds with his criticisms.

Harley attended the holiday ceremony, though, positioning himself close enough to the president that he would be in any photos, which were sure to get national and international exposure. When it came to publicity photographs, Harley was the polar opposite of Josiah. While President Josiah felt being photographed could lead to pride, Harley was more than happy to take that trip. He also wanted to be close enough to any and all reporters so that he could continue getting in a few under-the-breath jabs at his old rival.

"Funny, isn't it, how this president won't use electricity, but he'll participate in this grand display of electric power," he'd said to anyone close enough to hear him.

Harley knew Josiah would catch the remark on the news programs, but to Harley's annoyance, Josiah didn't take the bait. He seemed to have developed a knack for recognizing Harley's verbal traps and could navigate his way through the minefield quite skillfully.

That didn't stop Harley, though. Losing a debate or an election never seemed to stop Harley. His mouth could accommodate both feet quite easily.

When it came time to light the tree, Harley watched as White House staff lit the candles on the tree. Before everyone's eyes, the tree became an old-fashioned, elegant display of glowing, holiday cheer. The DC Fire Department monitored the situation carefully, but all went well. The crowd gasped and then applauded in awe.

Harley mumbled something under his breath and walked off in a bit of a huff. It wasn't a Christmas tiding. Scrooge would have been proud.

THE FOLLOWING EVENING, AS THEIR HUSBANDS DISCUSSED THE nation's issues in the Oval Office with the president's cabinet, Elizabeth and Cindy took a stroll through the Rose Garden.

"Elizabeth, would you mind if I asked you something?" Cindy said.

"Why, not at all, dear," Elizabeth answered.

"How did you keep from getting bitter over the things that have happened in your life?"

"I assume you're referring to our daughter?"

Cindy nodded. "You have such strong faith. But how do you hang on to it when things go so horribly wrong?"

"It hangs on to me."

"And if we had lost the election, you would have been okay with that too?"

"If that was God's will, then yes, I would have had to be okay with it."

"So how do you get to that place?"

"Contentment? You hang on ... and you let go. The fact that I've forgiven the driver doesn't alter the truth. But my not forgiving him would alter my future. That driver took a big part of my heart from me that night. I don't have to give him the rest of it."

"Then maybe that should be your cause."

"My cause?"

"Every first lady has a cause. Maybe yours can be forgiveness. Most of us have to forgive somebody for something, and we need to be forgiven ourselves."

"I could do that, *jah*."

"And you don't need any fund-raisers for forgiveness."

———

LATER THAT EVENING, AS ELIZABETH AND JOSIAH PREPARED TO turn in for the night, Elizabeth turned to her husband and asked, "So is it everything you thought it would be?"

"The presidency?"

"Jah."

"Harder. A lot harder," he said. It had been everything they'd thought it would be, and nothing they'd thought it would be.

Elizabeth nodded.

"The lines have blurred," Josiah said. "Hard to tell them apart anymore."

"Between the two parties?"

"No. Right and wrong."

"Trust what's inside you, Josiah," Elizabeth said. "Do what you know is right."

Josiah nodded. "Do you think I've made any difference here?" he asked.

"Time will answer that," she said.

The question of whether Josiah's presidency had made a difference in Washington could only be addressed by each individual's heart, but there was at least one tangible proof that it had made some difference in the world: the Nobel Peace Prize committee's decision to award the prestigious honor to President Josiah Stoltzfus. This gentle man had led by example, and the world had noticed.

Josiah didn't quite understand the honor. *Why give an award for simply promoting peace?* he wondered. *Isn't that what we all should be doing?*

Because of that belief, Josiah didn't attend the actual ceremony. Vice President Mark Stedman accepted the award for him. Josiah was grateful for the honor, of course, but he had work to do. Besides, it was meat-loaf night at the White House, and he had promised the kids a game of checkers after dinner.

CHAPTER 21

★

JOSIAH COULDN'T BELIEVE THAT IT HAD BEEN MORE THAN A year since he'd been elected president. Even though he'd held many press conferences throughout the year and kept the nation informed of what was going on in Washington, it was time now to deliver his State of the Union address. The president was gathering his thoughts on the eve of the big day when Elizabeth stepped into the Oval Office.

"Let's get away," she said. "Go for a ride. It's a beautiful night."

"That would do us both good, *jah*?" Josiah said, dropping his pen onto the desk, happy for the interruption. "I'll have them bring the limo around."

"No, not the limo," Elizabeth said, gently placing her hand over his. "Tonight, let's make it just you and me."

Josiah knew what she meant. The Secret Service had been performing their duties with outstanding professionalism, but sometimes they did too good of a job. Between the children and the Secret Service, Josiah and Elizabeth didn't seem to ever be alone these days.

"I've grown tired of our lack of freedom," Elizabeth said. "I can hardly trim the flowers in the Rose Garden without one or two Secret Service agents hovering over me or the staff trying to do it for me. I miss the openness of our farm in Lancaster County."

"No limo then," Josiah agreed. "The horse and buggy?"

Elizabeth shook her head and smiled.

"Then what?" Josiah asked, noticing the playful look in Elizabeth's eye.

Elizabeth led Josiah to the storage room and to their set of chainless bicycles, otherwise known as Amish scooters. Josiah was both surprised and pleased.

"I snuck our scooters onto the moving truck when we left Lancaster." Elizabeth giggled like a schoolgirl.

"When I was busy with the horses?" Josiah asked.

Elizabeth nodded. "And then, when the movers were unpacking the truck, I told them to tuck the scooters in the back of the storage room, and I covered them with a sheet. Think we can sneak out?" Elizabeth asked.

Josiah laughed. "We can sure give it a try."

The First Couple made their way down the hallway like two teenagers trying to sneak out of their parents' house.

"Now it won't be easy, but I have a plan," Josiah whispered. "Remember that secret passageway they showed us when we first moved in?"

"Jah," Elizabeth said eagerly.

"Take off your apron and put something over your bonnet. We can't look Amish, or we'll be recognized."

Elizabeth did as Josiah suggested, grabbing a cloth from off one of the side tables and draping it over her bonnet. They rolled their scooters through the secret passageway that snaked around before leading them to an outside guard shack.

"You won't say anything, will you, Howard?" Elizabeth asked the guard when they finally came up out of the tunnel.

"I don't know what you're talking about, ma'am," Howard said with a wink. "But wait, let me call an accomplice."

Howard made a call on his walkie-talkie and within minutes, a black SUV pulled up. It was Baylor, one of the security staff.

"Let him load your bikes and drive you out of traffic," Howard said.

"I'll drop you off at the National Monument," Baylor said.

Josiah and Elizabeth thanked the two guards as they loaded up the scooters. After Baylor found a fairly deserted parking lot and dropped off the president and the First Lady, they pushed their scooters along the streets of Washington, D.C.

Josiah noticed that the Secret Service had followed them — as he'd expected they would — but he chose not to tell Elizabeth. He enjoyed seeing the childlike joy on her face at thinking she'd outmaneuvered the Secret Service. But understandably, there they were, tailing the First Couple past various monuments that lit up the darkened sky. They stayed back just far enough that Josiah and Elizabeth could enjoy their presumed privacy. But they were there.

When it comes to the president's safety, the Secret Service was always there.

After about an hour, Josiah and Elizabeth returned to the black SUV, which returned them to the White House.

As Howard let them pass back through the tunnel, Josiah nodded at him, acknowledging that he knew Howard had called Secret Service and that it was okay. Howard went along with it, continuing to let Elizabeth believe the two had gotten away with their little escapade.

After Josiah and Elizabeth, mentally refreshed but cold and physically tired, returned their scooters to the storage room, they ran into Cindy. When Elizabeth told her where she and the president had been, Cindy laughed.

"So is that the secret to a good marriage? Sneaking out and going for bike rides together?"

Elizabeth smiled at Josiah before answering. "It can't hurt."

———

THE NIGHT OF THE STATE OF THE UNION ADDRESS ARRIVED. THE congressional chamber was filled with both houses of Congress and a good deal of anticipation. The House Doorkeeper entered the room and hushed the eager chatter of the crowd by announcing, "Mr. Speaker, the president of the United States!"

When President Josiah Stoltzfus entered, the people stood and cheered. Josiah shook hands with those closest to the aisle as he made his way up to the platform. With both the vice president and the Speaker of the House seated behind him, Josiah stepped up to the microphone, raised his hand to quiet the crowd, and then attempted to speak. But the place erupted in applause again. Finally, when the ovation died down, Josiah began his speech.

"Mr. Speaker, Vice President Stedman, members of Congress, and the American people, tonight I am most pleased to report that the state of the Union is *gut!*"

The people jumped to their feet and gave their president another resounding ovation. Then Josiah continued.

"All signs point to a robust harvest of all that we have planted this past year. And I'm not talking about the corn in the Rose Garden ... although that did quite well too. I'm talking about rebuilding trust in our government, taking steps to ensure our resources will be here for our children's children, and making our country safer by recalculating what it truly means to live in peace. You and I have traveled a long way together. We're no longer on the path to the right or the path to the left; we've stepped back to recalculate before taking the path to tomorrow. But our work is not done. There is still plenty more to do ..."

By the end of the speech, both sides of Congress were on their feet giving their resounding approval.

Emily Watson, the network newscaster who had originally reported from the "Welcome to Lancaster, Pennsylvania" sign when this first started, took her position at the back of the room and — with the members of Congress talking excitedly among themselves in the background — she began her report.

"The president, whose approval ratings had begun slipping a few months ago due to several unpopular decisions, needed to hit a home run tonight, and by all accounts he did just that. A powerful, moving speech. Whichever side of the aisle you're on, you've got to admit this president isn't afraid to speak his mind ..."

———

THE PRESIDENTIAL MOTORCADE WAS PARKED AT A SIDE ENTRANCE of the Capitol Building, and the public lined the street out front to catch a glimpse of President Josiah in person. The loyal had waited there for hours in the rain. Even Camo Man showed up, ever faithful in his attempt to get close enough to see President Josiah.

When the news spread through the crowd that the president would be leaving by the side entrance in just a few minutes, some rushed to that area to get as close as they could to the motorcade, but the police pushed them back.

With the rain beating down on their umbrellas and their cameras at the ready, the crowd watched as President Josiah Stoltzfus stepped out of the Capitol Building surrounded by members of the Secret Service.

One woman with a camera around her neck angled for the perfect position. All she wanted was one brief moment when she could get a clear view of the president rather than the men and women who encircled him. And then there it was. Her opportunity. One split second and—

BANG!

A shot rang out, and the president fell limp, collapsing to the ground. America's beloved Amish president had been struck in the chest by an assassin's bullet.

It was an image that would later be played in slow motion on every news show across the country for weeks, months, and years on end.

There was immediate pandemonium as Secret Service scrambled into position, some throwing their bodies over the bloodied president while others scanned the crowd to see if they could see anyone with a gun.

The lady with the camera around her neck backed away. She wanted to run, to escape the ruckus, but when she turned, she looked squarely into the face of the man who had been standing directly behind her, the man dressed in camouflage.

The woman saw Camo Man look down at the gun, glistening in the rain and the moonlight, clear enough for anyone close by to see. *He sees the gun! He knows I'm the shooter!*

"She's got a gun!" Camo Man yelled. People screamed, then instantly formed a human wall around the woman as Camo Man grabbed her arm, twisting it behind her until she dropped the weapon. Camo Man took her to the ground, laying his body across hers, where he waited for the Secret Service officers and the police. The shooter kicked and screamed, but Camo Man held her fast. She muttered something incoherent about allegiance to some misguided cause and then screamed, "I am StormCloud44! The storm clouds have gathered! You cannot stop them!"

"Shut up!" Camo Man screamed, his voice cracking with emotion.

The Secret Service team had arrived and cuffed her hands.

"You're crushing me! I can't breathe!"

"I CAN'T BREATHE," JOSIAH GASPED. A MAN OF PEACE, HE WAS now lying in a pool of his own blood.

"I'm here," Elizabeth said, trying to choke back her tears and be brave but failing at both. She held her beloved in her arms. "The ambulance is on its way. Don't talk, Josiah. Save your strength."

"I love you, Elizabeth."

"I love you, too, my husband," she said. "You've just lost a little blood, that's all. The doctors will fix you up, and then you'll come back home. We're going to grow old together, remember? You promised."

Some Secret Service officers did their best to calm Josiah's children and keep them back from their wounded and bloodied father, but the officers' efforts would never erase from the children's minds the scene they had just witnessed.

Josiah tried to smile at Elizabeth as he struggled for air. He tried to speak, but Elizabeth couldn't hear his weakened voice over the screams of protest coming from the heartless shooter, who was now being led to a police car.

Within moments, another mass of police swarmed the location, their blue strobe lights flashing in the rain. An ambulance quickly followed, pulling up as close as possible to the scene.

The police car with the suspect in it quickly left the area to protect the shooter from retaliatory action.

As precious minutes passed, the crowd gathered at the scene waited for news of the president's condition. Law-enforcement officers and emergency medical technicians surrounded him, making it difficult for the crowd to see anything.

Elizabeth remained at Josiah's side, holding his hand as the paramedics kept watch on his vitals and attempted to stop the bleeding long enough to transport him to the hospital. He was pale and weak but trying desperately to speak.

"Elizabeth," Josiah said, struggling for breath. "I'm sorry ..."

"For what?"

"That it's ending like this."

Elizabeth gently squeezed her husband's hand. "But it's not ending, Josiah," she said. "You have too much to do to leave us. The kids need you. The country needs you. I need you."

Josiah's blood pressure was dropping rapidly. He had lost an enormous amount of blood, and the look of concern on the faces of the medical team told Elizabeth more than she wanted to know.

Josiah slipped in and out of consciousness.

"Josiah!" Elizabeth screamed, desperately trying to call him back to her. "Josiah!"

Josiah opened his eyes, staring off to the side. Elizabeth wasn't even sure he could see her, but she leaned in as close as she could.

"Elizabeth," he said weakly.

"I'm here, Josiah. I won't leave you. I will never leave you, Josiah."

"Elizabeth ... it's beautiful! So beautiful."

Again Josiah struggled for breath, and Elizabeth's lips trembled as she wept openly.

"Elizabeth ..." he said.

"What is it, Josiah? What are you trying to tell me?"

Josiah gathered whatever strength he had left and spoke one final word: "Forgive."

Josiah coughed and gasped, and then he closed his eyes and died.

Elizabeth wept as the paramedics reverently removed their equipment from her beloved and placed his sheet-covered body onto a gurney before wheeling it into the waiting ambulance.

———

A STUNNED AND CONFUSED CROWD WATCHED IN SHOCK AS MARK and Cindy helped the grieving widow into the limo.

"Why isn't she going in the ambulance with the president?" one man wondered aloud.

"Noooooo!" wailed Camo Man, realizing what had happened to his beloved president. "Nooooo!"

The people wept and immediately began sharing the heartbreaking news with their friends and family via calls, texts, or tweets, but many in America had already seen the news alert on television and knew the horrible truth.

President Josiah Stoltzfus had been assassinated.

As the presidential motorcade and emergency vehicles drove away from the scene, reporter Emily Watson stood off to the side of the Capitol steps and looked into a camera, adding her tearful commentary of the night's events.

"This evening, following his inspiring State of the Union address, President Josiah Stoltzfus was assassinated. Our thoughts and prayers are with the Stoltzfus family and our entire nation. Tonight the world grieves the senseless loss of a Plain man who sacrificed his peaceful life to become one of America's great leaders. Tonight he has paid the ultimate price.

"Police have a suspect in custody, but that doesn't ease our nation's pain. We are stunned and saddened at the loss of this beloved man, dedicated father and husband, and most remarkable president. Josiah Stoltzfus will never be forgotten."

———

IT WAS WELL PAST MIDNIGHT WHEN MARK STEDMAN WALKED into the Oval Office and turned on the light. It looked different to him now. The Oval Office had always held a fascination for Mark. He had often imagined himself sitting in that chair behind the presidential desk, handling the day-to-day affairs of the nation, telling Congress and the lobbyists exactly what he thought, and delivering memorable speeches to the American public. None of that seemed as overwhelming a task as it did at this very moment.

"I figured this is where you'd be," Cindy said as she entered the room.

"I don't know if I can do this," Mark said, being painfully honest with himself. Reality sometimes clashed with the glamour of dreams.

"If only we could know the future, huh?" Cindy said. "I never thought it would turn out like this."

Mark nodded solemnly as he looked around at the various items in the Oval Office, at items that were so typically Josiah — the latest copy of the *Farmer's Almanac*, a dulcimer, the Bible that had been used for Josiah's inauguration.

"I used to think I was a good man," Mark said. "Sad what we settle for in ourselves, huh?"

"You are a good man, Mark."

"Not nearly good enough," he said as he walked toward the presidential chair and ran his hand along the back of it. But Mark couldn't bring himself to sit in that chair. He was the president of the United States. He had been sworn into office immediately following Josiah's death. But he did not, could not, would not sit in Josiah's chair. Not yet.

"How do you go from believing you know everything to knowing beyond any doubt that you know absolutely nothing at all in such a short amount of time?" Mark wondered out loud.

"Maybe that's the true definition of a great leader—someone who's not afraid to admit he doesn't have all the answers."

"There are no easy answers. I know that now," Mark said. "That's the only thing I know for sure anymore."

———

FROM SOMEPLACE DEEP WITHIN HER AND WITH GOD'S GRACE, Elizabeth found the strength to tell the children about their father's death. How difficult it was for her to explain such a violent act. It was one thing to lose a parent to disease or a car accident or some other catastrophe outside of anyone's control, but for her children to be robbed of their father through such a senseless and brutal act seemed incomprehensible.

From early childhood, Elizabeth—as with all Plain folk—had been taught to honor life. That was one of the reasons the Amish didn't drive vehicles—because the possibility of taking another person's life in an accident was too high. That was also one of the reasons the Amish opposed war—life was precious to them.

Now the Stoltzfus children would have to accept the actions of someone who didn't share their respect for the life of another. Because of this stranger's selfish actions, there would be no more running out to greet their father as his horse and buggy made its way up their drive. There would be no more baseball games or bedtime stories from him. The children would have to accept life without their father.

And they would all have to somehow, in some way, choose forgiveness.

Elizabeth assured her children that God was in control and that they'd make it through this time in their lives. Then she held them close and, together, they wept.

CHAPTER 22

★

OUT OF RESPECT, THE LATE-NIGHT COMEDY SHOWS TOOK A self-imposed hiatus and ran reruns in place of new programming. The nation was grieving. and there was little to laugh about.

Retrospectives of Josiah's life were hurried into production and aired nonstop across the airwaves. A few daytime news and talk shows dedicated their programs to looking into the twisted minds of assassins.

Most Americans, though, just wanted to weep. Their hopes of a better tomorrow had been snatched from them, and in spite of sound bites of President Stedman's giving sincere and encouraging words to the nation, the country felt horribly robbed.

Hundreds of thousands of people waited under overcast skies to watch as President Josiah's flag-draped coffin was taken in a six-horse-drawn caisson, with Samson and Delilah leading the other horses, down Constitution Avenue. The procession would end at the Capitol Building, where the coffin would lie in state on Lincoln's catafalque in the Rotunda.

A riderless DayBreak followed the caisson, Josiah's wide-brimmed hat hanging from her saddle. The stirrups on the saddle were reversed, and Josiah's boots, also reversed, were standing upright in the stirrups, symbolizing that Josiah would not ride his horse here again. The reversed boots also represented Josiah looking back on his beloved family and friends, bidding them a final farewell. DayBreak moved down the street with a slow, elegant trot out of respect for her fallen friend.

Over the course of the next few days, approximately one million people passed through the Rotunda to pay their respects to President Josiah. Millions more watched the ceremonies via television and the Internet, sharing in the nation's grief.

A formal ceremony was later held at the Washington National Cathedral, with world leaders and many of the nation's politicians and celebrities in attendance. Everyone wanted to honor the man they had grown to love.

The crowd was solemn, and both men and women wept openly. The chief justice expressed his condolences to the Stoltzfus family, and then President Mark Stedman addressed those who were gathered there and the nation who watched from their homes and workplaces.

"Less than two years ago," he began, choking back the tears, "just outside of Lancaster, Pennsylvania, I met a man who had wisdom not seen since ... well, perhaps not since another of our great presidents, Abraham Lincoln. Like Lincoln, Josiah Stoltzfus came to Washington a humble and decent man filled with common sense and uncommon courage. He has left behind some mighty big shoes to fill. Not just for me, but for every one of us. The question for us now is this: Are we up for the challenge?

"I will be the first to admit that I fall dreadfully short of the mark. But because of President Josiah Stoltzfus, I want to do better. I want our country to do better. I know you do too.

"We still have a lot of work ahead of us. Our course has shifted and our plans have been altered by circumstances, but they can be changed again. We can go back to where Josiah was leading us. Only we'll be wiser because of our experience and more appreciative of his vision.

"America is a blessed nation. An exceptional nation. A nation with a good heart. As Josiah would say to us if he were here, 'We just need to recalculate.'

"Less than two years ago I met a man. You met him too. And we're all better for it."

President Josiah had been an unlikely hero and a reluctant savior for a broken nation, although he would have rejected both of those titles. He had seen himself as neither a hero nor a savior. He was simply a man who followed a path he felt he was meant to follow. In his heart, Josiah believed he had been born "for such a time as this." And now his work was done.

After the ceremony, Josiah's body was taken to the Ronald Reagan Washington National Airport. A dulcimer played "Hail to the Chief" as President Mark Stedman and military personnel stood at attention and saluted Josiah's flag-draped coffin as it was loaded onto Air Force One, en route to its final resting place in Pennsylvania.

Josiah's interment was held at a small Amish cemetery in Lancaster County. Dozens of buggies parked alongside government vehicles, and a crowd of Amish friends gathered beside politicians to welcome their beloved friend home. Bishop Miller gave the funeral message, extolling his friend who had sacrificed so much for what he had believed was his mission. President Mark Stedman again shared a few words. At Elizabeth's request, the services closed with Josiah's favorite hymn:

> *When peace like a river, attendeth my way,*
> *When sorrows like sea billows roll;*
> *Whatever my lot, Thou hast taught me to say,*
> *It is well, it is well, with my soul.*

Following the Amish ceremony, Mark and Cindy gave Elizabeth loving and heartfelt embraces.

"I don't know if you feel the same," Mark said, "but I'm glad our paths crossed."

"Mark, you came into our lives, and everything changed," Elizabeth said, wiping the tears from her eyes. "But I know Josiah didn't have any regrets."

"And you?"

"I took a vow to follow my husband wherever he led us. And I would do it all over again."

Bishop Miller approached Elizabeth and extended his hand.

"Welcome home, Elizabeth," he said. Elizabeth had been accepted back into her Amish family with open arms. She and Josiah had never rejected their Amish faith, and even though they had disobeyed the rules of the *Ordnung*, and discussions of shunning had been ongoing, Bishop Miller felt, as did the community and church officials, that the family had suffered enough pain. It was time for healing and mercy.

As Mark turned and walked toward his car, a familiar voice called from behind him.

"Mr. President?"

Mark turned around to see Harley Phillips standing there. Mark was both surprised and pleased.

"Thanks for coming, Harley," Mark said.

"Look, I know we've had our differences, but ... he was a good man."

Mark nodded. "He was. Yes, he was."

Harley walked to his own car, and Mark stood for a moment taking in the familiar countryside. This is where it had all started. It seemed like so long ago, but it had been less than two years since Mark's car had careened off the road and into the ditch here. So much had happened since then. So much joy and so much pain.

Mark got into the presidential limousine and watched out the window as he left behind the little Amish community and the man and woman who had forever changed his life.

On the way back to the White House that night, the presidential motorcade passed by the Washington Monument. President Stedman looked out the window at the historic obelisk.

"I think I finally know why the tip of it remains in the shadows," he said.

Cindy looked up at the top of the monument. "You're right, it is in the shadows," she said. "I hadn't noticed that before."

"I think it's because we're not supposed to see it all. I think the shadows represent that part of life that will always be just out of our view."

"The part where we have to trust?"

Mark nodded, and the driver drove on, taking the president and First Lady back to their new home. Once there, Mark headed to the Oval Office again. Cindy followed.

"You're going to have to sit in it sometime, you know," Cindy said, turning the Oval Office chair around so that the seat of it faced Mark. He looked at it for a moment, hesitated, and then respectfully sat down in it.

"It's bigger than I imagined," he said. "Or maybe I just feel smaller."

Only those who had seen the country from the vantage point of that chair could fully understand what Mark was feeling at that moment. It was a private club, this society of presidents, and the password was *What in the world have I gotten myself into?*

"Throughout the years, incumbent presidents have offered some of their best advice to their successors," Mark added. "At Benjamin Harrison's inauguration, outgoing president Grover Cleveland was gracious enough to hold an umbrella over the new president so he wouldn't get rained on. I wonder what Josiah would be saying to me right now."

Cindy smiled. "He'd probably be saying, 'Don't lose your way.'"

"And President Reagan told President George Herbert Walker Bush, 'Don't let the turkeys get you down.'"

Most residents of the Oval Office respected the presidents who had gone before them and on some level felt empathy for those who followed. It took a person with a lot to give to sit in that Oval Office chair, and that Oval Office chair would take a lot from that person.

SPRING CAME, AND THE CHERRY BLOSSOMS WERE NOW IN FULL bloom in Washington, D.C. It was a spectacular sight — pinks and whites everywhere, as though some angelic artist had splashed vibrant and colorful paint at random all over the landscape. As usual, tourists arrived in droves to capture the beauty in their memories and through the lenses of their cameras.

It was a new season for Washington in other ways too. A different attitude was prevalent in the halls of Congress. The constant verbal wrangling between the two sides that had previously defined Congress had toned down. Each party, as well as Independents, now listened as the other side explained their position. Rare was the congressional member who would miss a vote, and rarer still was any filibuster.

Congress was working together, putting aside their various differences, to perform the work of the people. They were doing what they had been sent to Washington to do. And when it came to a ballot, they voted their consciences. They didn't fear losing a reelection because of a certain stand they had made on an issue. They voted the way their hearts told them to vote. They had recalculated their priorities.

In the halls of Congress, it was commonplace to see a Democratic member of Congress holding the door open for a Republican member, and vice versa.

People couldn't believe what they were seeing. And members of Congress couldn't believe what they were doing. The change seemed to happen naturally. Balancing the budget became a priority instead of a panic play to avoid a government shutdown. Everyone, it seemed, wanted to work a little harder, be a little bit better.

Even Harley Phillips was coming on board, ending one of his speeches before Congress with, "And that is why I propose we appropriate the six billion dollars for this project in my home state of … Ah, never mind. We don't need it."

What was happening to the country?

It was being healed.

The morning of President Stedman's State of the Union address arrived, but back in Lancaster County, Pennsylvania, a certain widow paid it no mind. Other than her personal memories, that chapter of her life was over now. She might read some brief mention of it later in the Amish newspaper or hear talk of it from the tourists, and she would, of course, wish her old friend well. But today she knelt in the graveyard and solemnly brushed a few blades of grass and some leaves off a tombstone, then lovingly ran her fingers along the carving. The stone read "Josiah Stoltzfus—beloved husband, father, son, friend." The words summed up her husband well—Josiah Stoltzfus, the Amish man who had represented hope for so many. The words fully described him. Almost. Tagged on at the end, listed in the order of Josiah's priorities in life, were two more words that completed the picture:

"And president."

———

Mark Stedman sat behind the desk in the Oval Office reviewing his State of the Union address one last time. He had aged more than the actual time he had served in office, but he wore the gray well. In honor of Josiah, he had also grown a beard. Josiah's well-worn Bible was at the top right-hand portion of the presidential desk. Josiah's Bible was a constant reminder of Mark's dear friend and the source of the Amish man's strength.

When the time came, the presidential limo picked up the president and First Lady and drove them to the Capitol Building, where the much-anticipated speech would take place.

"Mr. Speaker, the president of the United States!" the House

Doorkeeper said as President Stedman entered the congressional chamber, where both sessions of Congress were assembled.

The crowd cheered as the president entered the room, made his way up to the platform, and approached the microphone.

President Stedman waited for the applause to die down, then he smiled and said, "The state of the Union is *gut!*"

The standing ovation Mark received was said to be the longest in American political history.

EPILOGUE

★

IF YOU ARE EVER IN THE LANCASTER, PENNSYLVANIA, AREA, FOL-low the signs that say Josiah Stoltzfus Presidential Library. It's a small, modest building—exactly how Josiah would have wanted it. No fund-raisers were held to build the library. The Amish constructed it themselves, raising the frame in just one day.

When you get there, pull into the driveway and find a place to park. Then walk up to the front entrance and go inside. The cost of admission to the library is on the honor system.

A portrait of President Stoltzfus hangs on the wall just inside the entrance. It shows Josiah holding DayBreak's reins in front of the White House. The portrait view is from the back, but it is unmistakably Josiah. It's a striking pose.

Elizabeth Stoltzfus will most likely greet you herself when you enter, and she'll invite you to look over some of her husband's books and papers that he wrote while serving in the White House. The former First Lady might even invite you to her home for supper. If you have the time, take her up on it. She'll feed you well and will probably offer you some homemade shoofly pie for dessert.

Enjoy your visit. By the time you leave, you'll have learned a little more about Josiah, his presidency, and the Amish.

They are good people!

ACKNOWLEDGMENTS

M Y HUSBAND, RUSS, WHO HAS WALKED ALONGSIDE ME ON
this journey through life since we first met when I was fifteen
years old, and my children and grandchildren, who later joined us
on the journey and have made it all worthwhile.

My agent/manager, Dan Posthuma, for enthusiastically seeing
this idea through from its birth at Border's coffee shop to its publication, and for his friendship and encouragement along the way.

To Mel Riegsecker, owner of The Blue Gate Restaurant and
Theater in Shipshewana, Indiana, for his generous help, support,
and personal knowledge of Amish traditions and faith.

To longtime friend Lynn Keesecker, who said to me over lunch
one day, "Why aren't you writing novels?!" Thanks for the friendly
nudge. And to Carolyn McCready, Terry Glaspey, and others who
have also nudged me in that direction.

To the entire Zondervan editorial team, including Sue Brower,
Tonya Osterhouse, and Leslie Peterson, for your efficiency and
skill; Londa Alderink, Jennifer VerHage, Ben Greenhoe, and
everyone else on the Zondervan publicity team for your enthusiasm and creative talents; Verne Kenney, who believed in this
project from its beginning, and the entire Zondervan sales team.

Bill and Gloria Gaither, Beverly Lewis, Wanda Brunstetter,
Jerry Jenkins, Mike Huckabee, Congressman Marsha Blackburn,
Gene Perret, Mark Lowry, Ken Davis, Chonda Pierce, Michael
Catt, Bunny Hoest, Rick Eldridge, Lani Netter, Lord Taylor,

David Pendleton, Paul Aldrich, Charlie McCoin, Rick and Bubba, Judi Feldman, Scott Davis, Rik Roberts, Wayne Newton, Doug Wead, Nazareth, Taylor Mason, Jim France, Gloria Wallman, Joshua Katzker, Adam Lowe, Miranda Sloan, Sara Posthuma, Angela Hunt, Twila Belk, Kim Messer, Carter Robertson, Heidi Petek, Nan Allen, Bonnie Keen, and each one of you who has helped with promos, endorsements, and too many other ways to list, but most importantly, your encouragement and friendship. I sincerely appreciate you and can't thank you enough!

The casts, crews, and theater staffs of The Confession and Half-Stitched for all the wonderful time we've spent in Amish communities together (Indiana, Pennsylvania, and Ohio). A special thank-you to composer and director Wally Nason. A thank-you, too, to Robert Dragotta.

Paul Miller, who took me to the next level on this writing path with the publication of my first book back in 1985.

John Branyan and my friends in the Christian Comedy Association for their love and support over the years.

My "adopted" mom, Diantha Ain, for always being a loving and enthusiastic cheerleader.

Linda Aleahmad, Mary Scott, Margaret Brownley, Kathi Macias, and all my writing and speaking friends all over the country for their friendship and kinship in this craft (AWSA, WAN, WGA, and all the others).

Friends, family, work associates, and all you readers of books who have ever written or spoken words of encouragement to me over the years. Writers are an insecure lot and need all the positive input we can get. So many of you have provided that at just the right moment in my life. I do not take your words lightly. They (and you) mean the world to me!

Shipshewana Amish Mystery Series

Vannetta Chapman

There's more to the quaint northern Indiana town of Shipshewana than handcrafted quilts, Amish-made furniture, immaculate farms, and close-knit families. In her signature style, Vannetta Chapman crafts cozy Amish mysteries with a twist!

Available in stores and online!

Kauffman Amish Bakery Series

Amy Clipston

Take a trip to Bird-in-Hand, Pennsylvania, where you'll meet the women of the Kauffman Amish Bakery in Lancaster County. As each woman's story unfolds, you will share in her heartaches, trials, joys, dreams ... and secrets. You'll discover how the simplicity of the Amish lifestyle can clash with the English way of life—and the decisions and consequences that follow. Most importantly, you will be encouraged by the hope and faith of these women, and the importance they place on their families.

Available in stores and online!

Christian Fiction

Share your passion for books

Christian Fiction

✓ Liked ⚙ ▾

Welcome | Virtual Book Club | Bookshelf 7▾

Join a virtual community of Christian Fiction lovers.

Peek into the latest books, read reviews, chat live with authors, win free books and enjoy a virtual book club. Join the conversation with other folks who share your passion for books that tell great stories while pointing people toward the most important Story of all!

www.Facebook.com/ChristianFiction

ZONDERVAN®
.com

Amish Life

Celebrating the simple joy
of all things Amish.

Amish Life

✓ Liked | ⚙ ▾

Recipes | Bookshelf | Welcome | 7 ▾

Join an online community
for people who love all things Amish.

You long for a simple life, and you love reading stories about the
Plain Folk! At Amish Life, you'll find other folks who share your
passion for all things Amish. Join the conversation, interact with
top Amish Fiction Authors and share your stories, recipes,
recommendations and photos.

www.Facebook.com/AmishLife

Share Your Thoughts

With the Author: Your comments will be forwarded to
the author when you send them to *zauthor@zondervan.com*.

With Zondervan: Submit your review of this book
by writing to *zreview@zondervan.com*.

Free Online Resources at

www.zondervan.com

Zondervan AuthorTracker: Be notified whenever your favorite
authors publish new books, go on tour, or post an update
about what's happening in their lives at www.zondervan.com/
authortracker.

Daily Bible Verses and Devotions: Enrich your life with daily
Bible verses or devotions that help you start every morning
focused on God. Visit www.zondervan.com/newsletters.

Free Email Publications: Sign up for newsletters on Christian
living, academic resources, church ministry, fiction, children's
resources, and more. Visit www.zondervan.com/newsletters.

Zondervan Bible Search: Find and compare Bible passages in
a variety of translations at www.zondervanbiblesearch.com.

Other Benefits: Register to receive online benefits like
coupons and special offers, or to participate in research.

ZONDERVAN.com/
AUTHORTRACKER
follow your favorite authors